The Watcher in the Shadows

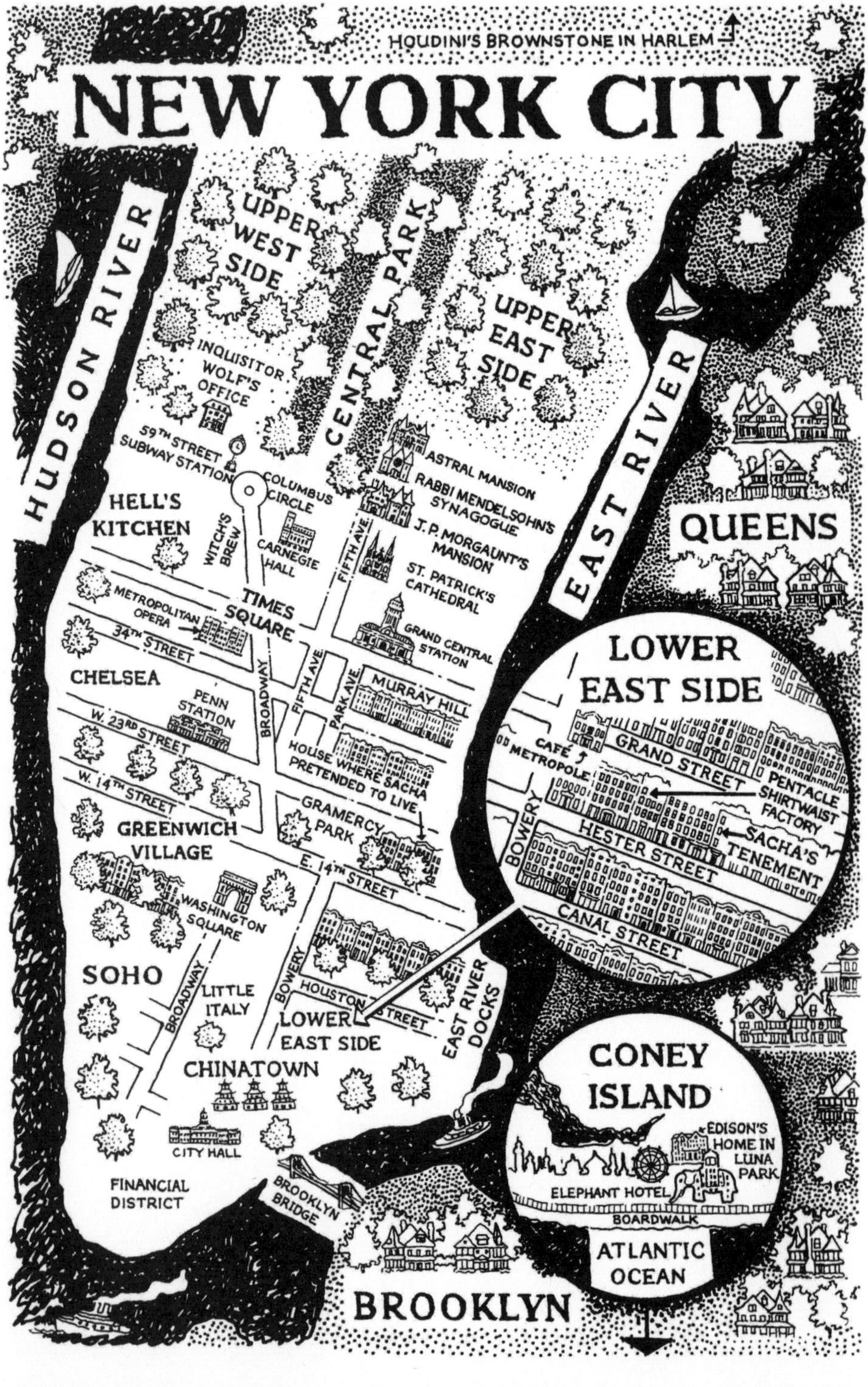

HOUDINI'S BROWNSTONE IN HARLEM

NEW YORK CITY

HUDSON RIVER
UPPER WEST SIDE
CENTRAL PARK
UPPER EAST SIDE
EAST RIVER
INQUISITOR WOLF'S OFFICE
59TH STREET SUBWAY STATION
COLUMBUS CIRCLE
ASTRAL MANSION
RABBI MENDELSOHN'S SYNAGOGUE
HELL'S KITCHEN
WITCH'S BREW
CARNEGIE HALL
FIFTH AVE.
J. P. MORGAUNT'S MANSION
ST. PATRICK'S CATHEDRAL
QUEENS
METROPOLITAN OPERA
TIMES SQUARE
34TH STREET
GRAND CENTRAL STATION
CHELSEA
BROADWAY
FIFTH AVE.
PARK AVE.
MURRAY HILL
PENN STATION
W. 23RD STREET
HOUSE WHERE SACHA PRETENDED TO LIVE
W. 14TH STREET
GRAMERCY PARK
GREENWICH VILLAGE
E. 14TH STREET
WASHINGTON SQUARE
SOHO
BROADWAY
LITTLE ITALY
BOWERY
HOUSTON STREET
LOWER EAST SIDE
EAST RIVER DOCKS
CHINATOWN
CITY HALL
FINANCIAL DISTRICT
BROOKLYN BRIDGE
LOWER EAST SIDE
CAFE METROPOLE
GRAND STREET
PENTACLE SHIRTWAIST FACTORY
BOWERY
HESTER STREET
SACHA'S TENEMENT
CANAL STREET
CONEY ISLAND
EDISON'S HOME IN LUNA PARK
ELEPHANT HOTEL
BOARDWALK
ATLANTIC OCEAN
BROOKLYN

THE WATCHER IN THE SHADOWS

CHRIS MORIARTY

ILLUSTRATIONS BY

MARK EDWARD GEYER

HARCOURT CHILDREN'S BOOKS
Hougton Mifflin Harcourt
Boston New York

Harcourt Children's Books is an imprint of Houghton Mifflin Harcourt Publishing Company.

www.hmhbooks.com

Text set in Mrs. Eaves
Book design by Christine Kettner

LIBRARY OF CONGRESS CATALOGING-IN-PUBLICATION DATA
Moriarty, Chris, 1968–
The watcher in the shadows / Chris Moriarty ; illustrations by Mark Edward Geyer.
pages cm
Companion to: The Inquisitor's apprentice.
Summary: In early twentieth-century New York, as thirteen-year-old Sacha Kessler, the Inquisitor's apprentice, faces enemies old and new that threaten him and his family, he changes his mind about learning magic.
ISBN 978-0-547-46632-3 (hardback)
[1. Magic—Fiction. 2. Murder—Fiction. 3. Apprentices—Fiction. 4. Jews—New York (State)—New York—Fiction. 5. Dybbuk—Fiction. 6. Spirit possession—Fiction. 7. New York (N.Y.)—History—20th century—Fiction. 8. Mystery and detective stories.]
I. Geyer, Mark, illustrator. II. Title.
PZ7.M826726Wat 2013
[Fic]—dc23
2013003919

Manufactured in the United States of America
DOC 10 9 8 7 6 5 4 3 2 1
4500399826

For Linus and Annika

PROLOGUE

Kidnapped, New York Style

THE TWO MEN lurked in the shadows across the street from the Pentacle Shirtwaist Factory. The lights were still on in the factory, where the foreman had kept everyone late to finish a big order for an uptown department store. But on this side of the street, there were shadows aplenty.

The last hour of the long workday seemed to drag on forever, but finally the sewing machines fell silent and the guards unlocked the great iron doors, releasing a flood of chattering, jostling girls into the darkening street. Now the two men craned forward, peering into one face after another in search of their victim. But they were still careful to keep out of the light. There'd been a strike brewing at the factory for months now, and anyone who saw their rough faces and gangsters' clothes would have known that they were starkers: men who hired out their fists—and worse—to the highest bidder.

Finally the starkers saw the women they were waiting for.

They were obviously a mother and daughter, but apart from their dark curls and pleasantly plump figures, you could hardly have found two women in New York who looked more different from each other.

The daughter wore the severe white shirtwaist, black wool skirt, and knitted necktie that were the unofficial uniform of the firebrand Wiccanist revolutionaries who preached strikes and rebellion down at the Café Metropole. And though she looked like a little girl dressing up in her big brother's clothes, there was a glint in her brown eyes and a pugnacious set to her pretty jaw that had already made the foreman at Pentacle mark her down as a potential troublemaker.

The mother, however, seemed to come from another century. She was as neat and tidy and proper as a woman could be, but her unfashionable dress and frumpy shawl belonged to Russia, not America.

"Are you sure you're going to be all right?" she asked her daughter. "I don't know if you should be wandering around alone at night with all this talk of a strike—"

"I'm not wandering around alone, Mama. I'm going to night school, like always."

"Maybe you shouldn't go until things quiet down at the factory. One of those girls who've been handing out flyers for the union got herself beat up just last week—"

"She's fine, Mama. She's already out of the hospital. And anyway, nothing will happen to me between here and night school." Bekah laughed, patting her mother's cheek affectionately. "And if you're still worried after dinner, you can send Sacha to walk me home."

The two women parted, the daughter walking off eagerly and the mother watching her go with a worn and worried look. Only then did the starkers step out of the shadows.

They stalked their prey for several blocks, cutting through the rush hour crowd as swift and silent as two sharks on the hunt. They made their move just after she'd passed the golden lights and steamed-up windows of the Café Metropole.

"Excuse me," the larger of the two men said, stepping in front of the woman.

The woman exclaimed in Yiddish and backed up—only to bump into his companion, who had sidled around behind her to cut off her escape.

"Are you Mrs. Kessler?"

"Who are you?"

Instead of answering, the starker grabbed a slender chain around her neck and yanked on it to expose the silver locket that hung from it. "It's her," he told his partner. "Let's go."

The two men grabbed her by the elbows and began hustling her along the crowded sidewalk.

"Where are you taking me? What do you want from me?"

"Don't worry about that. All you need to know is Mr. Morgaunt wants to see you."

She screamed then, but she might as well have kept her mouth shut. No one heard her. No one even turned to look at her. It was as if she and the starkers had dropped out of the ordinary city into a ghostly realm of silence where the thousands of New Yorkers thronging the Bowery could neither see nor hear them.

She shut her mouth and made the sign of the evil eye. She was the daughter and granddaughter of wonderworking rabbis—she knew magic when she saw it. And she knew the difference between the harmless household spells she'd learned at her mother's knee and Great Magic such as this. No pious Jew would have dared to perform such a spell, lest he upset the delicate balance of the universe. She had fallen into the hands of a *mekhashef,* a wicked sorcerer, and only God and His angels could protect her.

They turned south off the Bowery into the dark and narrow side streets, and she realized they were going to pass within a few short blocks of her own tenement on Hester Street.

Usually the Jewish Lower East Side was abuzz with activity at this time of night: shift workers making their way home, children playing in the gutters, housewives gossiping on the front stoops and fire escapes. But tonight all those people seemed to grow deaf or look the other way when Mrs. Kessler screamed for help. She and her kidnappers could have been deep sea creatures, cut off from the rest of humanity by the crushing weight of thousands of feet of dark water. And she knew somehow that the *mekhashef* had told them to walk through the tenements. He had wanted her to feel his power and to know that it reached right up to her very own doorstep . . . perhaps even into the heart of her very own family.

As the starkers hustled her down the steep stairs of the Canal Street subway station, she glimpsed a crooked sign that read

STATION CLOSED FOR LINE WORK.

They dragged her across the platform toward the subway tracks. The drop yawned before her, and the third rail glittered in the shadows like a deadly thread of silver—

—and then suddenly a lone subway car was coasting into the station and its doors were whispering open before her. The kidnappers pushed her onboard and into a deep armchair upholstered in oxblood velvet. Beside the armchair stood an ornate floor lamp, its crimson silk shade casting more shadows than light.

The car rolled north and picked up speed until, a few blocks past Grand Central, it turned off onto an unlit spur of track and coasted smoothly into a station with no name or street number. The station was as private as the subway car, and at least as luxurious. The vaulted ceiling was supported by ornate cast-iron pillars. The walls glittered with mosaics of leaping nymphs and satyrs. A fountain gurgled softly at one end of the platform. At the other end, a monumental marble staircase wound upward into a darkness lit only by flickering gaslight.

The two men hurried her up the stairs, through a dim entrance hall, and into a vast space that echoed like a cathedral.

It was a library. Books ranged around them in glass-fronted shelves that rose one, two, three stories high. All around the walls of the cavernous room hung the heads of slaughtered beasts—animals Mrs. Kessler had never seen, and some she'd never even heard of. They were *kelippot,* she told herself: husks, like the empty shells of people that dybbuks took possession of. Their dead eyes glittered like stars, at once dazzling and terrifying. But nothing in the room was as terrifying as the man who waited before the fire for her.

He was as gray as ashes, as cold as iron, as bitter as the death of a child.

He wore black, and at first she thought he was dressed in sorcerer's robes, like the evil *mekhashfim* in her father's books, an ocean away and half a lifetime ago. But then she made out the glimmering points of white at wrist and neck, and realized that he was wearing what people in America called evening dress.

The only point of color about the gray man—the only thing in the whole vast room that seemed to be part of the bright world of warmth and life at all—was the rich golden liquid swirling in the cut-crystal glass in his hand.

"Let her go," he told the starkers.

They released Mrs. Kessler's arms, and she sank to the floor, unable to keep her balance after being dragged along against her will for so long. She heard the starkers' boots on the marble floor and then the dry *snick* of the great doors closing behind them. She struggled to her feet and forced herself to look the *mekhashef* in the eye so he would know she wouldn't bend to him.

"Do you know who I am?" the gray man asked.

She nodded. He had visited the factory a few times since she'd worked there. And even if he hadn't, she'd seen his photograph in the newspapers often enough to recognize him.

"I apologize for the inconvenience," he told her, "but I had to see you in private about a matter of some importance to both of us."

"What do you want from me?" she asked.

"Just a little job. One well within the scope of your powers. But first I think we ought to understand each other a bit better than we do at present."

He raised one hand, and a slithery, witchy woman emerged from the shadows beside the great hearth. She held a small white and gold cylinder. It looked like a trinket, a mere child's toy . . . and yet a looming sense of power hung about it. Then the woman pushed something that looked like a phonograph out of the shadows, slotted the cylinder into the player, and turned the starting crank.

Mrs. Kessler had thought she was frightened before the music started. But that hadn't been real fear, not as a mother knows it. With the first haunting notes of the melody, she felt a terror worse than she had known in the pogroms, or huddled in steerage while waves crashed down on the shuddering hatches, or standing in the pens at Ellis Island while the health inspectors peered into her children's eyes and chalked strange symbols on them to say who would reach America and who would be turned away. For all those times, she had feared only for her children's lives. But now she was face-to-face with a man who had the power to destroy soul as well as body.

Finally the terrible music ended and the machine trailed off into a repeating suck of static. When the *mekhashef* spoke, his voice was quiet, and his words simple.

"You know what it is, don't you?"

"It's my son, my Sacha. You've taken his soul and you've . . . turned it into music."

"Rather good music too, don't you think? It has a depth and complexity that most etherograph recordings . . . well, but then I've listened to enough of them to become something of a connoisseur."

Mrs. Kessler couldn't speak.

"What would you do to win it back from me? You're a proud woman, I can see it in your face. But for your children, you would do anything."

"Yes," she whispered. "Anything." What was the use in denying it? She held her hand out for the cylinder.

"Not so fast!" He laughed. "There's someone I want you to meet first. You see, you're not the only one who wants this little trinket."

And then he was leading her back out of the library, back down the twisting staircase to the private subway station. At the far end of the platform, there was a door, small and plain, and behind it were more stairs. They plunged deep into the bowels of the earth, so far below the city that the air smelled of worms and time and darkness. And then they stepped into a room so thick with the stink of magic that it stole her breath away.

There was a little circle of stone at the far end of the room, just where the vaults shaded into gloom and shadows. As they grew closer, Mrs. Kessler realized it was the rim of a well, just like the one she had fetched water from in her childhood. It was so webbed over with spells and hexes that it was difficult to make out what was at the bottom. She couldn't see the spells the way Sacha would have been able to see them. But she still knew that she was looking at a prison cell for a demon so dark and dangerous that even a wizard powerful enough to kidnap souls was terrified of it.

Thinking back to the tales she'd heard her father tell in her distant childhood, she knew there was only one thing that could possibly be at the bottom of that well: a dybbuk.

"And you know whose dybbuk it is too, don't you?"

He gripped her shoulders and forced her to her knees. She struggled, but he was stronger. Her face broke the surface of the spells. And suddenly it was as if she'd thrust her head into clear water and could see straight down to the bottom.

But there was no monster at the bottom of the well. There was no nightmare creature from beyond the gates of death and life.

It was only her own Sacha. And though she knew the

dybbuk must pose a deadly danger to her son, it was still a part of him . . . and how could the mother in her not love every part of her child?

"What do you want me to do?"

"Not much. Nothing that will keep you from carrying on with your ordinary little life. I just need you to work for me—"

She blinked in confusion and dismay. "But . . . but . . . I already work for you."

"I know!" His harsh laugh echoed on the stone walls and rippled along the vaulted ceiling. "That's what makes it so amusing!"

Morgaunt rose to his feet, looking impossibly tall in his black evening dress. He loomed over Mrs. Kessler and put a finger to her mouth, silencing her. "And now, my dear, it's time to send you home. You're about to learn a spell I doubt your father ever taught you. A pity you won't remember the lesson."

He placed his hand on her head and began to speak in a cold harsh voice that seemed to scour her very soul.

"I conjure you, O Zachriel and Shabriri, Princes of Memory and Forgetting, to remove this woman's memory of myself and to cast it out into the waste and the wild."

And then the voice of iron began to chant the name Shabriri, dropping a letter each time he repeated it. It would have sounded like a child's game if it hadn't all been in such deadly seriousness. But there was no mistaking the black magic behind the chant, or the way it set her head spinning and whirling.

"Briri!"

She felt a tug behind her eyes, as if someone had knotted a string around her memories of the kidnapping and was yanking them out of her brain by sheer force of will.

"Riri!"

She tried desperately to hold on to the memory, but whatever was on the other end of that invisible string was stronger than she was.

"Iri!"

A sharp pain slithered through her mind—and then the memory broke free and drained away like water running through cupped fingers.

She looked around, blinking, and rubbed a hand across her eyes. What was this place? Whatever she'd come here for mustn't have been that important, or surely she would have remembered it.

"Ri!"

As the last echo of the final syllable faded, she turned, silent as a sleepwalker, climbed the marble stairs to the entrance hall, and walked out into the dark, sleeping streets of the city.

CHAPTER ONE

The Klezmer King's Last Matinee

"MOVE ALONG, FOLKS!" cried the manager of the Hippodrome. "There's nothing to see here!"

As he spoke, he tried to hide the Klezmer King's corpse with his own body—which was almost wide enough to do the job, Sacha reflected.

Maurice Goldfaden was a short man, but not a small one. Not that he was fat, exactly. There just seemed to be more of him than there was of most people. His big belly seemed to have a life of its own. It strained his shirt buttons to bursting and thrust out from under the bottom of his waistcoat, jutting over the top of his trousers so that it reminded Sacha of a tenement fire escape. In fact, everything about Maurice Goldfaden seemed to overflow normal bounds and limits. His hair stood up from his head in every direction, defying combs and brilliantine to break out into wild and frizzy curls with every shake of his head. He talked big too. His whisper reached the back row of the theater, and his hands gestured so dramatically that Sacha wondered if he'd been watching actors onstage so long he'd forgotten how real people talked in ordinary life.

The only thing about Goldfaden that wasn't bigger than life were his eyes. They were small and black and very bright, and they nestled in his jowly face like the poppy-seed filling in hamantaschen. Looking at those eyes, Sacha had a feeling that very little happened at the Hippodrome that Maurice Goldfaden didn't know about.

"Nothing to see!" Goldfaden repeated to the world at large. And then he turned to Maximillian Wolf and added in a quieter voice, "And certainly nothing that need concern you, Inquisitor!"

Frankly, Sacha was inclined to agree with Goldfaden. The cause of death was certainly clear enough. The Klezmer King lay sprawled across the stage of the Hippodrome with one long-fingered hand still clutching his clarinet. He had died onstage during the Friday afternoon matinee. He'd been in full song, right in the middle of a dazzling high E-flat solo riff, when his electric tuxedo had sputtered, flickered, and flared up in a blinding flash. He was still wearing the tuxedo that was billed on the marquee outside as his "world-famous electric tuxedo." No one had mustered up the nerve to turn it off. So now the Klezmer King lay at Wolf's feet, flashing and twinkling like a flurry of falling stars.

Wolf looked down at the dead klezmer player for a long moment without speaking. Then he walked backstage, following the wires that snaked away from the body into the shadows, and kicked the plug out of the wall.

"Oh," Goldfaden said sheepishly. "I guess I should have thought of that."

They walked back to the body and stared down at it. Wolf wore his usual bland and disheveled expression, but Goldfaden looked completely undone by the presence of a corpse on his stage.

"Pathetic," Goldfaden said. "Asher was a genius, an absolute musical genius, one of the all-time klezmer greats—even if his box office wasn't exactly to die for. And now look at him! Fried to death by a couple of strings of cheap Christmas tree lights!" Goldfaden shook his head mournfully. "That's not just tragic. It's worse than tragic. It's *bad showmanship.*"

Lily giggled, and Wolf let out a strangled sort of cough. But Goldfaden wasn't laughing.

"And to have it happen at the Hippodrome," he went on. "Terrible, just terrible! The poor old girl doesn't deserve this indignity. Why, the Death-Defying Dershowitzes defied death right here on this very stage! And that rascal Harry Heller practically invented smoke and mirrors here. I even had Houdini headline his disappearing elephant act—no illegal magic, mind you, just honest fakery, all totally kosher. But in all these years, I never imagined the Hippodrome would come to this!" He frowned at the spot where Asher had died, his mouth tightening in a way that confirmed Sacha's suspicion that Goldfaden—and maybe a lot of other people too—hadn't much liked Asher. "But isn't that Naftali Asher for you? Electrocuted by his own tuxedo because of some stupid publicity stunt that—mind you, I saw the nightly take, and I know for certain—didn't do a thing at the box office. What a *shlimazel*! If he ever makes it into heaven, everything will go wrong from the minute he gets there. The neighborhood will start going to pot, and the angels will move to hell to get away from Asher's Yiddish luck."

"Sounds like he wasn't the sort of fellow who ought to have been messing about with electricity," Wolf hazarded.

"Yeah, well, thank God he had Sam to do that for him, or he probably would have fried himself months ago."

"Sam?" Wolf echoed, scrounging in his baggy pants pockets for his ever-elusive pencil stub.

Suddenly Goldfaden looked like he could have bitten his tongue off for having mentioned the name. "Asher's dresser. A good kid. The best."

"And what's Sam's last name?" Wolf had finally scared up a disgracefully chewed pencil stub. Another search produced a dog-eared scrap of paper that looked like it might once have been a laundry ticket.

Goldfaden's eyes shifted around nervously. "I'm sure Sam'll turn up sometime. He's probably just too upset about the whole thing to—er—and anyway, Sam wouldn't hurt a fly!" Goldfaden glared fiercely at Wolf, as if daring the Inquisitor to contradict him.

"Ah," Wolf said in a soft voice that made Sacha's ears prick up. He looked sideways at Lily and saw that she had caught it too. Wherever Sam was—and whatever his name was—Sacha wouldn't have changed places with him for all the tea in China.

"Well, this certainly is an unpleasant business," Goldfaden said, as if eager to change the subject. "Pathetic, really. It's enough to make you wonder if all that crazy talk people made about him was true."

"What kind of crazy talk?" Wolf asked in a very quiet voice.

Sacha held his breath. Next to him he could feel Lily practically buzzing with anticipation. Something was definitely up. There might not be any magical crime involved in Naftali Asher's death. But there was a secret. And if Sacha had learned anything so far in his apprenticeship, it was that one way or another, Wolf would know what it was by the time they walked out of the Hippodrome.

"Oh, well, you know," Goldfaden said. "People always talk. Especially theater people. Can't believe everything you hear, can you?"

Wolf seemed willing to go along with Goldfaden's changes of subject—for now anyway, though Sacha had watched him at work long enough to know that he would eventually meander back to every dangling hint and unanswered question. "I understand that it was a lady who called in the Inquisitors?" he said.

"A lady!" Goldfaden cried, as if in all her storied history, the Hippodrome had never seen such a creature. "Oh, you mean Pearl! Well, I don't see why you need to talk to *her.*"

Wolf fished out his pencil stub again. "Pearl—?"

"Pearl Schneiderman, a.k.a. Madame Eelinda the Electrifying Eel Maiden."

"What?" Wolf sounded perplexed. "Did she dress up in light bulbs too?"

"Nah, she's a contortionist." Goldfaden twisted his arms up like pudgy pretzels. "But not the usual contortion shtick. Veeeery artistic is our Madame Eelinda! Anyway, the point is you don't need to know. This isn't a magical crime. It's barely a crime at all. More of a—a—an unfortunate happenstance. No need whatsoever for the Inquisitors to involve themselves."

Sacha looked at Wolf to see what he thought of this, but it was impossible to tell. Wolf stood stock-still, his handsome bony face impassive, and his dishwater gray eyes blinking mildly at Goldfaden through spectacles still fogged with cold. The only moving thing anywhere on Wolf's person was the icy rainwater dripping from his coat and pooling around his sodden shoes.

Sacha glanced at Lily Astral, who stood beside him. But his fellow apprentice just widened her bright blue eyes at him as if to say, *Don't ask me. I have no more idea than you do what goes on inside Wolf's head!* Then she reached into the pocket of her heavy winter cloak, fished out a delicate little lace handkerchief, and blew her aristocratic nose with a resounding honk.

It was February, in the middle of the worst New York winter anyone could remember, and if there was one small satisfaction that made up for Sacha's raw fingers and frozen toes, it was the sight of prim and perfect Lily Astral with her nose running all over the place.

Not that he wanted her to be *too* miserable. He liked her. And if she were just a little less rich and a little less of a know-it-all—and if she weren't a girl, obviously—she would have been the best friend a fellow could ever have. But still, it was nice to know that even Lily Astral was human enough to catch a cold.

"Seriously," Goldfaden insisted. "The guy was hopping around onstage strung up like a Christmas tree, sweating like a hog, and spitting into his clarinet. You think he needed *help* killing himself?"

"I do see your point, of course," Wolf said mildly. "But all the same, Miss Schneiderman did report a magical crime."

"Well, she was upset. People say all sorts of things when they're upset."

"And people say all sorts of things when they aren't upset too. But I've generally found that the things people say when they're upset turn out to be a good deal closer to the truth."

Goldfaden pursed his lips and narrowed his prune-colored eyes. "I could kill Pearl for making that phone call," he muttered. "I really could!"

"I hope you won't," Wolf said earnestly.

Suddenly Goldfaden seemed to remember the body lying at his feet. He turned a little green and tugged at his shirt collar as if he felt in need of air. "Pearl overreacted a little, that's all. Because Asher was involved . . . and . . . well . . . *you know.*"

"Actually, I *don't* know."

"Well, I'm not one to repeat malicious rumors. And Asher was a—well, okay, not exactly a *friend* of mine. Asher wasn't the kind of guy who *had* friends. But I felt sorry for him. He was tormented. Even for a genius. Which he certainly was, whatever people might say about how he got his talent."

"All the same," Wolf said, circling back to their earlier disagreement, "I would like to talk to Madame Eelinda—er—Miss Schneiderman. And of course Asher's dresser, Sam—what did you say his name was?"

"Oh—er—I didn't," Goldfaden blurted out. "I mean, I sent Pearl home. The strain of it all, you know."

"Shall I send an officer to her house to assist her?" Wolf asked solicitously.

"I'm sure that won't be necessary. I'll just ring her up."

"And what about Sam?"

"I . . . um . . . don't know where he lives, actually."

Wolf gave Goldfaden a blank stare that Sacha wouldn't have wanted to be on the sharp end of for love or money.

"No, I swear, really I don't! He was living with his family on Henry Street last I knew, right over the kosher butcher. But those Schloskys move around like gypsies. You know how it is in the tenements. Every month come rent day, there's kids whose home address is a pile of furniture on the sidewalk. That's the Schlosky boys for you: sent unshod into this sorry world with nothing to their name but red hair and empty bellies. So how's a man supposed to keep track of a family like that? I paid Sam in cash under the table, and we were both happier that way. And if you want to report me for *that,* go suck on an egg!"

But Wolf just laughed and told Goldfaden to call Pearl Schneiderman.

"For you, anything," Goldfaden proclaimed with a wink. "And in the meantime, you can always talk to the other eyewitnesses—all three hundred of them!"

For the next hour, while a Black Maria trundled Asher's body down to the Tombs, they heard from a parade of eyewitnesses. They talked to matinee-goers from every walk of life: Hester Street shopkeepers and Orthodox cantors, Wiccanist revolutionaries and sweatshop seamstresses. They talked to the sellers of seltzer water and candy and roasted chestnuts. And finally they talked to the vaudeville performers themselves—the contortionists and chorus girls and song-and-dance men who had watched from the wings in what turned out to have been the best seats in the house for the Klezmer King's final, fatal performance. But they all said the same thing—so much so that Sacha started to wonder if they'd all rehearsed it together before the Inquisitors showed up.

The Klezmer King had just embarked on his most famous solo—the great *Terkish,* with all the high notes—when the electric tuxedo sputtered and flared, sending out a shower of blue sparks. Asher staggered and cried out. And then he collapsed, stone dead before he hit the ground.

Or that was the story, anyway. And everybody who worked at the Hippodrome seemed pretty determined to stick to it.

Wolf was a subtle and delicate questioner. So subtle and so delicate, in fact, that he could usually interview witnesses—or even suspects—without them ever noticing when he moved from casual questions to the really important stuff. But Sacha had watched Wolf at work many times by now, and he could see that there were two burning questions on his mind: Where was Sam Schlosky? And what were Naftali Asher's dying words?

Sooner or later, more or less discreetly, Wolf asked every single witness those two questions. And one after another, from the fat lady to the midget boy, every single witness lied to him.

No one had heard Asher's last words. No one was even willing to guess what they had been. No one had seen Sam Schlosky after Asher died. And no one had the faintest, foggiest clue as to his whereabouts.

"This is absurd," Wolf said at last, sounding as close to annoyed as he ever got. "How can a man shout his dying words onstage in front of three hundred eyewitnesses without a single one of them hearing him?"

"Acoustics," Goldfaden intoned with a lugubrious shake of his jowls. "I always say acoustics is more art than science. Why, I worked at a theater in Moscow once where— But whaddaya know! Here's Pearl! Pearl can tell you everything!"

Despite Goldfaden's obvious doubts about her status as a lady, Pearl Schneiderman looked nothing like the "painted women" Sacha's mother was always accusing Uncle Mordechai of consorting with at the Yiddish People's Theater. She wore no makeup, and her prim shirtwaist and heavy wool skirt covered her from neck to ankle. In fact, Sacha couldn't see the slightest difference between her and any other nice Jewish girl on the Lower East Side—except for an odd nervous tic she had of cracking her knuckles by bending the fingers so far backward that they all but touched the backs of her alarmingly flexible hands.

"So," Wolf said when he had worked his way around to the subject at hand. "You are the young lady who called the Inquisitors. And Mr. Goldfaden here seems to think that you did so because of some rumors you'd heard about Naftali Asher."

"All nonsense!" Goldfaden interrupted. "What good can come of passing on such crazy talk?"

Wolf turned his dishwater gray eyes on Goldfaden. There was nothing threatening or intimidating about Wolf's stare. In fact, it was so absent-minded that you couldn't really call it a stare at all. But Sacha had been on the receiving end of that absent-minded gaze often enough to know just how uncomfortable it could make a person.

Goldfaden squirmed and swallowed nervously, but he was made of tougher stuff than most people. He clamped his jaws shut and glared at Wolf like a dog defending a bone.

It was Pearl who cracked first. "They said he'd sold his soul to the devil," she whispered. "They said he met the devil at the crossroads and sold his soul for a bunch of klezmer songs."

"See?" Goldfaden said. "Utter nonsense! People have

been saying things like that about great musicians ever since there *was* music. How many klezmer players were supposed to have traveled with gypsies and played with the devil in the Old Country? And how many times have we all heard about some blues man down south who met the devil at the crossroads and sold his soul for the magic in his fingers? But the very idea of such a thing happening in New York is ridiculous. I mean, honestly, how many crossroads are there in Manhattan?"

"Two thousand four hundred and sixty-seven," Wolf answered promptly. "If you count Five Points and Mulberry Bend."

Goldfaden shuddered—though whether it was at the idea of all those hitherto unsuspected crossroads or at the mere mention of the two foulest slums in Manhattan, Sacha couldn't guess.

"I still don't believe it!" he said stoutly.

Wolf turned to Pearl. "But you believed it," he said softly. "At least enough to call in the Inquisitors. And don't think I'm unaware of how very reluctant anyone who works here would have been to do that. So why did you?"

Pearl seemed to collapse into herself. She glanced desperately toward Goldfaden. But he was looking resolutely the other way, as if now that he'd failed to keep Pearl away from the Inquisitors, he was determined to show Wolf that he wasn't going to interfere with her telling her story.

"I—I heard Sam and Asher fighting," she whispered at last. "While Sam was dressing Asher for the show last night."

"What were they fighting about?" Wolf asked.

"I couldn't tell, really. I couldn't hear them all that well. And what I did hear didn't make any sense. Sam said something about Pentacle, which seemed strange, since Asher stopped working there years ago. Asher tried to laugh it off, and Sam said, 'Don't lie to me, Asher. I know where you go. I followed you.' And then Asher got really angry, but I couldn't hear anything much of what he said. He wasn't a shouter—he always got bitter and quiet when he was angry. He could say terrible things, things people never got over, in the quietest whisper." She put her hands to her mouth, and her eyes filled with tears. "I'm sorry! It's horrible to talk that way about him when he's—"

"Never mind," Wolf said gently. "You can't help it if that's the way he was. And people don't become angels when they're murdered. What else did they say? You'll feel better once you've told me."

"Not if it gets Sam in trouble," Pearl said darkly. "Anyway, the next thing I heard, Asher was telling Sam it was none of his business, and besides, he'd already quit. 'It's all settled,' Asher said. 'Tomorrow's my last day. They've found my replacement.'"

"And then?" Wolf prompted.

"And then—Sam laughed. You can't imagine that laugh. It was so *old* and world-weary. And he said, 'Don't tell me pretty stories, Asher. I *saw* that creature. I saw the watcher in the shadows. Do you think that *thing* will go quietly back to wherever it came from? Do you think you can sell your soul to the devil and not pay the bill when it comes due?' And then . . . and then it was time to go onstage. They didn't say another word to each other. But I saw Sam's face when Asher died. And one thing I can tell you for certain: Sam didn't think it was an accident."

Wolf looked from her to Goldfaden. "Is that what you've all been hiding from me? Why?"

Goldfaden looked sheepish but still defiant. But Pearl clasped her hands together with a pleading look on her face and almost seemed about to drop to her knees before Wolf.

"Because of Sam!" she cried.

"What about Sam?" Wolf seemed genuinely mystified.

"We were all terrified of getting him in trouble." Pearl grasped at Wolf's coat sleeve. "He's a good boy. He never hurt anyone. Whatever Asher was mixed up in, Sam couldn't possibly have been part of it! Can't you just . . . just forget we ever mentioned him?"

"Do you really think I can do that?" Wolf asked sadly.

Pearl dropped her head into her hands and sobbed. "Then it's all over! As soon as the newspapers get word of this, it'll all be 'Anarcho-Wiccanists' and 'subversive magical elements.' And that'll be the end of any justice for poor Sam."

Wolf frowned. "What on earth does this have to do with politics?"

"But—but don't you understand who Sam Schlosky *is*?" Pearl stammered. "He's Moishe Schlosky's little brother!"

Sacha's heart sank. Pearl was right, no matter how much

he hated to admit it. Moishe Schlosky had spent the last year trying to organize the workers at J. P. Morgaunt's Pentacle Shirtwaist Factory. If any reporter sniffed out the faintest hint that Moishe's own brother was mixed up in a magical crime, every paper in town would declare it an Anarcho-Wiccanist conspiracy. Sacha knew that as surely as he knew the sun would rise tomorrow. And he knew something else too—something that made the sinking feeling in his stomach even worse. Moishe was in love with Sacha's sister. And—though he couldn't fathom how his plump, pretty sister could possibly even look twice at a redheaded klutz who was skinnier than a starving chicken—Sacha was starting to have a sneaking suspicion that Bekah was sweet on Moishe, too.

At that moment, the door at the back of the theater burst open. Light footsteps tripped down the aisle, and a voice Sacha would have known anywhere called out, "Good golly, who canceled the second matinee? And what's all this about Inquisiduhs?"

He turned to look up the aisle—and sure enough, there was Rosie DiMaggio, a.k.a. Rosalind Darling, in all her gorgeous, auburn-haired glory.

Halfway down the aisle, she caught sight of Wolf and his apprentices. "Hey, whaddaya know!" she cried. "Sawshah! Lily! Inquisiduh Wolf!"

"Sounds like the elocution lessons are coming along swimmingly," Lily whispered in Sacha's ear.

Sacha tried not to laugh, but he had to agree. The purpose of Rosie's mother's life was to backstage-mother her dazzlingly beautiful daughter into fame, fortune, and a high-society marriage. But honestly, Sacha thought she ought to just give up and let Rosie follow her dream of becoming a famous inventor. Rosie had as good a head for business as any Wall Street Wizard. And Lily had a point about the elocution lessons too. Rosie might be a thousand times prettier than any of the society beauties who flocked to Maleficia Astral's dinner parties . . . but Sacha still doubted there was a speech coach or elocution spell in the world strong enough to conquer Rosie's New York accent.

"Well, well," Inquisitor Wolf said with the friendly smile that he always had for Rosie. "If it isn't Miss Little Cairo!"

"Nah, I got a new act this year. My mother decided I needed something more artistic if I was gonna break into high society. Now I'm doing 'Miss Rosalind Darling's Living Statue Exhibition.' A one-girl museum, complete with depictions of illuminated miniatures from Mr. Morgaunt's world-famous magical manuscript collection. Very classy. But the white paint's hard to get out of my hair. And I get the cramp somethin' awful havin' to stand still so long. Honestly, I preferred the belly-dancing."

Lily made a sound that Sacha would have called a snort if anyone but the heir to the Astral family millions had made it.

"Anyway," Rosie said, oblivious as always, "what are you guys doing here?"

Wolf stepped aside so she could see the chalk outline on the stage.

"Oh, no!" Rosie gasped and covered her mouth with her hands. "Who was it?"

"Naftali Asher."

Was it Sacha's imagination, or did Rosie suddenly look a lot less sorry? But all she said was "Ooh. Nasty. How'd it happen?"

"The electric tuxedo."

Rosie shook her head, tossing her auburn curls. "I never thought that claptrap thing was safe."

"See?" Goldfaden insisted. "Of course it was an accident!"

"Oh, sure, sure," Rosie replied absent-mindedly. "Wouldn't want to speak ill of the dead. Still . . . if there was one guy in vaudeville I *wouldn't* be surprised to see turn up murdered, it'd have to be Naftali Asher."

"Why's that?" Wolf asked quietly.

Rosie gave him a meaningful look. "I guess you never met the guy. Still, Mr. Goldfaden's probably right. Sam's a good kid, but he's no genius. I tried to tell Asher they needed to ground the thing properly, but he practically bit my head off. He shoulda listened to me, huh? After all, I got exploded and set fire to enough times back when I worked for Mr. Edison to know a thing or two about electricity."

"You're not working for Edison anymore?" Lily asked.

"Nah. After the fire at the Elephant Hotel, my picture got in the paper, and Mrs. Edison saw it and decided to take Mr. Edison on a long trip to California to promote 'his' motion-picture camera. As if! He can barely run the thing without my help! But two can play at that game. And the way I see it, since I already invented one motion-picture camera for Mr. Edison, there's nothing to stop me from inventing another one for myself!" She gasped again. "Oh, golly! If the camera was working right today, the whole thing must be on film!"

Suddenly Rosie was off and running. She dashed back up the aisle toward the exit. Wolf followed close at her heels, with Goldfaden waddling behind him and the two apprentices bringing up the rear. They made it into the lobby just in time to see the muddy tails of Wolf's overcoat vanishing through a green baize door that led to a steep flight of stairs.

As soon as Sacha stepped into the stairwell, he was surrounded by the soft whirring and clicking of some piece of machinery running overhead. It was a familiar sound—and not in a good way. It reminded him of Edison's etherograph. Morgaunt had used that machine to steal Sacha's soul and make a dybbuk of it. And then Sacha had played into Morgaunt's hands by recklessly summoning the dybbuk—a blasphemy that still made him cringe with guilt every time he thought of it.

He'd never seen the dybbuk again after that night; it had vanished into the flames of the Elephant Hotel, and he fervently hoped it was gone forever. But he still knew he wasn't finished with J. P. Morgaunt. Morgaunt had told Sacha that he had the makings of a Mage. He'd said that Maximillian Wolf had caused him so much trouble that he wouldn't tolerate another Mage-Inquisitor in the city. Then he'd offered Sacha a job—and laughed in his face when he refused it.

Ever since that night, Sacha had tried to forget Morgaunt's mocking laughter. And he'd tried almost as hard to avoid Wolf's efforts to get him to learn magic. He couldn't give up his apprenticeship, because his family needed the money too badly, but he was still determined not to become a magician. The one time he had worked magic—to summon his dybbuk—he had felt with every fiber of his being that he was doing wrong. And the magic that Wolf had used to defeat Morgaunt in the burning hotel had been even more terrifying than the summoning of the dybbuk. If that was magic, then Sacha wanted nothing to do with it.

Sacha had stopped on the stairs as the memories came to him, overwhelmed by the weak, sick feeling that always overtook him when he thought about that night. But now he realized that the others had gone on before him, and he forced himself to follow. At the top of the stairs hung a heavy red velvet curtain. Sacha pushed it aside—and stepped out into what felt, in that first instant, like midair.

They were in a private box: a little balcony that hung just to the side of the Hippodrome's stage, close enough that the actors could have stood onstage and struck up a conversation with the uptown ladies and gentlemen who could afford these seats.

But there were no audience members in the box now.

Instead, a spindly-legged steel spider crouched over the plush-upholstered seats—it was cobbled together from about five regular camera tripods. On top of the thicket of spindly legs, like a clockwork daddy longlegs, was the strangest camera Sacha had ever seen.

Or at least he thought it was a camera. It seemed to have all the parts and pieces cameras had. But it also had other parts: an extra-long adjustable lens, a speaker trumpet just like the one on Edison's etherograph, and a strange figure-eight contraption on one side that seemed to be doing nothing at all except rolling a long strand of shiny tape from one bobbin to another bobbin.

It was this part of the machine that was making the whirring and clicking noise. And now that Sacha stood beside it, he could hear a sort of scritchety sound as well: the sound of the shiny strand of tape catching in the little cogs and gears that sent it snaking through the belly of the machine.

Rosie flicked a hidden switch, and the machine sighed and wheezed and shuddered to a stop.

"What is it?" Lily asked in the soft silence that followed.

"It's my walking, talking motion-picture camera," Rosie said proudly. "The only one in existence—but not for long! This invention's gonna make me the toast of Hollywood!"

"Why I let her talk me into allowing the thing in my theater, I really couldn't tell you," Goldfaden kvetched. "It's unfair competition, the worst threat to real theater since the phonograph! The actors' union would kill me if they knew

I was aiding and abetting the enemy this way. But that girl could charm a stone into getting up and walking!"

"And you think you filmed Naftali Asher's death with it?" Wolf asked Rosie. "Sound included?"

"Hopefully. I'm still having a heck of a time making the sound match up to the pictures—there's a trick I used for Edison, but he's got the patent on it now, so it's back to square one on *that* little problem. Still, you can usually hear everything pretty good, even if it looks a little funny."

"Can we see it?"

"Well, not yet. You gotta develop the film just like with a regular camera, you know? I could do it for you. Let's see now . . . if I rushed it a bit, I could probably have it ready for you day after tomorrow." Then her face fell. "But wouldn't that be a conflict of something or other? I mean, I work at the Hippodrome. Ain't I a suspect?"

Wolf's eyebrows shot up in surprise. Then he smiled, a little ruefully. "You forget, Rosie. I know you. And out of all the millions of people in New York, you're about the last one I'd ever suspect of killing anybody."

"Oh!" Rosie seemed flattered and even a little flustered by the compliment, though Sacha couldn't figure out why. "Uh . . . I'll bring it to the Inquisitors Division on Monday. I always wanted to see where Sacha and Lily work. I heard so much about it, I got a real curiosity for the place."

"Anyone else I should talk to?" Wolf asked Goldfaden. "Besides Sam Schlosky, I mean."

"Well, you'll need to talk to Asher's wife, of course. And Ki—erm—" Goldfaden fidgeted for a moment, once again unable to meet Wolf's eyes. "Ahem, that is to say—no. Nobody who comes to mind, strictly speaking."

Wolf gave Goldfaden one of his blandest looks. "Everyone has enemies, Mr. Goldfaden, or at least people who don't like them very much. If you're worried that I'll jump to unwarranted conclusions just because you mention, say, a rival or a professional competitor—"

"Oh, heck!" Goldfaden erupted. "I guess you'll hear it sooner or later, so it might as well be from me and not the rumor mill. Asher had it in for the Kid. Thought he was trying to put him out of business. You know who I mean, don't you? Hottest klezmer clarinet in New York."

Wolf looked blank.

"That guy was the Klezmer King," Goldfaden said, pointing at the wavering chalk outline where Asher had lain. "And in my humble opinion, he was the greatest klezmer player who ever lived. But genius or not, he was finished. No one wanted to hear him anymore. They were all too hot for the new sensation that's sweeping the nation: Kid Klezmer."

"Oh!" Sacha gasped before he could stop himself. *"Him!"*

"You know about this person?" Lily asked, as if the mere idea were too absurd to be believed.

"Sure—um—my mother sort of has a thing for him."

Goldfaden snorted. "Your mother and every other live female on the Lower East Side between the ages of nine and ninety. If you ask me, he doesn't have a tenth of the talent poor Asher had. But the women are almost as crazy for him as they are for that talentless hack, Mordechai Kessler. I should be so handsome. I woulda been a millionaire!"

Sacha started guiltily at the sound of his uncle's name, but Wolf was too busy asking where he could find Kid Klezmer to even notice.

"We-ell," Goldfaden said doubtfully, "he spends a lot of time at the Essex Street Candy Shop."

"Oh," Wolf said, in a very different tone of voice. "I see."

Lily looked mystified, but Sacha knew exactly what Goldfaden meant—and why Wolf suddenly sounded as wary as a mouse who'd just caught wind of a new cat in the neighborhood.

Everyone on the Lower East Side knew that the Kid was Meyer Minsky's favorite klezmer player. He was practically the official clarinetist for Magic, Inc. And he hung out with all of New York's most notorious Jewish gangsters in the back room of the Essex Street Candy Shop. Mrs. Kessler wouldn't let Sacha or Bekah set foot in that store, even though it had the best candy in town and was only a mouthwatering block and a half from their apartment on Hester Street. But Meyer Minsky had once visited Benny Fein's mother in the apartment upstairs from theirs, arriving in his canary yellow limousine with his pockets full of candy for all the neighborhood kids—and the taste of that candy was one of the sweetest memories of Sacha's life.

"But I guess you wouldn't want to be seen walking into the candy store," Goldfaden said hesitantly. "It'd give people the wrong idea."

"Quite," Wolf agreed.

"But . . . uh . . . Meyer likes to have lunch at the Café Metropole. And it is almost twelve. And that might be . . . ah . . . neutral territory, so to speak."

"A very astute suggestion," Wolf agreed in his blandest voice. "And now we really should be going. Rosie? We'll see you Monday?"

"You betcha!" she called from the bowels of her walking, talking motion-picture camera.

A minute later, Goldfaden was hustling Wolf and the apprentices out onto the street under the blinking, flashing Greco-Roman awning of the Hippodrome. The weather was still appalling, and they hurried to button coats, twine mufflers around chilly necks, turn up their collars, and prepare for the freezing slush of the New York sidewalks in February.

But before stepping into the icy rain, Wolf turned back to Goldfaden for one last question. "You mentioned Harry Houdini earlier," he asked the theater manager. "Just out of curiosity, would you still hire him now?"

Sacha and Lily both knew what Wolf was asking: Would the Hippodrome still hire a magician who'd been unofficially blacklisted by ACCUSE, the Advisory Committee to Congress on Un-American Sorcery? Maurice Goldfaden knew what Wolf meant too. And from the look of things, he didn't like it much. His eyes narrowed, and his already flushed face turned a purpler shade of red.

"What kinda question is that? This is the Hippodrome, not just some garden-variety vaudeville joint. We started out in Yiddish theater way back when. We've had all the greats here: Adler, Thomashefsky, Kessler. I mean *David* Kessler, of course, not Mordechai the Meatball!"

Sacha jumped again at the sound of his Uncle Mordechai's name—and Goldfaden's poppy-seed eyes flicked his way with a twinkle in them that made Sacha suddenly suspect Goldfaden knew exactly who he was and was taking active pleasure in insulting Mordechai to his face. Sacha had seen his uncle Mordechai in several Yiddish People's Theater musicals—you had to catch them fast, since almost every show that opened at the Yiddish People's Theater folded before the actors even got their first paycheck. Still, he couldn't help feeling that Goldfaden was being a little unfair. But he wasn't going to argue the point, so he tried to copy Wolf's blandest expression, forcing out of his mind the very idea that he even knew anyone named Mordechai Kessler.

Wolf knew about Sacha's family, of course—though Sacha hadn't exactly gone out of his way to tell him more than was strictly necessary about his scapegrace Uncle Mordechai. But Lily still thought Sacha was a respectable middle-class boy who lived in the sedate row house near Gramercy Park, where the Astral family limousine dropped him off every day after work. And she'd go on thinking that as long as Sacha had anything to say about it. He'd die of shame if she ever found out that he lived in the tenements.

"Anyway," Goldfaden went on, "the point is the Hippodrome's got history. She's got soul. And the Hippodrome is not gonna stiff Harry Houdini just because a bunch of congressmen from states with square corners think being a rabbi's son makes him un-American!"

Goldfaden was shaking a finger in Wolf's face now, his big potbelly pushing the taller man backward step by step. Soon both were standing in the rain, Goldfaden in nothing but his suit jacket and waistcoat. But he was too angry to notice—and the finger that had been waving in Wolf's face was now jabbing at his chest.

"And you know what else, Mr. Fancypants Inquisitor? If you think you're going to lean on me to report my friends and neighbors for Wiccanist activities—"

"Actually," Wolf said mildly, "I'm quite a fan of Mr. Houdini myself. And he seems to be having a little trouble finding work lately. So I thought I might mention that if he did appear at the Hippodrome, I'd be happy to buy a ticket."

"—you've got another think—oh!" Goldfaden stopped short. "Really? You'd come see Harry? And the Inquisitors wouldn't shut us down if we had him back? D'you think we could get away with doing the elephant trick again? No, wait . . . that elephant's on tour in Saskatchewan. And trust me, you don't want to try that trick with the wrong elephant! So I suppose we'd have to come up with something new. A séance?

A death-defying escape? Something underwater, perhaps?" His eyes sparkled, and he rubbed his hands together excitedly. "Harry'd have to get back in training, of course. Nothing makes a good magician go to seed faster than testifying in front of Congress."

CHAPTER TWO

A Shtetl Love Triangle

AS THEY WADED through the dirty slush on their way to the Café Metropole, Sacha dropped back to talk to Lily.

"That has to be about the weirdest thing I've ever seen," he began.

"Maybe. But it's still not a job for the Inquisitors." She sniffed disdainfully. "And I have better things to do with my time than run errands for the ordinary cops."

"Crime is crime. And Naftali Asher's still dead, no matter what he died of."

"I suppose. But personally I'm getting sick of traipsing up and down Manhattan on the say-so of illiterate immigrants who can't tell the difference between Old World magic and perfectly ordinary machinery. I mean, are we training to be Inquisitors or public information officers? And how can anyone possibly make it through Ellis Island without figuring out the difference between a killing spell and an electrical circuit?"

Sacha was quite sure that Pearl Schneiderman could read very well and had never set foot on Ellis Island, but he bit his tongue and let it pass.

"And what was all that stuff about Kid Klezmer and the candy store anyway?" Lily asked as they forged on through the driving sleet. "Now there's some problem with Inquisitors going into a candy stores?"

"Rule five hundred and eighty-four in the NYPD Inquisitors handbook," Sacha teased. "No candy for Inquisitors. Wanna quit yet?"

Lilly elbowed him in the ribs. "Come on!"

"Everyone knows the Essex Street Candy Store is Magic, Inc., headquarters. So if an Inquisitor ever went in there and came out alive . . . well, the whole world would think he was working for Meyer Minsky."

Lily stopped in her tracks and stared at him. "That's completely ridiculous! You're telling me the most notorious magical gangster in all of New York runs his rackets out of a candy store? Why on earth would he do that?"

"Maybe he has a sweet tooth."

"Oh, *be* serious, Sacha!"

"I am."

"Well . . . but what parents would ever let their children buy candy there?"

"I don't know about that. But one thing I do know: they don't have much trouble with shoplifters!"

"Would you two like to come inside?" Wolf called back to them from halfway down the block, where he was holding open the big mahogany and plate-glass front door of the Café Metropole. "Or are you enjoying the spring weather too much?"

The Café Metropole was the legendary watering hole of New York's intellectual set—or at least the Jewish part of it, which pretty much amounted to the same thing. It was strategically located between the Eldridge Street Synagogue, the Industrial Witches of the World headquarters on Hester Street, and the several Yiddish theaters that competed for the hearts and wallets of Lower East Side theatergoers.

Each great Yiddish theater had its own stars, its own playwrights and songsmiths, and its own army of die-hard fans ready to come to blows with one another to defend their favorites. The Thalia had the great tragic genius David Kessler. The Windsor had the immortal Thomashevsky. The Grand had what seemed like an endless string of comic leading ladies, each shamelessly promoted as "America's Sweetheart," regardless of the fact that no one north of the Tenderloin had ever heard of her. And of course the ever-struggling Yiddish People's Theater had Uncle Mordechai. But the center of all this flamboyant Lower East Side *mishigas* was the gleaming main saloon of the Café Metropole. Here rabbis happily rubbed shoulders with actors and revolutionaries. Here the IWW organizers plotted strikes over tiny steaming glasses of strong tea. Here young men (and young women too, despite Mrs. Kessler's clucking tongue) debated deep into the night over the latest revolutionary pamphlets smuggled in from England or Russia.

Which made it strange that Sacha hadn't realized until this very moment just how much he *didn't* want Lily Astral to set foot inside the place. But there was nothing to do about it now. Wolf was holding the door open, and already getting irritated looks from the customers near enough to the entrance to feel the cold wind blowing in around him.

Lily marched inside, shaking off her sleet-spattered coat and looking around the place in wide-eyed curiosity. Suddenly, Sacha saw the Metropole through her eyes. The gleaming mahogany bar with its polished brass railing was as immaculate as ever, but everything looked a little shabby compared to the uptown places he'd seen in the last year as he followed Wolf from crime scene to crime scene. And, truth be told, the people looked a little shabby too. None of the Metropole's regulars bothered much with appearances. For one thing, they were mostly poor. And for another thing, they were all far too busy planning the coming Wiccanist magicworkers' paradise, or plumbing the mysteries of theoretical Kabbalah, or penning the next brilliant masterpiece of Yiddish theater. All of which could be done perfectly well in old, tattered, ink-stained clothes. But still—

"Who's *that?*" Lily asked, poking Sacha with her elbow.

Sacha followed her stare across the room—and to his horror, he saw that Uncle Mordechai had gotten up from his usual table in the corner and was headed straight for them with his hand out and a welcoming grin on his face.

Sacha glanced at Wolf—who was busy talking to the bartender, thank God—and then gestured desperately to Mordechai behind Lily's back.

Mordechai caught the gesture, wavered ever so slightly, and then kept advancing toward Lily as if nothing had happened.

"Let's go," Sacha said, trying to drag Lily toward Wolf and get away from Mordechai.

"Wait a minute—"

"Good afternoon," Mordechai said in his smoothest voice. And Sacha turned back just in time to see him sweep his hat off his glossy black curls and give Lily his most winning smile. "May I be of any assistance?"

"Uh . . . well . . . oh!" Lily opened and closed her mouth like a fish out of water, but she didn't seem to be able to make a rational sentence come out of it. What on earth was wrong with the girl?

Sacha gave Mordechai a pointed stare. "No help required, thank you very much. We're here with the Inquisitors."

"A nice Jewish boy like you working for the Inquisitors?" Mordechai said, with an absolutely malicious grin on his face. "You must have broken your poor mother's heart!"

"I don't discuss my mother with *strangers,*" Sacha snapped.

"I applaud your discretion." Mordechai's solemn smirk told Sacha he was going to be the butt of his uncle's jokes for many family dinners to come. "Good day, young sir. And please accept my utmost apologies for intruding upon you, Miss—er?"

"Astral," Lily gasped.

"Not *Lily* Astral!" Mordechai exclaimed as if he'd just heard that she was the goddess Aphrodite fresh off her clamshell.

"But—how do you know my name?" Lily asked breathlessly.

"Ah, well, I can be discreet too. Shall we say a little birdie told me? But they didn't tell me you were so very charming. Little birds can be so unreliable, can't they?" Mordechai gave Lily the smile that had broken the hearts of half the girls on Hester Street. And then—having tormented Sacha for long enough—he retreated to his table in the corner.

Sacha glanced back at Wolf to see if he'd noticed anything. But he had been talking to the bartender and was now making his way through the crowd toward the Metropole's back room.

"Come on," Sacha said brusquely, starting after Wolf. "Don't you know better than to talk to strange men in public?"

But Lily was too busy staring after Uncle Mordechai to hear him. "That is the handsomest man I've ever seen in my entire life," she said as Sacha dragged her along. "And I feel like I've seen him somewhere before too, if only I could remember where. He *must* be famous, Sacha. Who *is* he?"

"How should I know? Just some out-of-work actor."

"Don't be ridiculous. Actors are seedy and disreputable. And he's . . . well . . ." She cleared her throat and looked a little embarrassed suddenly. "You know what?" she asked brightly. "I think he must be one of those exiled Polish noblemen one sees around town these days. That would explain why he looks so familiar, too. I must have seen him at one of my mother's parties."

"I seriously doubt that!" Sacha muttered.

"As if you'd know anything about it!"

But what they saw when they stepped into the Metropole's private dining room stopped their argument cold. Kid Klezmer was sitting at a table full of food and drink far better than anyone in the front room of the Metropole ever got to eat. At the table's far end lounged Dopey Benny Fein, the most notorious starker on all the Lower East Side—a man bold enough (or, some people said, stupid enough) to hand out a professionally printed price list of his starking services. And between the Kid and Dopey Benny sat the king of the Lower East Side: Meyer Minsky.

Sacha had seen Minsky before, of course, but he still couldn't help staring at him. Sure, Kid Klezmer was handsome enough in that skinny Uncle Mordechai kind of way that girls seemed to like. And Benny Fein would have been a fine figure of a man if he hadn't broken his nose so many times that he talked like he had a permanent head cold.

But Meyer Minsky—now, *that* was Sacha's idea of what a real man ought to look like.

Minsky had grown up on the streets of the Lower East Side, among the poorest of the poor. But you'd never know it to look at him today. He wore the best clothes money and magic could buy, and he carried himself like a perfect gentleman. Yet the set of his broad shoulders would have demanded respect even if he'd been dressed in beggar's rags. That and the proud glint in his blue eyes that seemed to say, *Other Jews may be poor and powerless, but I'm not. Respect me, and we'll get along. Disrespect me, and I'll make you sorry you were ever born.*

That quiet but indomitable pride had made Meyer Minsky the idol of every Jewish boy in New York, and the closest thing the Lower East Side had to royalty. He was an honest-to-goodness made-in-America Jewish folk hero, and in the eyes of most Lower East Siders, he could do no wrong. If you called him a common criminal, they'd tell you he was a nice Jewish boy who treated his mother like a queen and made the streets safe for respectable girls. If you told them he abused magic in ways no pious Jew should tolerate, they'd look uncomfortable for a moment—and then ask if you wanted to let the Irish and Italians rule the streets. If you told them he was dangerous, they'd tell you that Jews had been slaughtered and persecuted for two thousand years, and maybe it was time for a dangerous man to step to the fore.

And so Meyer Minsky reigned over the Lower East Side, living off the fat of the land like a modern-day King David—and far more beloved by his subjects than most kings could ever hope to be. Of course the owner of the Café Metropole would have paid his protection money to Irish gangsters if he had to; there was no escaping life's harsh realities. But he would have felt ashamed. Minsky, on the other hand, he was proud to pay. And when Minsky deigned to grace the private back dining room of the Café Metropole, you could almost see every man in the place stand a little taller and breathe a little freer.

At the moment, however, Minsky wasn't looking much like a modern-day Jewish warrior king. He was just relaxing comfortably over lunch with a few friends. And when Wolf came into the room, Meyer gazed mournfully up at him as if to say that even an Inquisitor ought to have better taste than to mar pleasure with business.

Still, he greeted them graciously, called the waiter to set out plates for the three of them, and made polite small talk until the waiter was gone again. Then he turned to Inquisitor Wolf and asked, "What can I do for you, Max?"

"Oh, it's Max, is it?" Wolf replied with a hint of a smile. "I didn't think we'd parted on such good terms last time I saw you."

Meyer threw back his head at this and laughed merrily. "Ah, but we were young and hungry together, Max! And a man who's your friend when you're poor is your friend for life. Besides, even if I hated your guts, I gotta respect a cop I can't buy."

"And you can buy all the other ones?" Wolf asked with a solemn twinkle in his gray eyes. "I thought Mr. Morgaunt had already beat you to it."

"Ah, but they don't *stay* bought, that's the trouble, Max! They only rent themselves out until someone comes along with a better offer. Can't you talk to Keegan about trying to recruit a better class of rascal?"

"I don't think the Inquisitors pay well enough to hire

honest rascals," Wolf pointed out. "Maybe you'd be better off talking to Morgaunt. I'm sure the two of you could come up with something."

Minsky frowned and pushed back his chair a little. "I hope you're not here to pester me about Morgaunt," he told Wolf.

"What about him?" Wolf asked in his blandest voice.

"Don't play the little innocent with me. I don't see you for years on end, and then Morgaunt's facing a strike at Pentacle, and you suddenly show up on my doorstep? What do you expect me to think?"

"Ah," Wolf said, glancing at Dopey Benny. "I see. Morgaunt's asked Magic, Inc., to put down the strike."

"Of course he has. We're the best. And Morgaunt always hires the best."

"Then you've agreed to work for him?"

"Not yet. But I don't see why I shouldn't." Minsky set his jaw and narrowed his blue eyes. "Morgaunt may be a nasty piece of work, but his money's as good as another man's. And if he wants me to put a little magical muscle on the street, then I don't see why I shouldn't take his money. Unless, of course, the other side can pay me more."

"We both know they can't do that."

"No, they can't, more's the pity."

"Have you been down to the IWW offices yet?" Wolf asked.

"I have," Dopey Benny said in his adenoidal drawl. "It's

right upstairs from my mother's apartment. They seem like a nice bunch of kids. Someone oughta tell their parents they're fixing to get their heads bashed in."

Wolf didn't say a word in reply to this—just stared hard at Minsky, who shifted in his chair a bit.

"It's nothing personal," the gangster protested. "Those kids down at the IWW are as brave as lions, and I'd give any of them a job in a minute if they asked for one."

"I think they have other goals in life," Wolf said with the hint of a sarcastic edge in his voice. It was only the very slightest of hints, but Sacha still held his breath with shock at the mere idea of someone speaking to Meyer Minsky in such a tone.

Minsky had clearly noticed it too, judging by the dangerous glint in his eye. "Now, Max. Don't despise me or my choices. I've always respected you, even when I disagreed with you. Even after you joined the *Inquisitors.*" Minsky's voice sank with utter disgust as he pronounced the despised word. "But you need to respect me back, or we won't be friends, even though I *do* like you so much."

"Don't get your hackles up," Wolf said mildly. "I wouldn't insult you for all the world. I just don't like to see you even thinking about working for Morgaunt."

"I'd call it working *with* him, not for him, Max. And I have to think about it. A man has to think about staying on good terms with Morgaunt if he wants to keep doing business in this town."

"Oh, Meyer," Wolf said in a voice too soft and sad to give offense, despite the hard words. "I never thought I'd see *you* afraid of any man."

"Not afraid. Just realistic. Don't underestimate me: I'll go against him if I have to. But he has the cops in his pocket *and* the papers *and* City Hall. And lately he's been muscling in on my territory too. It's not just me that sees it. The Hell's Kitchen Hexers, the boys down in Little Italy, we're all seeing the same thing. There's—well, there's another thing I need to talk to you about, but never mind that now. The point is, if I go against Morgaunt openly in this Pentacle strike situation, it'll be absolute war. And that's not a war I can win, not yet anyway. You ever heard of the Maccabees? Look 'em up sometime. There's a fine line between being brave and being crazy."

Wolf sat silent for a moment, looking far from happy with this answer. But then he shrugged and said, "Well, I don't expect you to commit suicide for the greater good, Meyer. You know I'm not that unreasonable. Especially since I haven't quite worked up the nerve to do it myself."

"You've come pretty close a time or two, though, if memory serves me right."

"That was different. When a man drags women and children into trouble, he's got an obligation to stand up for them."

"Speaking of which, how is Shen Yunying doing these days? Damn fine-looking woman. There was a time when I even thought you two might—"

"Yes, well, that's all over now," Wolf said hastily, as if he were eager to avoid any further mention of Shen.

Sacha glanced sideways at Lily—and sure enough, she practically looked like she was going to explode. She had a serious case of hero worship for their martial arts instructor, Shen Yunying, who she was convinced was some sort of modern-day female version of the wandering Shaolin Monks of Imperial China. And she also had a lot of silly ideas about Shen and Inquisitor Wolf—ideas Sacha usually did his best to squash. He could tell that Lily was going to be all but irrepressible after this juicy tidbit.

"Actually," Wolf went on, "I'm not even here to see you today. I came to talk to Mr.—er—ahem." He turned to Kid Klezmer.

"Murray Gellman," the Kid said. "And what do you need to talk to me about?"

"Naftali Asher, actually."

"What about him?" Gellman asked, his handsome face darkening.

"He's dead," Wolf said baldly.

Gellman sprang to his feet, his eyes wild and the blood draining from his face.

"Sit down," Minsky said quietly.

"No," Gellman said. "Why should I involve anyone else in my misfortunes? It'll be better if I just go quietly."

"It'll be better," Minsky said in a voice that brooked no disobedience, "if you just do what your friends tell you to do."

Gellman sat down so quickly that Sacha suspected his knees had given out in terror. But it hardly mattered; Wolf's attention had already turned back to Minsky.

"You knew Naftali Asher was dead before I ever got here, didn't you?" he asked the gangster—and his question sounded dangerously close to an accusation.

"You think something like *that* could happen without my knowing about it before the cops do?"

"You could have told me!"

"Why should I have? I assumed you were here about the Pentacle strike. Since when did the Inquisitors ever care about a dead Jew or two?"

Wolf didn't try to argue the point—wisely, Sacha thought, since judging by what he had seen of the NYPD Inquisitors Division since his apprenticeship started, the best defense Wolf could have come up with was that they didn't care two straws about *any* poor people, Jew or gentile.

Meanwhile, Kid Klezmer seemed to have screwed up his nerve to defy Minsky. He stood up again and thrust his hands out to Wolf, offering them up to be handcuffed. "You might as well just throw me in the Tombs and have done with it. I'm an innocent man, as God is my witness. But no one will ever believe it. And if Naftali Asher's dead by magic, there isn't a lawyer in town who can save me from the electric chair."

"But . . . why?"

"Because I swore in front of our entire shtetl back in Russia that I would get Naftali Asher for stealing my girl—even if I had to follow him all the way to America to do it."

Wolf blinked owlishly at Gellman for a moment. Then he took off his spectacles and searched for a clean spot on his tie that he could wipe them on. Not finding one, he pulled out his shirttail and used that. And then he stood blinking at Gellman with his shirt hanging out and his tie askew. "Do you think I could get a cup of coffee?" he asked. "This looks like it's going to take a while."

"Yeah, me too," Kid Klezmer said. He sounded much more cheerful suddenly. "And maybe with a splash of slivovitz. It's a thirsty story. By the way, is it okay if Meyer stays to listen?"

"Do I have a choice?" Wolf asked ruefully.

Meyer just smiled and puffed at his cigar. "I wouldn't miss this for all the borscht in Bohemia," he said in a voice as silky smooth as the cloth of his spell-fitted three-piece suit.

"So," Kid Klezmer began, when the coffee had been served and the waiters were gone, "I was born in a small shtetl near Zhitomer, the oldest son of the oldest son of the oldest son of a famed family of *klezmorin.* From the time I was born until I was eighteen years old, my life was perfect. I played my music. I studied Torah. I grew up, and I fell in love with our rabbi's youngest daughter. And I mean real love, like in the storybooks. The kind of love kids today don't know a thing about."

"Don't let the schmaltz get in your eyes," Sacha muttered.

"Shh!" Lily hissed back at him. "I think it's romantic."

Sacha made a rude noise—but he was careful to make it quietly enough that none of the grownups heard him.

"Life was perfect," Gellman went on. "Until Naftali Asher came to town. And then everything started to go wrong for me. Boils, rashes, split reeds . . . you name it! But the worst was what happened to poor Rivka!"

"She fell in love with Asher?" Wolf guessed.

"As if!" Kid Klezmer cried. "Asher was nothing back then! Nothing as a man, and less than nothing as a klezmer player! How poor Rivka ever could have left me for such a *nudnik*—well, it's obvious, isn't it? He cast a hate spell on her!"

"I've never heard of a hate spell!" Lily exclaimed.

"And I hope a nice young lady like you never will," Gellman told her. "It's bad enough to cast a love spell on an innocent girl instead of letting the best man win! But a hate spell—ah, may you never know the misery *that* kind of magic can make! Anyway, there was no help for it. Asher may have been a dud as a klezmer player, but when it came to magic, he was a genius. The next thing I knew, Rivka was standing under the *huppa* with Asher. And I—well, I got drunk and crashed the wedding. And you know the rest."

Wolf drew his breath to speak, but he was interrupted by a snort loud enough to make Sacha wonder if someone had snuck a carthorse into the room with them. But it wasn't a horse. It was Dopey Benny, who was blowing his nose and weeping great, glistening tears. "Id's eduff to break a fellow's heart," he sobbed in the adenoidal tones that every kid on the Lower East Side knew how to imitate by the time they were old enough to see over the counter of the Essex Street Candy Store. "Excudze me . . . I gotta blow by dose again."

Benny blew his nose like a bugler sounding a trumpet. Even Minsky cringed at the noise—and then he cast a sharp look around the room, as if to say, *You wanna make fun of my right-hand guy and personal starker, you better have the guts to do it to my face.*

"So then what happened?" Lily asked the Kid.

"Nothing," he said sadly. "She married him. And they emigrated to America."

"And you followed them," Wolf prompted. "Just like you said you would."

"I didn't *follow* them!" Gellman sounded exasperated, as if he was tired of explaining himself. "There happens to be this little thing going on in Russia at the moment called pogroms. And not to make light of the larger tragedy or anything, but it's hard to make a living playing klezmer when the Cossacks keep burning down your venues!"

"So you came here looking for work," Wolf said in a placating tone. "That's reasonable enough. And what about Asher and Rivka?"

"Oh, Asher had the worst luck in America that a jilted lover could wish on a rival. I would have loved it—if he hadn't been dragging poor Rivka down with him. He gets to Ellis Island, and what do you think they do? They fumigate his clarinet! Have you ever heard of such a thing? Anyway, that's the end of his klezmer plans. So he gets a job at Pentacle. Not that I blame him for that; he wasn't the first one to fall back on magic when he figured out that a poor man can't earn an honest living in New York. He works at Pentacle for two years, saving every penny to buy a new clarinet.

But when he finally gets the clarinet . . . well, great horn blowers are dime a dozen in this town, and Asher wasn't all that good in the first place. Until—until whatever happened happened." Kid Klezmer laughed nervously. "He used to tell some schmaltzy story about sharing a rear tenement room with some old Hasidic mystic and nursing him through his final illness. He claimed the Hasid taught him all his *nigun* before he gave up the ghost—you know, the holy songs the mystics sing. But it always sounded like a bowl of borscht to me." Kid Klezmer gave a bitter laugh. "Asher wasn't exactly the type to selflessly nurse a perfect stranger through his final illness."

"Well, maybe Rivka nursed him," Lily pointed out.

"Oh!" Kid Klezmer seemed never to have thought of this. "Maybe she did at that. Still, no one would ever believe Asher did it."

"But they believe he sold his soul to the devil," Wolf said.

Kid Klezmer gave him a sharp, almost frightened look. "Who told you that? Goldfaden? Does *he* believe it?"

Wolf shrugged.

"*I* believe it." Gellman's voice dropped to a nervous whisper. "Naftali Asher hexed the woman I loved and destroyed all my hope of happiness in this world. And then, to add insult to injury, he turned himself from a mediocre hack into the greatest klezmer player I've ever heard. But you know what? Even though he had everything I ever wanted in the world, I felt sorry for him. He made a bargain with *someone*—

man, devil, or magician. And whatever he got, he paid a price for it that I never would have paid." He shuddered. "At least I hope I wouldn't. I guess a man can't ever know what he'll sell until the devil waves a check in his face."

A long silence fell over the room when Gellman finished, as if his tale were so dark and strange that even the two hardened gangsters were struck dumb by it.

It was Meyer Minsky who finally broke the silence. "Well, that's that," he said, taking out a cigar as if to signal that the conversation was over, as far as he was concerned. "If you're going to arrest the Kid, you'd better do it now. I gotta go mind the store."

"I don't think I am going to arrest him," Wolf said slowly, talking over Gellman's head as if Minsky were only person whose word counted for anything. "If he tries to run, I'll have to arrest him, of course. But I'd rather not. It's not so easy to get a man out of the Tombs once you've put him in."

"You don't have to tell me that!" Minsky said feelingly. "I left two teeth down there!"

Dopey Benny didn't say anything—but he fingered his crooked nose and looked a little green around the gills. The Tombs was what most New Yorkers called the underground holding cells at the Police Department's main headquarters down on Mulberry Street, and their reputation was so bad that hardened criminals had been known to confess at the mere mention of the possibility that they might have to spend a night there.

"Anyway," Wolf said, turning back to Gellman, "don't do anything foolish. If you can manage that, I may be able to help you."

"Then you believe me?" Gellman asked with pathetic earnestness.

"I don't believe or disbelieve you. But there's no law against going to a wedding without an invitation, is there?"

"You're a *mensch,* Wolf," Meyer Minsky said as he cut his cigar with a dainty little pearl-handled pocket knife. "A real Jew. We oughta make you an honorary member of the tribe."

"I'll take that as a compliment."

"It's the best compliment there is," Meyer said with fierce pride. "And I wouldn't say it if I didn't mean it. So don't be a stranger. Drop by the store sometime."

"Maybe I will, if only to keep up with the all the news that's not fit to print."

"We give out free candy to cops, you know."

"Ah, but candy always tastes sweeter when you buy it for yourself."

Minsky lit his cigar and snuffed out the match between his thumb and finger. "Personally, I always think candy tastes sweeter when you steal it."

Wolf smiled and rose to leave. But then he sat back down and frowned at Minsky. "What was that other thing you wanted to tell me about, Meyer?"

"I'm not sure I do want to tell you," Minsky said, toying with the change in his pocket. "Maybe I thought better of it."

He glanced at Sacha and Lily. "Or maybe you should come down to the candy store so we can talk privately."

"Come on, Meyer, you know I can't do that."

Meyer flattened his lips into a frustrated line. He pulled a buffalo head nickel out of his pocket—one that legend said he'd taken off the body of the man who'd run Magic, Inc., before he took over. Minsky frowned at the nickel for a moment and then flipped it, throwing it high into the air and letting it fall on the table without even trying to catch it. The coin rolled down the polished wood, bumped into a half-empty seltzer bottle, and finally came to rest in front of Dopey Benny.

"It's tails, boss," Benny said morosely.

"I know," Minsky said without even looking at the coin. "I hate it when it does that. That son of a gun's been dead twelve years, and his damned nickel still has it in for me. I *hate* hexes that don't die with the hexer. There oughta be a law against 'em."

"What's got you so jumpy, Meyer?" Wolf asked.

Meyer sighed. He held out his left hand, and the buffalo head nickel slid along the table and landed in his open palm with a soft smack.

"Have you heard anything on the street about . . . well, I don't know what to call them. I'd call them hits if there was any hitting involved. But it's more like guys just dropping dead for no reason."

"Gangsters, you mean. Yes, I've heard something about that."

"Gyp Saminowsky died last week. And Bloody Martin O'Shea. And . . . well, there's a couple of others, but who cares about the names? The point is, someone's knocking off gangsters all over town and getting away with it. It's like New York's turned into a different city in the last few months. It used to be safe to walk the streets at night—for us, anyway. And now it's not."

"Who do you think is behind it?"

"I don't know. Or why would I be asking you? The thing is, a couple of my guys have been hit. And they both saw someone following them before they died."

"Did they get a look at his face?"

"No. One of them said he saw a shadowy figure that he could never quite get a real look at. 'The watcher in the shadows,' he called it. And the other one . . . the other one said he *did* see the guy, but what he said made no sense."

Wolf, so still in his chair that he was barely breathing, kept his eyes on Minsky's face. "What did he see?"

"He saw . . . a man made out of flies."

The two men stared at each other for a moment. Sacha couldn't tell if Minsky's words meant anything to Wolf or not. Finally Wolf shrugged and stood up. "I'll keep my ears open," he said.

"That's all I wanted, Max. Just keep a lookout. Better not say anything officially for now. And if you'll take an old friend's advice, stay out of this Pentacle mess too. It's going to be a bloodbath."

CHAPTER THREE

The Devil's Bargain

WHEN THEY FINALLY left the Café Metropole, the afternoon shadows were lengthening and rush hour was almost upon them. Normally—that is to say, when they had no pressing cases—Wolf would have chosen this moment to head back to the office and relinquish Lily and Sacha to the care of the Astral family chauffeur for the long ride home across the park. They took that ride almost every day because, though Lily had managed to defy her mother effectively enough to become Wolf's apprentice, she had yet to convince her that the sky wouldn't fall if her daughter ever rode public transportation.

Today, however, Wolf turned off the Bowery into the narrow, thronging streets of the Lower East Side. At first Sacha was afraid they were going to find Moishe Schlosky at the Industrial Witches of the World office—which would have meant braving the stairs of his very own tenement building in Lily Astral's company. But instead Wolf was following up

Goldfaden's half lead about Sam Schlosky's old apartment on Henry Street.

Pearl turned out to be all too right, however; they did manage to find a neighbor at the building who remembered the large family with the skinny redheaded son who'd turned into an IWW rabble-rouser. She pointed them to a building on the corner of Grand and Orchard. And someone at Grand and Orchard remembered that the Schloskys had moved away about a year and a half ago, and thought they'd taken one of the cheap second-floor apartments that fronted on the Allen Street elevated tracks. But the apartment at Allen Street was the end of the line. Allen Street was the heart of the Lower East Side's thriving red-light district, and apparently no one there paid enough attention to politics to even know what the IWW was.

At this point, Wolf gave up on finding Sam Schlosky and hurried the two apprentices north into the mostly German-Irish neighborhoods between Astral Place and Tompkins Square. This neighborhood had once been the center of New York high society. The original Astral mansion was there, as were the ancestral homes of half the old New York dynasties. But now all the rich New Yorkers had moved north toward Central Park, and the sedate colonial homes were broken up into disreputable boarding houses whose shiftless lodgers drifted in and out of the saloons and loitered on street corners.

It wasn't a neighborhood Sacha knew much about, except by reputation. For though the people who lived here were no poorer than people on Hester Street, they were still looked down on. They lived rootless, shiftless lives, cut off from the larger Jewish community and surrounded by Irish and German and Bohemian neighbors, who were, Sacha imagined, equally adrift and cut off from their fellow countrymen. And though Sacha's grandfather and Meyer Minsky probably didn't have anything like the same definition of a "real Jew," they would both have agreed that this neighborhood was just about the last place in New York to look for one.

"Where are we going now?" Lily asked—a little breathlessly, since she had to practically run in order to keep pace with Inquisitor Wolf's long strides.

"To see Naftali Asher's widow."

Sacha felt surprised—and a little dismayed—at the idea that Naftali and Rivka Asher had lived in this neighborhood. He thought of the way Gellman had described Rivka: a modest, quiet rabbi's daughter. Looking around at the stale beer halls and the slatternly women and slovenly men lounging on every street corner, Sacha couldn't imagine that any halfway decent husband would have brought such a girl to live in this place.

Still, he thought, people did strange things in New York. And Naftali Asher had obviously been a strange and difficult man. Perhaps he'd found comfort in the rootless anonymity of this drifter's neighborhood.

As they passed by Astral Square subway station, the piercing cry of a newsboy caught Sacha's ear. Had there been a familiar name in that cry, or had he just imagined it? He scanned the crowd and caught sight of a ragged newsie brandishing the evening edition of the *New York Sun* overhead.

"Murder at the Hippodrome!" the boy cried. "Read all about it!"

Wolf stopped short and turned to stare at the newsie, his gray eyes so piercing that Sacha wondered the boy didn't feel the force of his stare across fifteen feet of sidewalk.

"Murder at the Hippodrome!" he repeated. "A Vaudeville Love Triangle Gone Deadly! Read all about it!"

Wolf strode over to the boy and bought a copy of the paper, and the three of them retreated to the relative quiet of a side street to scan the headlines and see how bad the damage was. What they read was enough to make Sacha's stomach churn and Wolf's face grow pale with fury.

"A BLOODY TRAIL OF LUST AND REVENGE," blared the headline. And if the headline was bad, the article was worse:

> Inquisitors reported to the scene of a magical murder this afternoon, only to discover a bloody trail of lust and revenge leading from the bright lights of the Bowery to the muddy shtetls of Russia.

Sacha supposed he shouldn't have been surprised that the papers had already gotten hold of photographs of Kid Klezmer and the Klezmer King. They'd caught the Kid in a nightclub sharing a table with Meyer Minsky and Dopey Benny, and the caption under his photo read "The Jilted Lover Who Pals

Around with Gangsters." That was bad enough, but the caption under the Klezmer King's photo was even worse:

Did Naftali Asher Make a Deal with the Devil?

But worst of all was the third photo—not a publicity shot but a blurry picture of an old-fashioned Jewish wedding party. This photo was so blurry, and the bride so far away from the camera, that all Sacha could have said about her was that she was young and shy-looking. But the groom standing next to her was a younger and even skinnier version of the Klezmer King. And the caption below the photo read "The Shtetl Enchantress Who Bewitched Two Klezmer Stars."

The article told the same story Kid Klezmer had told them. But somehow it managed to make it all sound completely different. Instead of a young man in love who lost his temper and got over it, Kid Klezmer came across as a depraved libertine who consorted with gypsies and Satan-worshippers and had spent the last ten years plotting and scheming to destroy his rival. And instead of a great musician with rotten luck, the Klezmer King came across as a man so desperate for fame and money that he'd bragged about selling his soul for a song. In fact, the whole article made it seem as if the reason they'd all acted so crazy was simply because they were Jewish. It sounded like Jews in Russia lived in some kind of alternate reality where people were cutting deals with the devil every chance they got and flinging killing spells around like confetti at a ticker-tape parade. And it made it sound as if they'd brought all their Jewish black magic with them through Ellis Island and were just waiting for the Inquisitors to look the other way before breaking out in a wild magical crime spree.

The funny thing was, Sacha could almost swear he'd seen this story before. In fact, it was the same exact story the papers ran every time anyone got stabbed in Little Italy, where every bump on the head turned out to be a "desperate crime of passion" committed over a "black-eyed Madonna" who "drove men to insanity with her hot Sicilian love spells." Sacha had read those stories without thinking much about them, but suddenly it all sounded very different. And he couldn't help wondering how ordinary law-abiding Italians felt when they opened up their morning paper to read about yet another violent vendetta.

"Why do they tell such horrible stories?" Sacha asked.

"Because they sell newspapers," Wolf said wearily. "But what I'd like to know is how they got hold of *this* story so quickly."

"Hmph!" Lily snorted. "And I'd like to know who owns the *New York Sun* these days."

"Morgaunt owns it," Wolf said flatly. "He bought the *Sun* right after they broke that story about him and Rosie DiMaggio. They broke the only unbreakable rule in this town: Don't print a blessed word about J. P. Morgaunt without having his lawyers sign off on it before you go to press."

They got to the Ashers' apartment, only to find it dark and empty. They were about to turn away when they heard slow, shuffling footsteps coming up the stairs behind them. One look at Rivka Asher's face told Sacha that she already knew about her husband's death.

Wolf introduced himself, speaking in the gentle murmur that he always used when people were in real trouble.

"Ah," Rivka Asher said in strongly accented but clearly fluent English. "They said at the Hippodrome that you would need to speak to me."

"I'm afraid I have many questions," Wolf admitted, "none of them very pleasant. But there's no help for it."

"No, I suppose not." She sighed.

Her apartment key hung from a little silver chatelaine pinned to her shirtwaist—the sort of thing observant women wore on *Shabbes* to avoid carrying their keys when they went out. She unlocked the door and went in, gesturing to them to follow her. The front door opened directly into a cluttered little dining room, and Rivka sank into a chair and propped her head on her hands, leaving them to stand or sit wherever they chose. A pale glow of gaslight spilled in through the windows of the front room beyond, and Sacha could see the *Shabbes* candles and candlesticks lying on the table before her. There was a polishing cloth too, which looked like it had been cast down hastily before she'd last stood up from the table. She must have been preparing for *Shabbes* when the news of Asher's death came, he realized.

After a moment, she looked up and seemed to remember their presence. "Are you by any chance Jewish?" she asked Wolf in her softly accented voice.

"No."

"Then would you be so kind as to turn on the lights for me?"

Wolf looked a bit confused, but he found the switch and turned on the lights without comment.

Wolf and Lily sat down at the table then, but Sacha slipped into the kitchen and scrounged around in the cupboards until he'd found bread and cheese and a half-empty bottle of wine. He began to take the food out to Mrs. Asher—but then on second thought, he checked the cookstove and found that, though it had gone out, there was a full water kettle and a big pot of half-stewed *cholent* on the cooktop. So he rekindled the fire and stoked it back into a respectable blaze before he went back into the dining room.

Rivka was now telling Wolf her version of the same sad story Kid Klezmer had told them. Sacha handed her the bread and cheese, and she gulped it down in a way that made him sure she hadn't eaten since breakfast. He gave her the wine when she seemed ready for it.

"Gut Shabbes."

She looked up sharply. "But—are you?—you shouldn't have—not for me—"

"I'm already working," he told her. "And anyway, you need to eat, or you'll be ill."

She stared at him for a moment, but her brain seemed too overwhelmed to hang on to any single idea, and after a moment, she looked away and went on with her rambling story.

Rivka Asher was hardly the kind of woman Sacha would have pictured at the center of a celebrity love triangle. She must once have been pretty, though she was so worn and thin now that it was hard to tell. And she was so shy and mousy that he couldn't imagine any man really working himself up into a full-blooded passion for her.

Still, the tale she told was full of passion, and of magic too. And as Sacha listened to it, he began to feel as if the world outside the tenement were giving way to another world: one where dybbuks stalked the crooked shtetl streets, and Great Magic hung in the air, and God and the devil played dice for men's immortal souls.

As she talked, Sacha began to understand her tale in a way that he never would have been able to a year ago. Then he would have thought that Rivka Asher was mad or superstitious. But now he had seen enough of the ways that unscrupulous people could abuse magic to suspect that she had been the victim of an insidious but devastating crime. Her life had been torn out of its intended track. Her heart and mind had been twisted until there was little hope of setting them straight again. And, worst of all, the criminal who had violated her was her own husband.

"Do you really think he was murdered?" she asked Wolf, with a doglike devotion in her voice.

"I don't know yet. I *would* like to talk to Sam Schlosky, though. Do you know where he lives?"

"I'm afraid I don't. I don't know that Naftali ever went to his apartment to see him. You could always ask Sam's brother, of course."

"Moishe," Wolf said in a flat tone of voice.

"Yes. Moishe is easy to find."

"Too easy," Wolf sighed. "If I go to the IWW headquarters, every newspaper in town will know it by tomorrow morning, and Sam will be suspect number one by lunchtime."

"Well, I don't know what else I can say to help you," Mrs. Asher said. "Ah, wait. There is one thing I remember: Sam's aunt keeps geese."

"You mean, on the roof, in coops?" Wolf asked. He didn't seem to think this was much of a clue—and Sacha had to agree with him. So many poor people in New York kept poultry that practically every tenement rooftop on the Lower East Side hosted a village-worth of homemade coops.

"No, no," Mrs. Asher said. "*Hundreds* of geese. It's a huge business. She sells the feathers and I don't know what else all over town. Everybody knows her."

"Wait a minute," Sacha interrupted. "Are you talking about Mrs. Mogulesko?"

"Yes, that's her name!"

"The *goose lady? Moishe Schlosky is the goose lady's nephew?*" Sacha couldn't seem to get his mind around the idea.

"Yes," Mrs. Asher said. "Sam used to work for her during the day and then come work for Naftali at night. And he would miss work every now and then because he had to help move the geese to keep them hidden from the health inspectors. So . . . well . . ." She trailed off as if she had forgotten what she planned to say.

"Do you know where this Mrs. Mogulesko lives?" Wolf asked Sacha.

"No. No one does. She's—she's a wanted criminal.

The police spend more time chasing her than they spend chasing Meyer Minsky. Everyone still buys her feathers, of course. What else are they going to do if they want real goose down? But it's like the gypsies rolling into town when she shows up. There she is at the door, and the next thing you know, the feathers are flying and the feather beds are stuffed and then—*pfft!*—she's gone! They say she travels on the rooftops and has keys to every subbasement between the Bowery and the East River, and that Colonel Waring practically foams at the mouth every time anyone mentions her name around him." Colonel Waring was a notorious martinet and the top man in the sanitation department.

"And Moishe Schlosky's her *nephew?*"

"What do you care whose nephew Moishe Schlosky is?" Lily asked.

"Never mind about that," Sacha snapped, glad that the lights were too dim to show the embarrassed flush on his cheeks. "The point is, you're never going to find Mrs. Mogulesko. And if she's hiding Sam, then you're never going to find him either. That woman has been publicly flouting the New York City Public Health Department for twenty years, and I don't think she's ever going to be caught!"

Wolf cleared his throat. "What about old friends from Pentacle?" he asked. "Didn't Sam and Asher meet when they were both working at Pentacle?"

"Yes, but—"

"Was Asher involved with the IWW when he worked there?"

"Oh, no, I'm sure not. Naftali never cared about politics. Only his music mattered to him."

Suddenly Sacha felt desperate to get out of the dingy apartment. The way Rivka Asher talked about her husband had made his skin crawl from the beginning. But now . . . was that *magic* he saw playing faintly about her features when she spoke the name? Was this just the normal grief of a newly widowed wife? Or had Asher laid a hex on the poor woman that would shackle her to him even after death and condemn her to a hellish half life for the rest of her days?

"Was he involved with anyone else that you were worried about? Anyone . . . dangerous?"

"Of course not! Naftali would never have had anything to do with such people!" Yet even as she spoke, her voice wavered and doubt swept across her face like a shadow on the sun.

"Sam said something to him before he died that suggested he feared he was . . . entangled."

"With whom? I don't understand you."

"Sam mentioned a—a watcher in the shadows."

"Ah!" Rivka cried out. "Then I did not dream it!" Her face grew deathly pale, and she wavered in her chair so that Wolf leaped up to catch her in case she fainted entirely.

"Tell me!" Wolf demanded. "Who did Asher meet every night? Where did he go? What magic bound him?"

"I don't know! I don't know anything! I only suspect and fear!"

"Then tell me your fears," Wolf whispered.

"People said he sold his soul to the devil. And God help me, as his wife, I should not even listen to such evil rumors. But . . ."

"But you believed them."

"I did, God forgive me! We were poor when he was working at Pentacle, very poor. But I would give anything to go back to that time! The moment he told me about his new job, I knew—oh, how can I explain to you what a wife knows, what she hears in the silences between the words a husband speaks to her? He said he was going to be a great musician, that all our dreams were going to come true and we would never be hungry again. And when I asked him what he had given to gain such riches, he told me not to worry. 'They don't want my soul,' he told me. 'All they want is for me to sew a few shirts for them. And what could be the harm in that?'

"But I knew it was a devil's bargain. I knew it the first time I heard that terrible, beautiful, cursed music!" She was weeping openly now, and it took her a moment to gather her breath and keep speaking. "After he became famous, he turned into a different man. He was obsessed with his reviews, his fans, his critics, with everything and anything but the music itself. And it used to be only about the music for him. He loved his music. He loved it humbly and truly. And he loved me too. With all his faults, he loved me.

"But then came the new job that he would not tell me about, the one he went to at night, sneaking off like a thief who was ashamed to be seen by honest people. And then suddenly he was a success, a star, a celebrity. But still, he would go to this other job at night, in secret, after his concerts were over. I asked where he went, but he wouldn't tell me. I asked him to stop, but he grew furious. He told me it was none of my business—me, his own wife, can you imagine?—and I'd better keep out of it or I'd be sorry. And I did keep out of it . . . well, mostly. One night I waited outside the theater and followed him to see where he was going. He met someone underneath the Elevated tracks on the Bowery. I never got a good look at the other person, if it even was a person. It stood in the shadows. It seemed to be a creature made of shadows. But I heard its voice. It was the most terrifying thing I've ever heard in my life."

Rivka Asher looked over her shoulder, as if she imagined that the creature might be hidden in the shadows of the little room that the faint lamplight didn't penetrate.

"They were fighting," she whispered. "Naftali sounded angry and terrified. I've never heard him speak so. He was saying that he was finished, that he wouldn't do it anymore and they must find a replacement—"

"A replacement for what?" Wolf asked, leaning forward tensely. "Can you remember his exact words?"

"I remember them all," Rivka said. "If I lived a thousand years I would still be hearing those words and wondering what I could have done to save him. He said, 'Tell your boss I won't do it anymore. I have to live here—it's not just about money

to me. And I can't trust you to keep the secret forever, can I? So find someone else to do your dirty work!'"

"And then what?" Wolf asked.

"Then the shadow spoke. If you can call it speaking. It was just a whisper, so quiet that I couldn't make the words out. But it was still horrible. It made your head hurt just to hear it."

"And you heard what it said?"

"No. But Naftali did. And whatever the answer was, he didn't like it."

"And then?"

"Then he said, 'I don't care what he does to me.' And then—then he laughed. A horrible laugh. 'Some things are worse than death,' he told the watcher. 'You ought to know that better than anyone!' And that was that all. Naftali walked off, and I had to leave to make sure I got home before he did."

"But you never got a look at the man in the shadows."

"No."

"Can you tell me anything else about him? Anything at all? Even what his voice sounded like?"

Rivka shuddered and passed a hand over her brow as if it were a physical pain to remember the sound. "It sounded like the Baal Zaabeb."

Sacha gasped.

"Beelzebub," Wolf said. "The devil."

"That's just a name," Rivka said with a wave of her frail

hand. "Do you know what Baal Zaabeb means? I mean, what those words mean in Hebrew?"

Wolf shook his head.

"It means 'the Lord of the Flies.' And that is exactly what I heard: a voice that sounded like the buzzing of a thousand flies."

CHAPTER FOUR

Trouble on Hester Street

BY THE TIME they left Rivka Asher's apartment, dusk had deepened into night and it was long past time that both the apprentices should have been home. Still, Wolf hesitated in the building's dingy lobby. "I don't like to put the two of you in a cab this late, but I really think I ought to try to find Sam Schlosky before—before anyone else does."

Lily and Sacha glanced at each other. Wolf had just managed to keep himself from saying that he needed to find Sam before Rivka's Lord of the Flies found him, but they were all thinking of the whispering figure she had seen under the elevated tracks—and of the uncanny similarity between it and Meyer Minsky's watcher in the shadows.

"You really don't know where that goose woman lives?" Wolf asked Sacha.

"No. But if you really want to find her, the best person to ask is Meyer Minsky. At least since you two are such—er—whatever."

"That's probably as good a name for it as any other," Wolf said with a sly grin.

"So ask him. He could round up every goose in Manhattan before we could even figure out where Sam's parents live now."

Wolf looked blank.

"Uh . . . kosher poultry?" Sacha prompted. "Litvaks?"

Now Wolf and Lily were both staring at him like he was speaking a foreign language.

"Okay, all the big Jewish gangsters either come from Latvia or Galitzia. Ever since anyone can remember, the Galitzians ran the numbers rackets, and the Litvaks—that's Minsky and Magic, Inc.—ran the kosher poultry business."

"I take it there's big money in kosher poultry?" Wolf asked, with a bemused look on his face.

"Well, I don't know about that. But right around the time Minsky took over Magic, Inc., the Litvaks took over the numbers runners too."

"And what happened to the Galitzians?" Lily asked.

Sacha grinned wickedly. "We don't talk about that."

Wolf laughed, but his narrow face soon grew solemn again. "All right," he said. "I'll ask Meyer. And in the meantime someone should go talk to Moishe Schlosky, too. But if I go down to the IWW offices and the papers get hold of it, Moishe's going to be declared the main suspect and Commissioner Keegan's going to be howling for me to arrest him."

Sacha cleared his throat. It seemed like there was an obvious solution to Wolf's problem, even if it wasn't one he particularly wanted to mention in front of Lily Astral. "Well," he said reluctantly, "I could always go talk to Moishe."

Lily and Wolf both stared at him—but with very different expressions on their faces. Lily looked astounded. Wolf looked—well, Sacha couldn't exactly read his expression, except to say that it wasn't comfortable.

"No one would notice *me* walking through that neighborhood. So I could just go over and tell him—well, what *should* I tell him?"

"I don't want to put you in the position of—" Wolf broke off and chewed his lip for a moment. "Well, just tell him to keep his head down and not make trouble at Pentacle until this blows over. And tell him that Sam will be much better off if he comes in on his own. Especially now that it's been splashed all over the papers. Just don't promise Moishe anything stupid, okay?"

"Like what?"

Wolf frowned at Sacha over the top of his spectacles. "Like that I can protect him."

"Is it really that bad?" Lily asked, her eyes wide and horrified.

"Yes."

"But we've only just begun to investigate! We don't even know that Asher was actually murdered!"

"Yes, we do," Wolf said quietly. "Naftali Asher died just after three o'clock. And the *Sun*'s evening edition goes to press at two thirty. Of course they can always hold the presses when they know there's a big headline coming in that they'll want to cover. But they still have to know it's coming. And there was a lot of research behind that article—photos, life stories. Someone must have had time to find all that."

"But how could anyone in his right mind take such a risk?" Lily protested. "Wouldn't they know we'd see the story and go straight to the paper to find out who gave them the information? And then *that* person would look as guilty as anything!"

"So one would imagine," Wolf said mildly.

"You're telling us the whole case is rotten," Sacha said. "You think Asher was murdered by someone who isn't afraid enough of the police to even care if he looks guilty."

He didn't have to say the name; he was sure Wolf had been thinking of Morgaunt ever since the moment they'd heard that Asher and Sam had met at Pentacle. No magical crime was just a crime to Wolf. No case was just a case. They were all part of the One Big Case: the case against Wall Street Wizard J. P. Morgaunt. Wolf's quixotic struggle against Morgaunt was the guiding light of his life—as far as Sacha could tell, it *was* his life. And it was a struggle that could only end in one of two ways: with Morgaunt in prison or Wolf in the morgue.

Wolf shrugged and began buttoning up his coat. "Oh, well. That's as it may be. But whatever mess we're going to be landed in tomorrow morning, right now I need to get you two safely home before your mothers come looking for me."

"Oh, I'll walk," Sacha said quickly.

"Is that safe?" Wolf asked.

"Why not? It's only a few blocks."

Wolf gave Sacha a pointed look, but all he said was, "I'd like to talk to you a bit anyway. Why don't you ride up to Lily's house and then we can have a chat while I take you home?"

Lily was obviously consumed with curiosity, and Sacha was going to have to come up with something to tell her by Monday. But after all, it wasn't nearly as bad as having Wolf expose his secret right then and there. So he supposed he ought to be grateful.

"Shen's told me about this ridiculous masquerade," Wolf said as soon as the door had closed behind Lily and the cab had driven on. "I really would have thought that woman had better sense than to play along with such foolishness."

"It's not foolishness! I couldn't go to work with Lily every day knowing that she knew how poor I was! I couldn't bear it. I'd quit first."

"I don't think you're fair to her, Sacha. She's not the kind of girl to despise a man for being poor. She wouldn't look down on you."

"No, she'd feel *sorry* for me."

Wolf's eyes widened in surprise, and he stared at Sacha for a moment. "I see," he said finally. "Well, I won't give your secret away. But I do think Shen ought to have tried a little harder to talk some sense into you." He snorted. "I hope you know the Inquisitors Division just ran up a whopping cab bill to keep your little secret."

"I'm sorry!" Sacha said earnestly. "I—I could pay it back."

"With what?" Wolf asked. And he was right, of course; that cab ride had probably swallowed up a week of Sacha's wages.

"Don't look so horrified," Wolf said. "And you *can* make it up to me by running upstairs as soon as you get home and trying to talk to Moishe Schlosky tonight instead of tomorrow morning."

Sacha thought of the watcher in the shadows and shuddered slightly. "I was already planning to do that."

"Good boy," Wolf said approvingly. And then he rapped smartly on the door of the cab until the driver pulled to the curb, jumped down, paid the fare all the way to Hester Street, and stalked off in a swirl of muddy coattails.

Sacha looked around curiously as the cab drove on, wondering where Wolf was going. But they were just south of Grand Central Station, in a nondescript region of shops and offices that formed a sort of crossroads between the Upper East Side, the Hotel District, and the Tenderloin. Most likely Wolf didn't live anywhere near here and had just gotten out in the hopes of finding Meyer Minsky at one of the semi-legal high-roller clubs in the Tenderloin. And yet it suddenly struck Sacha as odd that he had worked with Wolf for months without having the faintest idea where he lived. Other than the fact that he was in love with Shen Yunying—which was a mystery in itself—Wolf seemed to have a total blank where most people had a personal life.

When Sacha finally reached Hester Street, he ran past his own apartment, taking the stairs two at a time, and straight up to the sixth-floor headquarters of the Industrial Witches of the World. But a quick look around told him Moishe wasn't there, so he sighed and trudged back down the stairs, thinking he would talk to Moishe tomorrow.

It was very late indeed by now—so late that the *Shabbes* candles had burned low and the meal was long over. The two families who shared the apartment were still mostly gathered in the front room, which doubled as the Kesslers' kitchen and parlor. Their tenants, Mr. and Mrs. Lehrer, always shared the Sabbath meal—and of course the little family sweatshop that the Lehrers ran out of the apartment's back room would lie still and silent until after sunset on Saturday. But tonight Sacha's father and grandfather had retreated to the relative quiet of the back room and were sitting together on a pile of half-finished suits reading tomorrow's Torah portion.

Friday nights were the only time Sacha ever saw his father acting like a rabbi's son. The rest of the time, Mr. Kessler worked twelve hours a day at the East Side docks and came home far too exhausted to do anything but glance at the evening papers and stumble into bed. But on Friday nights, he made an effort. Everyone made an effort on Fridays—even Uncle Mordechai, who came home on time for dinner and stayed until the last possible moment before he had to be off to the theater. That said, there were strict limits to Mordechai's sense of family duty; the one time Mr. Kessler had tried to convince his younger brother to humor their father by reading Torah on Friday nights, Mordechai had declared that he would rather paint his face like a savage and dance around a bonfire—much rather!

Rabbi Kessler and Sacha's father both glanced up when Sacha came in—and they both looked so glad to see him that it only made him feel more guilty for being late. "I'll just grab a quick bite and come back in here," he muttered as he headed toward the kitchen.

"Nonsense!" Grandpa Kessler said. "You're a growing boy. You need your food. You can sit with me tomorrow afternoon after synagogue instead. I've been wanting to have a serious talk with you about something, and that Inquisitor of yours has been running you so ragged lately that I've started to wonder if you even live here anymore."

Sacha tried to act cheerful about the prospect of a serious talk with his grandfather, but he must not have done a very good job of it, because his grandfather burst out laughing at the look on his face.

"Don't worry. I'm not going to scold you for missing *Shabbes* again. Your mother, on the other hand, seems to think that the electric chair is too good for young men who let her Friday-night chicken get cold!"

Sacha groaned and went into the kitchen, where his

mother was still sitting around the table with Mrs. Lehrer, Uncle Mordechai, and Bekah. Mordechai was picking the last scrap of meat off a chicken wing and casting hungry looks at one of Mrs. Kessler's majestic honey cakes. And Sacha's mother and sister were doing what all Kesslers did best: arguing.

Mrs. Kessler had gone to the stove and started serving out a heaping plate for Sacha as soon as she'd heard him come in. She set it at his place before the seat of his pants even hit the chair and then passed the challah—all while stalwartly holding her ground in the raging battle.

"Strike, shmike!" she said as she poured Sacha's tea. "You forget this political nonsense and stick to your studies, young lady! Go ahead and eat, Sachele. I saved you the back fat!"

"Well, actually, Mama," Bekah replied, in a reasonable tone that Sacha knew from long experience was perfectly calculated to drive their mother up the wall, "the strike will give me a lot more time to study."

"Allow me to point out that sarcasm is not a quality *nice* men consider attractive in a wife!"

"Oh, Mama," Bekah said. "We're not in Russia anymore! American boys expect girls to have brains!"

"And what did your father think I had in my head when he married me? Matzo meal?"

"He wasn't thinking about your head," Uncle Mordechai teased. "His mind was entirely occupied with your other charms!"

Sacha's mother crossed her arms over her chest and smirked at her brother-in-law. "I'm not one of those theater floozies you have to flatter into cooking for you, Mordechai. You're family, remember? I *have* to feed you."

"And far be it from me to deprive you of the satisfaction of doing your duty!" Mordechai proclaimed. "In the words of the immortal bard, 'They also serve who only sit and eat!'"

"Stop flirting with my wife!" Sacha's father called from the next room. "What'll happen when you abandon her and she only has me to cook for? Oh, and by the way, that's Milton you're mangling, not Shakespeare."

"Don't grow up to be a know-it-all like my brother," Mordechai told Sacha in a piercing stage whisper.

"And don't grow up to be a mooch like *my* brother!" Mr. Kessler retorted.

As soon as the laughter had died down, Sacha's mother circled back to her original argument with Bekah. "All I'm saying," she insisted, "is that respectable girls shouldn't flaunt themselves on the streets, giving speeches and getting arrested. It's a *shande far di goyim,* it is!"

"I don't see how it's a *shande* to stand up for my rights," Bekah said. "When the strike starts, I intend to be there. Grown women with home responsibilities might have an excuse for staying on the sidelines. But any single girl who won't stand up to those bullies is a yellow-bellied dog—and I'd tell her so to her face, even if she weighed two hundred pounds and had eight big brothers!"

"Oh, great," Sacha muttered. "Then I'd get to fight the

brothers. And in case you haven't noticed, I *don't* weigh two hundred pounds!"

"So eat something already!" his mother cried, piling yet more food onto his plate. More food was Ruthie Kessler's answer to every one of life's little emergencies. Her daughter's pleasingly plump figure and her husband's five foot ten of solid workingman's muscle were her two proudest accomplishments in life, while Sacha's ability to swallow acres of potato *kugel* without putting any fat on his slender frame was a never-ending source of maternal humiliation.

"Mama," Sacha asked, suddenly struck by an awful thought, "what are you going to do when the strike starts?"

"Mind my own business and keep going to work as usual. Tell your father his tea's ready."

"Pops," Sacha called without getting up, "tea's ready."

"You can't go to work during a strike," Bekah told their mother in a long-suffering voice. "That's what a strike is, Mama. No one goes to work."

"That shows how much you know, little miss too-intellectual-to-listen-to-her-mother-and-marry-a-dentist!"

"Who's marrying a dentist?" Sacha's father asked as he came in from the back room with Grandpa Kessler leaning on his arm and got the old man settled back at his normal place in the big feather bed.

"No one, more's the pity!" Sacha's mother snapped. "How many times do I have to ask you to talk some sense into that girl?"

"What kind of sense?" Sacha's father asked slyly. "The

kind you showed when you married a penniless student who couldn't even put a roof over your head?"

"That was different," she said primly. "We were in love. And you can take your hand off my waist and stop making cow eyes at me, Danny Kessler. As if *love* hasn't gotten me into enough trouble already!"

But she wasn't fooling anyone—even before she ruffled her husband's hair and shoveled three normal slices' worth of cake onto his plate.

"So," Sacha's father said, tucking into his cake, "what desperate crimes were you so busy fighting today that you couldn't make it home for Shabbes?"

Sacha cringed. "I know, I know—" he began, only to have his father interrupt him with a gentle smile.

"Then you know that I have to give you a hard time about it, even though we both know it wasn't your fault. And *I* know that you'll try harder to be on time next week. There! The lecture's over. Was that so painful?"

"No," Sacha admitted sheepishly. And then he told them about the death of the Klezmer King and the crazy scene at the Hippodrome.

To his surprise, Mo Lehrer turned out to be an unexpected fount of klezmer knowledge—and a die-hard fan of the Klezmer King. "Can you imagine?" he asked the room at large. "The greatest klezmer genius of our age lighting himself up like a Christmas tree in order to sell tickets?"

"Genius, my big toe!" Mrs. Kessler scoffed. "You know what his playing always sounded like to me? A cat who fell in a rain barrel and was howling to get hauled out again! And the man's pride was beyond ridiculous! Refusing to play weddings and insulting people on the street as if anyone who didn't buy a ticket to see him was some kind of beetle-browed philistine! If you ask me, Kid Klezmer's five times better than cranky old Asher ever was!"

"Now, Ruthie, you know that's not fair!" Mo protested. "I won't say a word against Kid Klezmer's playing—though the company he keeps is another matter. But Naftali Asher was more than an ordinary klezmer player. His music expressed the existential tragedy of exile. It came from the depths of the Jewish soul; it was the highest expression of central tenets of our faith. He was a genius, a visionary! Those divine songs—"

"Nonsense!" Mrs. Kessler replied. "Who do you think he was, Gustav Mahler? He was a run-of-the-mill klezmer player who decided to put on airs and act like he was too good to play weddings. *Kid* Klezmer on the other hand—"

"Should *definitely* not be playing any weddings! At least not unless the girl's safely married *before* they let him in the building!"

"Well, if that isn't the pot calling the kettle black!"

And meanwhile, Bekah and Uncle Mordechai were going at it over the Pentacle strike like poker and tongs.

"But that's exactly my point!" Mordechai was saying with the passionate enthusiasm that his older brother was always saying would have stood him in good stead in the world if he'd ever applied it to anything useful. "The Industrial Witches of the World just can't understand that they'll never solve anything by negotiating with the anti-Wiccanist oligarchy. It's revolution we need, I tell you! A true Wiccanist utopia is the only hope of freedom for the huddled magical masses yearning to be free—"

"And in the meantime we should do nothing?" Bekah asked with mock incredulity. "Why? Because if your huddled magical masses aren't actually *starving,* they'll be less likely to go along with whatever harebrained schemes you and your friends dream up next at the Café Metropole? Honestly, Uncle Mordechai, just because *you* can't think about more than one thing at a time doesn't mean no one else can!"

"So why shouldn't Naftali Asher play at his neighbors' weddings?" Rabbi Kessler asked, startling Sacha. "Not that he was the most upbeat guy I've ever heard blow a *hora,* but still . . . playing at weddings is what klezmer is *for.* And a pious Jew puts family at the center of life. There's something . . . *un-Jewish* about this whole idea of turning klezmer into concert music."

Mo Lehrer looked confused and bewildered—not an uncommon state of affairs, since Mo was not even remotely in the Kessler league in terms of arguing talent. "Wait a minute," he said, turning to Rabbi Kessler with a sad and betrayed look on his face. "You're *agreeing* with her?"

"Of course not," Sacha's grandfather quipped without skipping a beat. "She's my daughter-in-law. I never agree with her, even if I have to change my mind to not do it!"

Sacha laughed so hard at this that he snorted up a lungful of tea and his father had to pound him on the back until he coughed it up.

"Look on the bright side," Danny Kessler said when Sacha had his breath back. "If the strike happens and your mother and sister lose their jobs, maybe Goldfaden'll hire your grandfather at the Hippodrome."

The idea of Rabbi Kessler doing a vaudeville comedy act was so ridiculous—and yet at the same time so strangely plausible—that Sacha choked on his tea all over again.

"The thing I can't believe," Mo was saying when Sacha recovered, "is that the police haven't dragged Kid Klezmer into the investigation already. Talk about a *shande far di goyim*! Hanging out with gangsters and hired killers—"

"I've known Meyer Minsky's mother for years!" Mrs. Kessler insisted. "And he's a nice boy, no matter what anyone says. So don't talk to me about hired killers!"

Sacha swallowed and started to explain about Wolf's trip to see Minsky at the Café Metropole.

"Too late," Mordechai cried. "I already told them *all* about it!"

"All about *what?*" Sacha asked in a perfectly calm tone that made him feel that the ensuing gale of laughter was thoroughly unreasonable.

"Oh," Mordechai said blithely, "you, me . . . the fair Miss Astral."

"In other words," Bekah told him, "you're never going to live this down."

CHAPTER FIVE

A Soul Like Clear Water

THE NEXT MORNING, Sacha woke up to the comforting Sabbath ritual of walking to synagogue and walking back home again for a long, rich, lazy lunch. This was Rabbi Kessler's busiest day of the week, of course—and one that taxed his waning strength to its limit—so everyone waited on him hand and foot. But he seemed to take a special pleasure in having Sacha serve him.

In fact, Sacha was almost beginning to feel that it was a perverse pleasure. The old man had practically made a habit out of forgetting his prayer shawl and *tefillin* when he went to synagogue and making Sacha run back to fetch them. For months, Sacha had been telling himself it was just a coincidence, but lately he was starting to wonder. Could his grandfather possibly know about the terrible thing Sacha had done with them last summer?

He had known even as he was summoning his dybbuk that it was the worst thing he'd ever done in his life. Indeed, he'd spent the week before Yom Kippur last year half believing that God would strike his name from the book of life for such a crime. Yom Kippur had come and gone, and he was still alive. Yet week after week, when his grandfather forgot his prayer shawl, or asked for help with his *tefillin,* or just looked at Sacha with his quick, bright birdlike eyes, Sacha felt certain that the old man could see how ashamed and miserable he felt.

He had examined the prayer shawl and phylacteries more than once for any sign of damage. There was nothing that he could see. But he had a nasty feeling that he must have contaminated them in some invisible way, so that all his grandfather's prayers were as nothing—blown away like dead leaves before the wind.

"Put my prayer shawl away, would you?" his grandfather said as soon as the rest of the family had gone out on their Saturday afternoon walk and the two of them were alone together. "It's right there."

Sacha started guiltily. He looked around and saw that the prayer shawl was hanging over the bedstead. What on earth was it doing there? It wasn't like Rabbi Kessler to be careless with it. Had the old man discovered Sacha's crime after all? And if so, how could he still be speaking to him—let alone smiling and joking with him?

He picked the prayer shawl up and began to fold it hurriedly, eager to get it safely into the drawer and out of sight for another week.

"No, no, not like that!" Rabbi Kessler said. "What do

you think you're doing, crumpling up a hot dog wrapper to throw it in the garbage?"

Sacha sighed and refolded it more carefully.

"That's better," his grandfather said approvingly. But when Sacha started to get up to place it in the special drawer next to the Elijah cup and the other small family treasures, his grandfather put out a hand to stop him.

"That's a funny Torah portion we read this morning," the old man said after a moment.

"Oh? How so?"

"Well, what was it about? In its essence, I mean—not on the surface."

"Oh, Grandpa, you know I'm no good at this! Don't you remember what a struggle it was just to get me through my *bar mitzvah*?"

"Nonsense. You're a late bloomer, that's all."

"Well . . . I guess it was about forgiveness."

"Yes! Exactly! It's really the sort of thing you'd expect to be reading before Yom Kippur, isn't it? And yet here we are at the dog-end of winter, starting to think about spring cleaning and Passover. It makes me think I need to talk more about forgiveness this Passover."

"I wouldn't think there was much forgiveness to talk about in a holiday that celebrates God smiting our enemies with boils and frogs," Sacha said.

"Ah, but there is! And the older you get, the more you'll see it. Forgiveness is at the heart of our faith. Christians believe their god can wash away men's sins. But we believe that God can only forgive sins against Himself. When we sin against another person, we must make peace with the person we have wronged before we can hope to stand right with God again. We are all our brother's keeper, you see. Our immortal souls are in one another's hands—for who can go through this world without needing to forgive and be forgiven? Hey, listen . . . get me a cup of water, will you?"

Sacha crossed through the slanting mid-afternoon sunlight that filled the little kitchen to scoop a glass of water out of the bucket that his mother always kept covered with a clean cheesecloth in the corner behind the stove.

Grandpa Kessler muttered the appropriate prayer and drank deeply. "Ah!" he sighed as he set the glass back on the table. "Is there anything more satisfying than a glass of water when you're thirsty? What was I saying just now?"

Sacha felt a brief twinge of hope that his grandfather might have forgotten what they were talking about, but he should have known better.

"Oh, right. Forgiveness. The rabbis of old were so convinced of the power of forgiveness—freely asked for and willingly offered—that when anyone did them a wrong, they would find excuses to be near that person, do little things to remind him of his crime, not to make him feel guilty but to give him a chance to confess and ask for forgiveness." Rabbi Kessler smiled ruefully. "I, unfortunately, am not as patient as the rabbis of old. I'm getting tired of remembering to forget my *tefillin* every week. And I'm getting even more tired of having my only grandson act like someone died every time he has to spend half an hour alone with me. So I'm just going to ask you now: what spell did you work when you stole my *tefillin* and my hidden books last summer?"

Sacha's hands went numb, and he felt the ancient cloth of the prayer shawl sliding through his fingers. Rabbi Kessler caught it before it hit the floor, and they sat like that for a moment, both leaning forward, their hands on the prayer shawl and their faces no more than a handbreadth away from each other.

"Don't lie to me," his grandfather said softly. "There's nothing you could have done that I won't forgive you for. But if you lie to me now, you'll break an old man's heart."

So Sacha took a deep, shaky breath and told him everything. He told him how he had summoned the dybbuk to his grandfather's little *shul* on Canal Street because he was furious at Lily and desperate to prove that it wasn't *his* dybbuk after all. He told him how he had fought the creature—and how it had seemed to become stronger and more solid with every minute he struggled against it. He told him about Morgaunt's plot to frame him for Edison's murder, and about how the dybbuk had killed Antonio's father and almost destroyed Antonio himself when he tried to avenge his father's death.

Rabbi Kessler seemed to sink under the weight of the horrible tale. "This is very bad," he said when Sacha was finally done. "This creature has hurt many people, and I fear will hurt many more. And you . . . you've made some terrible mistakes. But you didn't summon it, Sacha. All you did when you stole my books and my *tefillin* was let the creature know where you were." He shuddered. "It was Morgaunt who committed the unforgivable sin. And yet perhaps, after all, it is not unforgivable. You are the only one who can say. Remember what I said about holding one another's souls in our hands?"

"As if Morgaunt would ever come to *me* for forgiveness!"

"Stranger things have happened, my child."

"But how could Morgaunt have had the power to summon it?" Sacha said, brushing aside his grandfather's talk of forgiveness. "He's no Kabbalist."

"You don't have to understand fire to burn a house down! And that's all Morgaunt is: a child, playing with matches. Men like him have the greatest power in the world—the power of greed and ignorance."

"But still," Sacha said, unable to quite give up hope. "Maybe the dybbuk *isn't* a real dybbuk. Or . . . or maybe Antonio killed it."

"No, child, I'm afraid your shadow is real enough. And for it to have taken your shape so clearly—to have become a sort of doppelgänger—it must have been very, very close to possessing you entirely. And once a dybbuk has come that close to possessing a man, it never leaves him. I fear that mastering this creature will be the great work of your life. And though such struggles make for some of the profound lessons in the lives of the Kabbalists, I would not wish one on any man."

Sacha stared at his grandfather in mute despair. The old

man sat silent for several minutes, then shook his head and laughed bitterly.

"I blame myself for this," he said at last. "I blame myself more than you can know. What a judgment it is on my vanity! It broke my heart that neither of my sons had the talent to follow in my footsteps—or rather, I thought in my youthful pride that it would break my heart. And then when your father defied me over your mother, I was furious. Yet still . . . I knew her father was a powerful wonderworker. And when I learned that she had borne a son, I began to dream, almost without admitting it to myself, that you would be a fitting heir to both your grandfathers. You see, Sacha, this is how God rewards the vanity of old men! Never let anyone tell you He doesn't have a sense of humor!"

"Did you never meet my mother's father?" Sacha asked.

"Once," Rabbi Kessler answered, "long ago, when your parents were both still children. But later on, we were both too pigheaded to meet again, and, well, you know the rest of the story."

Indeed, Sacha knew every line of the story, for it was the same one his grandfather told every year at Passover. He always began the tale by saying that he had been the firstborn son of one of the great Ashkenazic rabbinical dynasties and that he had been raised to be pious and learned—but also to take overweening pride in his noble lineage. But then his firstborn son had defied him by running off to Moscow to go to the university. And worse still, the young Danny Kessler had run afoul of the Czar's secret police, been kicked out of school, and fallen in love with the daughter of a humble Hasidic wonderworker — a man who stood for everything the Kesslers had always despised. That was the last straw. Rabbi Kessler had threatened to disown his son if he married the girl. ("Boy, was I a jerk back then!" Grandpa Kessler always exclaimed at this point in the story.)

Danny Kessler hadn't even tried to argue with his father. He'd just walked out of the house and vanished. ("And I was an even bigger jerk," Sacha's father always said when Rabbi Kessler got to *this* part of the story.)

He didn't come back for six years—not until a wave of pogroms swept the land and thousands of families were being burnt out of house and home. Then he walked back into his father's library one night, looking like he'd been sleeping in a ditch for a week. He pulled out his pocket watch, laid it on the rabbi's desk, and told him he had fifteen minutes to pack whatever he wanted to take to America.

"Where's your wife?" the rabbi asked.

"Hiding in a field outside of town with your grandchildren."

"And what will she say to taking a slow old man along with her to America?"

"She's the one who made me come get you in the first place."

This was where the story always ended. The Rabbi would hold up the Elijah cup—an ancient *Kiddush* cup that had been passed down from Kessler to Kessler for centuries. "This is the only thing I took with me," he would say. "I spent the

next three months walking across Europe. And during that walk, I watched the girl I disowned my son for marrying save my grandchildren's lives a hundred times over. If it weren't for her, there wouldn't be any Kesslers left to hand this cup down to. So I thank God for delivering me from Egypt—and for giving my son a far better wife than I ever could have chosen for him."

"Put my shawl away now," Rabbi Kessler said. "And get the Elijah cup out while you're at it. I want to look at it. It's foolish to take comfort in pretty things. And yet . . . perhaps there *is* some comfort to be had there."

Sacha went back to the dresser, lifted out the carefully folded cloth that held the cup, and carried it to his grandfather. The old man unwrapped it and held it up so that it glistened and flashed in a slanting shaft of afternoon sunlight. It was a pretty thing: a small, slender-stemmed silver cup covered with an intricate filigree of twining grapes and pomegranates.

"This cup was made in the Loire Valley, where our family went after they were expelled from Spain. It first belonged to a very great scholar—a man who was said to have been a student of Isaac Luria himself. From that time on, it has passed from son to son in our family, even as we fled from France to Germany, from Germany to Russia, from Russia to America. Many great scholars have held this cup—and some who would have known how to undo the damage Morgaunt did when he summoned your dybbuk. It is their wisdom you must look to.

The wisdom of men who made it their life's work to repair the universe. That is where your answers lie, and not in the rough spellsmithing of men who see magic only as a tool to slake their selfish appetites."

"Then help me," Sacha pleaded. "Teach me!"

"But *how* can I help you? What am I to teach you? There's a reason those books you stole are hidden in the back of a closet and not left unguarded in the *shul* where anyone can read them! There's a reason that the great Kabbalists refused to teach men until they were so steeped in the study of Talmud that they had some defense against the overwhelming temptation to misuse such power!" Rabbi Kessler shook his head. "I have racked my brain for knowledge that might help rather than harm you, but it is hard. It is very hard."

It was several minutes before Sacha's grandfather spoke again. And even then, he picked his words with painful caution, as if terrified of accidentally revealing more than he intended to say.

"Perhaps after all, I was right to think of the Elijah cup," he said at last. "Tell me, Sacha, have you ever heard anyone speak of the doctrine of *gilgul ha-neshamot*?"

Sacha shook his head no.

"But you understand the Hebrew?"

"*Neshama* is 'soul,'" Sacha said hesitantly. "And *gilgul* . . . is that the word for 'wheel'?"

"So you do have room in your head for something besides baseball," his grandfather said with a dry chuckle. "Yes, that is the bare meaning of the phrase. The wheel of souls. Or, as Isaac of Luria called it, the doctrine of rolling souls."

"But I thought that was just superstition."

"You mean the saying that a soul lives as many lives as it takes for it to fulfill all six hundred and thirteen *mitzvot*?" Rabbi Kessler asked. "Well, yes, that does seem a little too neat and tidy. But there's a fine line between little superstitions and great truths. And the one great truth about dybbuks that I can tell you is this: when someone asked Isaac Luria what a dybbuk was, he said that spiritual possession was one of the deepest mysteries of our faith—and that it was inextricably entwined with *gilgul.* Under this doctrine, at least in the way that Luria taught it, there are harmful possessions—dybbuks, or clinging ghosts. But there are also beneficial possessions—which he called *ibbur.* Luria and many other Kabbalists throughout the ages have actively sought *ibbur* by prayer, fasting, and study, sometimes even by sleeping on the graves of holy men. And the belief also survives in the folk superstition of ordinary Jews, who will often name a baby after a dead relative whose good qualities they hope to see reborn in the child."

"But how does that help me?" Sacha asked. "It doesn't change anything!"

"Ah, but it does. Morgaunt may have called forth this clinging spirit. But he did not make it. Magicians *can* make golems and such earthly creatures. But a soul can only be made by God Himself. And each soul has a purpose in creation that no human mind can encompass. Morgaunt will never grasp that truth. But such wisdom is part of the birthright of every Kessler who has ever raised that cup at a Passover Seder. Morgaunt may think that the dybbuk is his creature. But you must remember that a soul belongs only to itself and to God. And if you do remember that—if you can bring yourself to think of the dybbuk not as a curse inflicted upon you but as a child of God, with its own destiny to fulfill in the world—then I do not see how it can ever entirely devour you."

Sacha looked at the pale silver *Kiddush* cup glinting in the wintry sunlight. He felt his grandfather's eyes on him, but he was strangely reluctant to meet the old man's gaze. "Has that ever worked?" he asked. "I mean, has anyone ever . . . repaired a dybbuk?"

"Not that I know of," Rabbi Kessler said in something like his normal cheerful tones. "But don't let that discourage you!"

"Wolf wants me to learn magic. To protect myself."

"I'm sure he thinks it's a good idea."

"But you won't teach me."

"Of course I will. When you're married and over forty!"

"Gee, thanks."

"Don't look like that, Sacha. Worse things have happened to people. Not often, but still . . . and anyway, I'll talk to Mo and see what he thinks. There are things that we *can* teach even to one as young as you are. I don't know that they're what your Inquisitor Wolf would call magic, exactly. But understanding the true nature of souls may be of more real help to you than any practical magic." Grandpa Kessler shook himself and struggled to his feet. "Enough of that, anyway. You look green. Go outside and get some fresh air, will you?"

But Sacha had just gotten to the front door when his grandfather's voice called him back again.

"Hey, wait a minute! Come back and get me another drink of water! I'm still thirsty!"

Instead of going outside when he finally left his grandfather, Sacha trudged upstairs to look for Moishe Schlosky.

He found Moishe and Bekah sitting out on the fire escape together, oblivious to the cold and so deep in some profound political discussion that their heads were practically touching. Sacha stared at Moishe until the older boy's face flushed almost as red as his hair.

"Mind if I borrow your boyfriend?" he asked Bekah.

"Don't!" Bekah warned him. "Don't even think about calling him that!"

"Whatever you say. But I still need to talk to him. Not about you," he said when he saw Bekah's glare. "About work stuff. *Secret* work stuff."

A look passed between Bekah and Moishe that made Sacha suspect his secret might be less than safe in Moishe's hands. But that wasn't *his* problem.

"Where's your brother?" he asked as soon as Bekah was out of earshot.

"Are you asking? Or is Inquisitor Wolf asking?"

"He's asking. And if you want to keep Sam safe, you'll tell him."

"I don't see it that way."

Sacha wasn't entirely sure that he didn't agree with Moishe. Still, he did his best to pass along Wolf's message.

"I'll tell . . . anyone who might know where he is," Moishe said. "That's all I can promise."

"Okay." Sacha started to turn away.

"You know," Moishe said, "you could have threatened to tell your parents that you caught Bekah out on the fire escape with me unless I told you where Sam was."

Sacha didn't know what to say to that. The idea hadn't even crossed his mind.

"But you're too nice to do that, aren't you, Sacha?"

"Or maybe just too dumb to think of it. And anyway, you weren't even *doing* anything."

"You think your mother would have cared about that?" Moishe asked with a lopsided grin. "Nope. You *are* nice. And I might as well warn you now that I plan to take shameless advantage of it. Your sister—"

"Don't push your luck!" Sacha said, putting out a hand to silence Moishe. "I'm not *that* nice!"

CHAPTER SIX

Naftali Asher's Last Words

ON MONDAY MORNING, Sacha arrived at Inquisitors Division headquarters just in time to hear Wolf get a blistering tongue-lashing from Commissioner Keegan.

Lily was in the front office with Philip Payton, a boy only a few years older than Sacha who was something in between Wolf's office clerk and a sort of unofficial inquisitor. But neither Lily nor Philip was working this morning. Keegan had walked into Wolf's room as some sort of gesture toward privacy but he was so mad he'd forgotten to shut the door. So now Payton and Lily were hovering beside the half-open door listening to every word, and they could hear everything.

Sacha knew it was Keegan in there without even asking; every beat cop in the NYPD prided himself on imitating Tommy Keegan's rollicking Irish brogue. Keegan had made his career—and, some whispered, a private fortune as well—by ensuring that poor New Yorkers didn't interfere with the business or pleasures of their richer neighbors. His first act as police commissioner had been to draw what he called a "dead line" around the Wall Street business district. All pickpockets, street peddlers, and conjure men had been warned that they could do what they pleased in the poorer neighborhoods of the city, but if they crossed the dead line, they would be made examples of. A few criminals crossed the line despite the warning; examples were made—or, more precisely, found floating in the East River—and no one ever crossed the line again.

Keegan's supporters boasted that he had made New York a great place to do business. Keegan's enemies—well, Keegan's enemies usually disappeared into the police lockups in the Tombs before they had a chance to say much of anything. Even Meyer Minsky had once confessed that he'd rather brave a gun battle with his worst enemy than risk a night in the Tombs with Tommy Keegan.

"Mark my words, Wolf!" Keegan blared from the other side of the door. "Ye'll solve this Klosky case, and ye'll solve it fast!"

"I think you mean Klezmer, sir," Wolf suggested.

"Klosky, Klusmer, do ye think I care what they call their infernal caterwauling? The main point is—when are ye goin' to arrest someone?"

"Well, I generally wait to start beating confessions out of people until I actually have a crime for them to confess to—"

Keegan stomped hard enough to rattle the door in its frame. "It's no joking matter, Wolf! People have their eye on this case! People who matter!"

"People whose money matters," Philip Payton muttered under his breath, just low enough that Keegan couldn't hear him. Sacha knew exactly who Payton meant: J. P. Morgaunt, owner of just about everything in New York that was worth more than a wooden nickel. Morgaunt was the only man in the city who could have Keegan in the office hollering at Wolf instead of relaxing with his betters in the oak-paneled gentlemen's lounge of the Union Club. But why on earth would J. P. Morgaunt "have his eye" on this case? Why would he even care one fig about some ridiculous vaudeville scandal?

"How long has this been going on?" Sacha whispered.

The older boy just rolled his eyes.

"They were already going at it when I got here," Lily said, "and that was at least ten minutes ago."

"And what about that Schlosky boy?" Keegan snapped in the next room. "When are you going to bring him in?"

"Whenever I find him," Wolf answered mildly. "I'm trying to track down anyone who knew him and Asher when they worked at Pentacle."

"Pentacle? Pentacle's not the problem, man! The problem is that immigrant trash down on Hester Street!"

"Excuse me, sir?"

"Don't play the meek little innocent with me, Wolf! You know who I'm talking about. Those godless Wiccanists won't rest till they've brought every factory owner in New York to his knees. Mr. Morgaunt says they've plans afoot for a general strike. Every magicworker in New York is going to walk off the job and shut down Manhattan from one end to t'other!" Keegan snorted. "But that's what we get for lettin' these damned foreigners into the country!"

"Quite so, sir. I can't think why we let any foreigners in at all."

"Aren't we clever today? I'll tell ye what, Wolf—why don't you go arrest Moishe Schlosky before I decide to let you laugh all the way to a job in Yonkers?"

"What for?"

"For being an arrogant dev—"

"No, I mean what am I supposed to arrest Moishe Schlosky for"—Wolf paused infinitesimally—"sir?"

"Look, man, you've got a point. But don't push it too far. Sometimes a man has to face reality."

"Unless he wants to end up working in Yonkers?"

"Just so. Mr. Morgaunt has made it clear how he wants this case handled. I know what you think of him. And I admit he's a hard man. But he's also a man who's done a lot for the city, and when he takes it in mind to speak, he has a right to be listened to. And frankly, Wolf, I think he's right about this case. When he asked me what the hell you'd been doing all weekend, I didn't have a word to say to him. So why don't you go down to Hester Street and roust out those IWW rascals? Even if they've nothing to do with this case, it'll be a public service to put the fear of God and the NYPD into them. And while ye're at it, change clothes, will you? You look like you've been sleepin' in the subway for a month of Sundays!"

"Well," Payton said dryly as soon as Keegan was gone, "I guess Mr. Morgaunt is a little more worried about the strike at Pentacle than he's letting on in public."

Sacha looked around to see what Inquisitor Wolf made of that comment—but Wolf was still staring after Keegan. The fake dumb cop look that he always put on to annoy the police commissioner was gone now, and he just looked tired and defeated. He glanced Sacha's way, caught him staring—and blinked at him for a moment as if trying to remember who he was and where he'd seen him before.

"Come into my office, Sacha," Wolf said after a moment, sounding brusque and unusually serious. "I need to talk to you."

Sacha goggled at him. So did Lily. And while Philip Payton would never have stooped to goggling, it was pretty clear that he was just as curious.

Sacha stepped into the office nervously and pulled the door closed behind him. Then he told himself that Wolf probably just wanted to know if he'd spoken to Moishe over the weekend, and his heart lightened. "If it's about Moishe—" he began.

"It's not about Moishe. Sit down."

Sacha started toward Wolf's desk with a feeling of doom in his heart, but before he got there, the door to the outside corridor slammed open again and Rosie DiMaggio's voice rang in the air.

Wolf ducked back out into the front room, and Sacha

followed just in time to see Rosie at the door with her arms full of heavy boxes. He leaped to help her. So did Philip Payton—and they collided in mid-leap. Lily rolled her eyes, stepped over them, and took one of the packages herself.

"Thanks!" Rosie said. "Boy, that lobby's really something! It boggles the mind the things people think of doing with magic in this city! And what's with the guy I just met coming down the stairs? That fella's got a serious liver problem. I worked with a girl who worked at Ziegfeld's, and she said Mr. Ziegfeld's brother-in-law's youngest sister knew a big director out in Hollywood who got red in the face like that every time he got mad, and his doctor told him to meditate twice a day and eat only non-bile-promoting, non-liver-aggravating food. And he didn't listen. So one day—pow!—dead as doorknocker! See? Somebody really oughta tell that fella about it!"

Sacha's head was spinning—a state of mind that Rosie usually produced in males between the ages of fifteen and eighty-five. "What's non—whatever you just said—food?" he asked.

"They make it in Battle Creek, Michigan, and it comes in a cardboard box—which is about what it tastes like, if you ask me. Anyway, here's the film. I brought it straight over as soon as it was developed, just like I said I would. And I brought the projector too, because I figured you might not have one. So now all we need is a nice, clean, empty piece of white wall to . . ."

She trailed off and glanced around the impossibly cluttered office, whose walls were stacked with files straight up to the cobweb-festooned ceiling.

"How 'bout if I just move these?" Rosie asked. She poked at one of the piles. For a moment nothing happened. Then the pile trembled and tottered and came slithering down in an avalanche that buried them all to the ankles.

"Oops!" Rosie said.

Wolf muttered something hopeful about taking advantage of the chance to reorganize—but Payton just groaned. And really, Sacha couldn't blame him. Wolf shed notes, letters, and random scraps of paper so quickly that Sacha still couldn't figure out how the paperwork hadn't smothered them all at their desks long ago. In fact, Sacha was starting to think that either Payton was one of the most powerful magicians working for the Inquisitors Division or he was secretly throwing old case files out the window into the alley to get rid of them.

As Sacha helped scoop up the files on the floor and clear the space Rosie needed for her projector, he couldn't stop himself from glancing constantly at Inquisitor Wolf, feeling vaguely sick to his stomach, and wondering what on earth the man wanted to talk to him about—and how long he was going to have to wait now to find out about it. But finally the projector was set up and a little square of space was cleared on the wall. Wolf climbed onto the windowsill and pulled down the rolling blind, releasing a collection of mummified bugs that looked like they ought to be donated to the Natural History Museum. They sat down to watch the final performance of the Klezmer King. And Sacha forgot all about Wolf wanting to see him, and Keegan wanting to arrest Moishe Schlosky, and Rosie and her non-bilious anti-aggravating cardboard breakfast food—and in fact everything else in the world except Naftali Asher and his strange, haunting, impossible music.

As the projector started up, the makeshift screen flickered and went black. Then a little circle of light appeared at its center—and Sacha realized that someone had just lit a spotlight, and they were looking down at the stage of the Hippodrome. The picture jiggled, and he heard a thump, rustle, and scrape—and then Maurice Goldfaden's voice muttering, "Testing, testing! Where is the damn thing anyway? Oh, there it is."

Then Naftali Asher appeared onstage, clutching his clarinet and walking in that hurried, jerky way that people in moving pictures always seemed to do. The clarinet glistened in his hand. The lights of the electric tuxedo flashed and winked. He stopped in the middle of the stage and gave the audience a long, baleful look—as if he already knew that his music was going to be completely wasted on them. Then he turned his back on the audience, put his clarinet to his lips, and began to play.

For the rest of his life, Sacha would struggle to describe that music. Indeed, years later, he would wander the record stores on Broadway, listening to the klezmer greats of the day and trying in vain to find anything to match the music he remembered Naftali Asher playing.

Asher had been a fine klezmer player. He coaxed from his clarinet all the quavering tones, heartbreaking sobs, and sweeping glissandos that made people call klezmer music the voice of the Jewish soul. But it was Asher's *songs* that really made him extraordinary. They seemed to meld the ancient traditions of four thousand years with the new joys and sorrows of life in America. And suddenly Sacha knew exactly where the Klezmer King had gotten his mysterious melodies. These were the same ones he had heard played on Mr. Worley's Soul Catcher and Thomas Edison's etherograph. They were the souls of real, living, breathing people, carved into the little wax cylinders that Morgaunt kept locked up in his library. Sacha had forced those songs out of his mind ever since that horrible night in the flaming ruins of the Elephant Hotel.

But now, as the cold tinkle of the etherograph was replaced by the rich warmth of a fine clarinet in the hands of a great musician, Sacha remembered the strange beauty of that music. He remembered the almost painful rush of pity and tenderness he had felt when he'd heard the lonely, wistful, waiting sound of Lily's song. And when Inquisitor Wolf had submitted himself to the machine? Well, Sacha had no words for that. A man would have to live a lifetime—and a very extraordinary lifetime at that—before he grasped the wellsprings of Maximillian Wolf's very private and complicated being.

Wolf stood up abruptly and stopped the film.

It took Sacha a moment to come out of the spell of the music. He looked around, still a bit surprised to find himself at Inquisitors headquarters instead of at the Hippodrome. The others were looking around in the same way, shaking themselves as if they'd just been diving in dark waters and were trying to remember what air and sunlight were. But while Payton and Rosie seemed to come back to themselves without any trouble, Lily and Wolf both wore the same confused and troubled look that Sacha could feel on his own face.

"Wasn't that—" Sacha began.

"Did that remind you of anything?" Lily asked at the same moment.

"Yeah, I know," Rosie said. "That's what I always thought. But why would Mr. Edison have let Asher listen to his etherograph recordings? I mean, it doesn't make any sense. Where would they even have met each other?"

"Was Edison still working on the etherograph when he left for California?" Wolf asked.

"Oh, no! That was always Mr. Morgaunt's project. Mr. Edison mighta had some of his own money in it, but honestly, he was pretty broke even before the Houdini Challenge. And after that . . . well, I think he must have had some idea what really happened that night. He sold out to Mr. Morgaunt so fast it was like he was too scared of the guy to even haggle about it."

"I think," Wolf said, "that we need to have another of our little talks with Mr. Morgaunt."

Wolf started the film again, and soon Sacha was so enthralled by the haunting music that he almost didn't notice the faint flicker of motion at the edge of the screen. It was

Sam Schlosky, Sacha realized, watching Asher in the final moments before his death.

Then the electric tuxedo flared and surged. Sparks flitted across Naftali Asher's chest. And as he flailed and clawed at the suit, Asher let out one final howl: the last words that everyone had admitted he had spoken but no one had been willing to admit to having understood.

On Rosie's tape, they came through loud and clear.

"Sam!" Naftali Asher howled. "No! Sam!"

The film finished. The strip crackled and slipped out of the spool so that its loose end slapped against the table like a fly battering itself against a windowpane.

The five of them stared at one another for a long time before anyone could manage to speak.

"Did he say what I think he said?" Lily asked finally.

"He couldn't have meant it the way it sounded," Rosie protested. "Sam never woulda—"

"That won't help him one bit if Commissioner Keegan ever gets hold of that tape," Payton pointed out.

"I've been looking for Sam all weekend and getting nowhere," Inquisitor Wolf said. "So I guess Keegan's right. It really is time we went down to Hester Street and paid Moishe Schlosky a visit."

Lily jumped up and started pulling on her coat.

"In a minute," Wolf said, turning back to Sacha, whose heart was sinking fast. "There's something else I have to take care of first."

CHAPTER SEVEN

No Easy Answers

SACHA FOLLOWED WOLF into his office, feeling like a lamb going to slaughter.

"Shut the door," Wolf said.

Sacha did—though it was all he could do not to dash through it, slam it behind him, and flee the building.

They stood there for a moment, staring at each other.

"You can sit down," Wolf suggested.

Sacha sat.

Wolf sat down on the other side of his desk, sighed, and took his glasses off. He peered at them, holding the lenses up to the light and squinting sideways at them as if they hadn't been working right lately and he was trying to figure out why. He picked up his tie, dabbed halfheartedly at the glasses with it, and then suddenly seemed to notice the motley collection of food stains that always bespeckled his ties. He frowned, sighed again, shrugged . . . and gave up on the glasses-cleaning project.

"Did you ever find Mrs. Mogulesko?" Sacha asked.

"What? Oh. Yes. And she told me where Sam's family was. But it didn't do me any good. None of them have seen him since Friday afternoon. He might as well have dropped off the face of the earth. The thing is, Sacha . . ." Wolf trailed off into a brooding silence.

"What—" Sacha began.

"What—" Wolf said at the same instant.

"Sorry, you were saying?" Wolf asked.

"Nothing! I didn't mean to interrupt."

"Mmmm," Wolf murmured, as if this were extremely worrisome news. "Well, I was going to ask you what you thought of the Klezmer King's music."

"I thought it was a little creepy—I mean that it sounded so much like the etherograph recordings."

"I agree," Wolf said. He looked down at one of the files that littered his desk. "Naftali Asher became an overnight success a little less than a year ago. Before that, he was an amateur klezmer player who couldn't get a gig to save his life, and other than that, he was just a stone-broke, out-of-work tailor."

"That's odd," Sacha said before he could stop himself.

"The timing, you mean."

"No. That he was a sewer, not a presser. I mean, there are plenty of tailors, of course. But in the factories, sewing is mostly women's work."

Wolf leaned forward in is chair, frowning. "Why? Can't men sew?"

"Well, a skilled man can usually find work as a tailor. That pays a lot better, you see. Whereas even the most skilled seamstresses at Pentacle only make ordinary magicworkers' wages."

"Ah," Wolf cleared his throat—and was Sacha imagining it, or did he seem a little stiff suddenly? "Thank you. That's helpful, actually."

"Is that all you wanted to ask me about?" Sacha said hopefully.

"No. Actually, I want to talk about you, Sacha."

"Oh."

"Have you ever thought about studying magic, Sacha?"

Sacha stared at his toes, trying to still the pounding of the pulse in his throat before he answered. "It would break my grandfather's heart."

"And how would your grandfather like to see you doing Morgaunt's dirty work?"

"What's that supposed to mean?" Sacha asked angrily.

"Don't play games with me. I know what he said to you in the Elephant Hotel that night."

"How?"

"Oh, Sacha," Wolf murmured sadly, "I know because he said the same things to me the year after *I* joined the Inquisitors Division. Morgaunt was trying to take over Chinatown then. He was going after the Spellbinders the same way Minsky's afraid he'll go after Magic, Inc., if they fall out over the Pentacle strike. I can't tell you what it was to walk the streets of this city then, and I hope you never see such a time."

"Is that when you fell—when you met Shen?"

Wolf seemed to shrink in upon himself. When he finally answered, his voice was little more than a whisper. "Her husband was my first teacher. Everything you're now learning from Shen, I learned from him. That and more. For unlike you, I was all too eager a student. Shen's husband taught me. He believed in me. He trusted me when I promised the police would protect him."

Wolf bowed his head and covered his face as if the memories passing before his eyes were too terrible to bear. "Morgaunt murdered him at Shen's very feet while I stood by without the skill to stop him. And that's what he'll do to everyone you care about, unless you make yourself strong enough to stand against him. Would your grandfather still tell you it was wrong to study magic if he knew all that?"

"It wouldn't change anything," Sacha said. "*Thou shalt not smite so much as a hair on a man's head by magic.* That is the law as far as he's concerned. Not *Thou shalt not smite so much as a hair on a man's head by magic unless he tries to smite you first.* And I guarantee you he's got a list of rabbis as long as your arm who've died for that principle."

"So you think it's right to obey to him in this?"

"It's not a matter of obeying, exactly," Sacha said. He hesitated, not being able to explain it even to himself. "If it were only a matter of small magic, the sort of thing my mother and sister do to keep their jobs at Pentacle, or even the sort of hexes that common criminals use. But I've seen what Morgaunt does. That's a different thing. Meyer Minsky himself wouldn't dare work such spells. He can spend every Friday night drinking, gambling with five showgirls on his lap, and still call himself a good Jew. But he wouldn't do what Morgaunt does." Sacha hesitated.

For a long moment Wolf just stared past Sacha with a haggard expression on his face. "No," he said finally. "I suppose he wouldn't. He'd say it was against his religion. And I would have said much the same thing back when I was within spitting distance of being a good Catholic."

Wolf stared at his desk as if he expected to find some answer in the piles of paperwork. "I really don't know what to tell you, Sacha," he said. "Maybe your family would be safer outside of New York."

Sacha felt a wave of dizziness sweep over him. Leave? Again? They'd already left one home to come to America. And at what cost? How could he tell his mother she wasn't safe here either? And where on earth were they supposed to go *now?* Would the wandering never end?

But he didn't know how to say any of that to Wolf, so he only sighed and said, "Morgaunt would find us no matter how far we went."

Then a strange idea struck him. "That's really why Meyer's afraid of Morgaunt, isn't it? Not because he thinks Morgaunt's actually a stronger magician, but because Morgaunt's willing to break the rules. And Minsky isn't."

"Yes, Sacha. Men like Meyer follow a sort of magician's code of honor. And Paddy Doyle and the Hell's Kitchen Hexers and all the other gangsters in New York are the same.

They're romantics. But Morgaunt is the ultimate cynic. You could almost even say he doesn't believe in magic. To a true magician, a device like the etherograph is practically anathema. The men of Magic, Inc., may not agree with Shen or your grandfather about anything else, but they all agree that power should be earned, not stolen."

Sacha tried to imagine his grandfather and Shen sitting down together to talk about Great Magic . . . but he couldn't get past the image of how his grandfather would look if he ever even heard of such a thing as a woman wearing pants in public.

"Well," Wolf said finally, "let me think on this. And in the meantime, keep going to your kung fu lessons with Shen, will you? She's not teaching you magic. But she's teaching you the kind of discipline that will help you use magic wisely should you ever change your mind and decide to learn it. And"—he hesitated—"she can teach you things that will help you grow into your . . . gifts. Whatever they may turn out to be. She wouldn't teach you what you call magic anytime soon, even if you asked her to. She isn't a woman who deals in easy answers." He grinned ruefully. "Or any answers at all, if she can possibly help it. But she's the best teacher—and the best friend—you could possibly have right now."

"But why—" Sacha stopped, not wanting to seem nosy.

"Go ahead," Wolf said. "I'm in a confiding mood. Even though I know you'll run straight to Lily with everything I say to you."

"Why does Shen help you? I mean after—what happened."

"You mean why does she want to help the arrogant fool who got her husband killed? I don't know. Maybe she feels sorry for me. If you ever find out why that woman does anything, you let me know about it."

CHAPTER EIGHT

Manhunt!

SACHA SPENT MOST of their long trudge downtown to the offices of the Industrial Witches of the World wondering whether Moishe Schlosky was going to be at IWW headquarters when they got there—and the other half thanking heaven that it was the middle of the workday so Bekah definitely wasn't going to be there.

Normally Moishe Schlosky was a pretty friendly guy, but today when he opened the door and saw who was waiting for him, he put his hands on his hips, blocked the door—or at least as much of the door as his skinny body could block—made a sour face, and said, "Oh, great! You again! Who am I supposed to have murdered this time?"

"No one," Wolf assured him. "I just need to ask you abou—"

"So you don't even need an excuse anymore? Now Morgaunt's just sending you down here to intimidate us?"

"When Mr. Morgaunt sends the Inquisitors to intimidate

you, I doubt they're going to knock on the door politely and wait for you to let them in."

Moishe made a rude noise at this—but he did step aside.

"Actually," Wolf said, looking around absent-mindedly, "what I really need to talk to you about is your brother Sam."

At the mention of Sam, an extraordinary change came over Moishe's face. Usually he wore an open, guileless, almost pathetically nice expression on his skinny features. But suddenly his eyes narrowed, and his mouth froze into a stiff line, and he grew completely still except for a nervous twitch to his fingers.

Sacha almost burst out laughing. He'd never seen anyone over the age of five look so obviously like they'd just gotten caught stealing candy.

"I haven't seen him," Moishe said. "Why would I have seen him?"

"I don't know," Wolf said. "Why would you think I was going to ask if you'd seen him? Is there something you want to tell me, Moishe?"

"Of course not!" Moishe's fingers twitched some more. "Do I look like I want to tell you something?"

"Well, actually . . . Good heavens, what on earth happened in here? Has Keegan already sent someone to turn the place upside down?"

Sacha looked around the room—and for a minute he, too, wondered if the Inquisitors hadn't already paid Moishe a visit.

The place was a mess. Books and papers were scattered

everywhere. But when he looked more closely, he realized that most of the papers were hot off the presses, still bundled into big stacks and waiting for volunteers to carry them around the city to hand out to passersby. Wolf glanced at a nearby folding table and fingered a freshly printed flyer.

"SHOCKING!" Sacha read in the middle of the page. "SCABBALIST SCANDAL! READ ALL ABOUT J. P. MORGAUNT'S ILLEGAL SCHEME TO DEFEAT THE UNION!"

"What's a scabbalist?" Lily asked curiously.

"A scab plus a Kabbalist," Moishe said with a possessive pride that made Sacha suspect he himself had coined the word. "A magicworker who stabs the union in the back by working for the bosses. And not just as strikebreakers, either. You see, we happen to have good evidence that Morgaunt has had a scabbalist working for him for months and months now, building up a secret stockpile so he can keep shipping shirtwaists even after the strike starts. Morgaunt found a magician so powerful that he could do the work of a hundred regular magicworkers—and he hired him to make Pentacle strike-proof!"

"Listen, Moishe," Wolf began, "I need to know—"

"Who the scabbalist is? I'll never tell! My lips are sealed!"

"Never mind the scabbalist," Wolf said dismissively. "Where's Sam?"

"I'll never tell that, either!" Moishe declared.

Wolf sighed. "I'd threaten to throw you in jail until you're ready to talk to me, but you'd probably be overjoyed about being turned into a martyr for the magicworkers' revolution."

"As if I need your cooperation for that!" Moishe puffed his chest out proudly. "I'll have you know I've been to jail three times just this month."

"Good God!" Wolf said. "What on earth for?"

"Making speeches about magicworkers' rights outside Pentacle Shirtwaist Factory."

Wolf hit the end of his patience. "Look, Moishe. I really need to talk to Sam. And you obviously know where he is—"

"I never said that!"

"You obviously know where he is."

"Not that I'm admitting anything!"

"Moishe!" Wolf shouted. "Shut up!"

"Well, gee," Moishe said in a wounded tone, "you don't have to shout."

"Do you know where Sam is? Yes or no!"

"Okay—if you insist—yes."

"And?"

"And I can't tell you. Don't look at me like that! It's not my fault. I promised him!"

"Listen, Moishe," Wolf said. Sacha could see his frustration at Moishe's uncooperativeness struggling with his knowledge of just how quickly Keegan would turn Moishe into a suspect if Wolf actually acted on his threat of dragging him in for questioning. "Sam's in danger. I need to talk to him. For his own good."

"No can do," Moishe said cheerfully. "But I will tell you this. You're going to hear from Sam pretty soon now. We've just got to find a newspaperman in town who Morgaunt doesn't own lock, stock, and barrel. And then Sam's gonna talk. And when he does, I promise you, what he has to say is going to expose Morgaunt for the scheming criminal he really is!"

Wolf seemed to feel he'd heard enough at this point. He stuffed his pencil and paper back into his pocket without having done more than doodled, and soon Sacha and Lily were following him back out into the stairwell.

"Psst!" Moishe whispered just as Sacha was about to start down the stairs behind them.

Sacha tried to silence him with a furtive hand gesture, but it did no good; Moishe was too honest to take a hint unless you knocked him over the head with it.

"Has Bekah talked to you about that little favor we need from you?" Moishe whispered, loudly enough that Sacha thanked his lucky stars Lily was already clattering down the stairs half a story below them.

"No," he answered.

"Well, come upstairs tonight so I can ask you about it."

"I might not be home early enough."

"So come tomorrow. Anyway, before the weekend."

Sacha just sighed and started down the stairs without answering.

* * *

For the rest of that week, Wolf turned Manhattan upside down looking for Sam Schlosky—or at least he turned Manhattan as thoroughly upside down as he could without naming Sam as a suspect or splashing his name all over the papers.

They went through every hospital, every cheap hotel and lodging house, every five-cent flophouse. They talked to everyone who'd ever known Sam and a lot of people who hadn't. But it really was as Wolf had said. Naftali Asher's dresser seemed to have vanished as completely as if God Himself had reached down and plucked him from the face of the earth.

On Thursday morning, Wolf made a final just-in-case round of the Bowery flophouses and then, having found zilch, struck north with nothing more in mind that Sacha could see than walking and brooding. As they neared the south side of Washington Square, the streets began to ring with the sounds of the garment trade. Banks of sewing machines clattered and rattled in the soaring lofts of the factories. Cutters and drapers shouted to each other, their voices spilling into the street through windows that were propped open even in February to cut the punishing heat of the flatirons and sewing machine crank engines. Wagons rumbled over the cobblestones and double-parked outside the garment factories while schleppers with shoulders as broad as Harry Houdini's tossed up the heavy bolts of cloth to the cutters who leaned out the second-story windows with arms outstretched to catch them.

Sacha had tagged after Wolf on a lot of these apparently aimless walks by now, and he had begun to sense that they were part of Wolf's way of thinking through a case. So he just kept his mouth shut and dropped back to walk next to Lily.

Lily was still full of the story about Shen's husband—which Sacha had naturally repeated to her almost as quickly as Wolf had predicted he would.

"I still can't believe Morgaunt killed Shen's husband right in front of her!" she exclaimed. "How awful! Wolf must feel so guilty about it. And no wonder she's never married him after that!"

"Yeah, that must be it," Sacha said sarcastically, "'cause it's not any problem that he's white and she's Chinese."

"Half Chinese," Lily corrected.

"Oh, right. How could I have forgotten? Maybe the police department would just half fire Wolf if he explained that to them."

"Poor Wolf," Lily sighed. "Horrible things do seem to happen around him. Did I tell you what my mother said the other night? She thinks he's cursed. She says he was born under the sign of fire, and death and disaster follow him." Lily glanced at Wolf and lowered her voice. "She thinks the fire at the Elephant Hotel was his fault."

"But, Lily! You know better! That's a malicious lie!"

"We-ell," she said hesitantly, "of course I know Morgaunt was the one who burned down the hotel. But it doesn't change the fact that bad things do seem to happen to anyone who gets too close to Wolf. Besides, my father believes it. And he's usually very skeptical about that sort of thing."

"So then why would they apprentice their precious daughter to such a dangerous character?"

She bit her lip, and if the idea of Lily Astral crying hadn't been completely unthinkable, Sacha could almost have thought there was a tear in her eye. "My father wants me to quit," she whispered. "I don't think my mother meant it to go that far. She was just spreading malicious gossip about Wolf because"—she hesitated—"because he doesn't fall over her like most men do, and she hates him for it."

"Lily!"

"Don't sound so shocked. I can't help the way she is. And you've met her, so you know what I'm talking about."

Sacha couldn't help blushing. He had an uncomfortable memory of his only meeting with Maleficia Astral; unlike Wolf, he *had* fallen all over her. And he had a sneaking suspicion that Lily had neither forgotten nor forgiven his behavior.

"But that's not the point," Lily went on. "The point is, once my father heard it, he asked some of the men at his club about it. And—and he won't say what he heard, but he said last night at dinner that he thought I ought to quit."

"So what happens now?" Sacha asked with a miserable feeling in the pit of his stomach that he didn't want to think too hard about.

"Nothing right away. For some reason I can't fathom, my mother doesn't want me to quit. I can tell she wishes she'd never mentioned the whole business in front of my father."

"So . . . they argue about it?"

"They never argue. They'll just give each other the silent treatment for a few weeks. And whichever one of them is willing to be silent longer will end up winning."

This seemed like a very odd way of resolving disagreements to Sacha, but he thought he'd better not comment on it. Lily could say the most appalling things about her own family, but Sacha had learned long ago that she could be as touchy on that subject as a pit bull with a sore tooth.

"Anything the matter?" Wolf asked, turning back to see why they'd lagged behind.

"No!" they both practically yelped.

"Good," he said, looking back and forth between the two of them. "Let's go, then."

They reached Greene Street and dodged the traffic in order to cross into Washington Square. Sacha could see a little cluster of newsboys picking up their papers beneath the white marble arch at the northern end of the park. Wolf veered toward them; he never missed a chance to buy a paper, and the Klezmer murder had been front page news all weekend.

"Who's this thing named after anyway?" Lily asked Sacha as they scurried under the arch behind Wolf's flapping coattails. "I never studied anyone named Washington in school."

Before Sacha could do more than stare quizzically at her, a newsboy jumped into their path, shaking a paper in their face and shouting, "Extra, extra! Read all about it! Manhunt on for the Klezmer killer!"

NY DAILY NEWS
EXTRA!
Gangsters & Anarchists!
Police Track Klezmer Killer
From the Bright Lights to
the Tenement Back Streets
Wanted
Dead or Alive

"GANGSTERS AND ANARCHISTS!" the headlines screamed up at them. "Police Track Klezmer Killer from the Bright Lights to the Tenement Back Streets!"

Beneath the headlines, the front page article was all about poor little Sam Schlosky. Except that it wasn't Sam at all, but an imaginary villain who seemed to be half Magic, Inc., gangster and half Anarcho-Wiccanist terrorist. To hear the papers tell it, it was a wonder that anyone on the Lower East Side had survived living next door to Sam Schlosky with lungs and liver intact. And right smack in the middle of page one was a picture of Sam Schlosky—a smaller, skinnier version of his big brother Moishe—with the words WANTED DEAD OR ALIVE! stamped across it.

Wolf threw down the paper and stalked off up Fifth Avenue. Every time he passed a newsboy, he bought a paper. And with every paper, he looked more furious.

Sacha hurried along behind Wolf, thankful he'd never given his boss reason to be angry at *him.* He didn't know if Keegan had actually ordered the manhunt for Sam Schlosky or if the papers had just made it up out of thin air. But whoever was responsible for those stories, Sacha did know he wouldn't want to be in that person's shoes when Wolf caught up to him.

CHAPTER NINE

Payton's Luck

BACK AT THE Inquisitors Division, Wolf stalked through the antechamber of Keegan's office without even stopping to acknowledge the nervous flutters of the secretary, flung open the Commissioner's office door, and caught Keegan talking on his private telephone with his feet up on his desk.

"What is the meaning of this?" Wolf demanded, flinging the papers onto Keegan's desk.

"Well, Wolf, it's been a week since the man died, and you haven't even located the main eyewitness," Keegan pointed out, showing a hint of the guile and quick-footedness he was famous for. "How long did you expect me to wait?"

A faint flush crept across Wolf's normally pale cheekbones. "So you decided to hurry me up by setting off a city-wide manhunt for a child who's more likely to be the next victim than the killer?"

"Schlosky may not be much of a suspect," Keegan said airily, "but he's the only one we've got, so we'd better make the most of him."

Wolf looked as if he was about to argue with Keegan. But then the look of anger vanished, as he seemed almost visibly to will his face back into its usual bland and nondescript expression. He thrust his hands into his coat pockets and stared down at the floor for a moment. When he looked up, he looked as unflappable as ever.

"Quite so," he said. "If you don't mind, I'll get back to work again. Excuse the interruption."

"Er—right," Keegan said, caught off-guard by Wolf's sudden change of tone. "File a report as soon as you find anything."

"Of course," Wolf answered with his blandest smile. "Though you're so well-informed about this case that there hardly seems to be any point in filing reports at all." Then he turned on his heel and walked out of Keegan's office, giving the apprentices so little warning that they barely managed to scramble through the door behind him.

Back at his office, Wolf swept through the front room without more than a brief nod to Philip Payton and vanished into his inner sanctum. The door closed behind him with a decided *snick.* Sacha had never seen Wolf slam a door in all the time he'd worked for him, but Wolf seemed to be able to put more expression into a quietly closed door than most people put into slamming and stomping. They heard Wolf's coat hit the floor in a heap. Then they heard him settling into his chair. A moment later, they heard Rosie's walking, talking picture projector starting up. And the only sound after that was the soul-searing wail of the Klezmer King's swan song.

Payton broke the silence first. "Well, *he's* madder than a wet hen," he said, then thought for a minute. "Tell me again what Moishe said about Sam's secret?"

"That it would cause a scandal," Sacha said.

"And expose Morgaunt as a scheming criminal," Lily added.

"Mmmm," Payton murmured. And then he clammed up and stopped talking to them entirely.

Lily stamped impatiently. "Come on, Payton! You can't just say 'mmmm' like that and then make like grass growing!"

"Can't I?" Payton drawled. And then he sauntered across the office, pulling old case files out of the towering mounds of paperwork here and there. Despite the eternal chaos of Wolf's office, Payton was always able to lay his hands on exactly the piece of paper he wanted at a moment's notice. He took his gleanings back to his desk, sat flipping through them for a few minutes, and then scooped the files up in his arms and knocked on Wolf's office door.

A chair creaked. The eerie music stopped.

"Who is it?" Wolf called.

"Me," Payton answered.

"Oh. Come in, then."

Payton went into the office, hooking the door closed

behind him with one ankle and giving the apprentices a final sharp look as if to say he'd better not catch them cramming their ears against the keyhole the minute the door was closed.

Which, naturally, was exactly what they both did.

Inside Wolf's office, they heard only the shuffling of papers for a few moments, as Payton showed Wolf the contents of the files he'd collected.

"What's your point?" Wolf asked. "And even if you are right, what can we do about it? Keegan would give me a warrant to search City Hall sooner than he'd give me a warrant to search Pentacle."

Payton cleared his throat. "You know," he said in a musing tone of voice, as if he were just thinking aloud to himself, "I haven't had a vacation in a long time."

"Payton—"

"I think I'd like to take some time off, if you don't mind."

"What? Now?"

"I have some personal business I'd really like to take care of—"

"I'm not having you running off and putting yourself in danger just to—"

"And I haven't called in sick or taken one day of vacation in almost three years of working for you."

"Payton!"

"And actually, I'm feeling rather ill, come to think of it. Don't you think I look a little pale?"

"Ha ha, very funny. Do you know what they'll do to you if they catch you? They'll throw you in the Tombs!"

"And you'll get me out," Payton said coolly.

"I'll *try*. That's a hell of a gamble, Payton."

"I'm feeling lucky," Payton said blithely.

"You and Paddy Doyle really are two birds of a feather, aren't you?" Wolf grumbled.

But a moment later, Payton came out of Wolf's office, pulled on his coat, tucked a few more files under his arm, and walked down the hall whistling a jaunty tune. Sacha and Lily waited until his footsteps had faded away down the corridor outside. Then they crept back to the door of Wolf's office. Payton had left it ajar on his way out, so they could see Wolf sitting at his desk, brooding and watching Rosie's film.

They watched the Klezmer King flash and sparkle. They heard the haunting music. They saw Sam Schlosky's white face peeping out from backstage. And as Wolf played and replayed and played the tape again, they heard Naftali Asher shout, "No! Sam!" over and over.

Suddenly Wolf sprang out of his chair and scooped his coat off the floor.

"Come on," he said, turning to the apprentices. "I'm going to pay a social call I ought to have paid the minute that first article hit the papers on Friday evening. Mr. Morgaunt's probably at home dressing for dinner now, and if he wants to tell me how to do my job, I might as well go over there and let him do it face-to-face instead of waiting for tomorrow's newspapers."

CHAPTER TEN

A Bookcase with a Bad Attitude

THEY WERE HALFWAY across Central Park when they heard the explosion. There was a sharp thud that reminded Sacha of the *crump* of someone stomping on a cardboard box to squash it flat. And then a wall of sound rippled through the falling dusk like floodwater rushing downstream below a broken dam.

Wolf glanced briefly up from his paper and then went back to the crossword.

"What on earth was that?" Sacha whispered to Lily.

Lily shrugged. "They've been blasting all week for the Harlem subway line. Or it might be some work they're doing at Morgaunt's house."

"It's *still* not finished? What's he doing now?"

The last time Sacha had been to J. P. Morgaunt's Fifth Avenue mansion, there had been an automated parking garage in the works and an entire village of Italian stonemasons living on the roof. "Is it true he has his own private subway stop?"

"Yeah. He took my parents down to see it last time we went to dinner. But my mother wouldn't let me go." Lily made a rude face. "She thought the sculptures in the fountain were unsuitable for young ladies."

"There's a fountain?"

"Well, of course there is! What else would they do with the water?"

Sacha shook his head, trying to dispel the dizzy feeling he got whenever Lily started trying to "explain" to him how "regular people" lived.

"What on earth are you talking about?" he managed to ask as they climbed the monumental granite steps that led up to Morgaunt's front door.

But Lily just gave him one of her best know-it-all looks. "We're on an island, Sacha. Think about it. And don't you ride the subway to work every morning? Honestly, how unobservant can a person be?"

Sacha opened his mouth to argue with her—but then he gave up because he didn't even know where to start. And anyway, they were pulling up at Morgaunt's front door already.

Wolf skipped up the steps, opened the heavy front door as if it weighed nothing at all, and sauntered into Morgaunt's entrance hall as confidently as if he were walking into his own office. Lily leaped up the steps behind him, grabbed the door just before it swung to—and pointed at the lock with a look of wonder on her face. It dangled from the door at an odd angle, and the wood around it was as twisted and splintered as if Wolf had just shot the lock out with a police revolver.

A black-clad butler flung himself in Wolf's path before he'd made it halfway to the library.

"Sir! You can't just—"

Wolf didn't even break stride. "I'm sure Mr. Morgaunt will be happy to see me."

"But Mr. Morgaunt isn't at home at the moment, so—"

"That's all right," Wolf said, pushing open the great bronze doors of J. P. Morgaunt's famous library. "I'll just wait in here for him."

Sacha had been here before, but he still felt the same sense of uneasy awe at the soaring height of the gothic vaults and dizzying spider's web of wrought-iron balconies. Wolf settled into one of the two armchairs before the great marble hearth, while Sacha and Lily stood around awkwardly, wondering what to do with themselves. Sacha scanned the bookshelves. Who knew what secrets were locked inside them? Perhaps the answers to many of the mysteries that Rabbi Kessler and his students debated at the little *shul* on Canal Street. Perhaps even the answer to the mystery that Sacha had lain awake so many nights wondering about. Morgaunt must have learned the spells that had created Sacha's dybbuk from one of the books in this very room. And if Sacha could get into this library alone—just for one precious half-hour—then maybe he could find that book and learn how to banish the creature back into the outer darkness, no matter what his grandfather said.

Almost without being aware of what he was doing, he began to drift toward the nearest bookshelf. The panes in its leaded-glass windows seemed to wink and beckon to him. As he drew nearer, he could see that the glass itself rippled and flowed like dripping amber.

There were spells worked into the glass, but they were like no spells he'd ever seen before. They had a sort of quelling force that damped the magic of the books inside the case like a candle snuffer. He peered through the glass, squinting, and realized that he could still catch a bit of the magic of the books themselves even through the smothering spells. Some of the books in there were just books, meek and silent. But others had a life of their own. They seemed to call to him, almost to beg him to take them down and read them and give their words life in his own brain, his own hands.

He reached out and took hold of the clasp to open the door—

"Gar!" shrieked the bookshelf. "Whaderyer think yer doin'? Quit pokin' me!"

"You want to watch out for that bookshelf," said a cool, amused, sultry voice from the doorway. "It's got an inflated ego and a bad attitude."

Sacha whirled around, his face flaming, and saw Morgaunt's librarian standing in the doorway laughing at him.

Bella da Serpa was one of the most talked-about women

in New York. Rumors flocked around her like art collectors around a priceless Renaissance Madonna. Rumors about her complicated relationship with J. P. Morgaunt. Rumors about her friendships with the famous sons of Europe's great magical dynasties. Rumors about her father, the mysterious Count da Serpa, a Portuguese enchanter whom everyone had heard of for years, but no one could quite remember having seen in person.

None of the rumors were even remotely as interesting as Bella da Serpa herself. She was a tall, elegant woman with a rich olive complexion and dark hair that was always pulled severely back from her face in a style that would have made any ordinary woman look pinched and plain. Her fashion sense was legendary—along with her dry sense of humor and her ruthless business smarts.

"My mother won't invite her to our house because she's not respectable," Lily had once told Sacha, "but she says that if Bella de Serpa had been born a man, she'd be the biggest Wall Street Wizard of them all."

Instead Bella da Serpa had chosen to work behind the scenes. She was the artistic genius behind Morgaunt's world-famous collection of magical manuscripts. Looking at her now, Sacha couldn't help wondering how many dark secrets she could have revealed to Wolf about Morgaunt's plans for New York.

If she'd wanted to, that is. But nothing in her dark eyes or her beautiful face suggested that she had any interest at all in helping Wolf.

"Where's Morgaunt?" Wolf asked her in a tone that made Sacha think they must know each other better than he'd realized.

"Well, wherever he is, you can't wait for him here." She swept across the room in a rustle of dove gray silk and sank gracefully into the chair behind Morgaunt's desk. "This is *my* library, and I prefer that it not be turned into a public waiting room."

Her voice was as soft and feminine as ever—but there was an edge of steel behind the words that Sacha didn't think even Wolf would dare to test.

"Then tell me where he is," Wolf retorted.

"That's just what I was about to do. There's no need to be rude about it."

Wolf's mouth compressed to a thin line.

"And no, actually, I wasn't going to call you a guttersnipe," Bella da Serpa said, as if she were plucking the thoughts out of Wolf's head and answering a question he hadn't even asked out loud. "But I do think it's interesting that that's how you see yourself. I suppose it must be quite difficult to be an orphan. One must be called upon very early to rely on one's own resources."

"I'm not impressed by your parlor tricks."

"And I'm not impressed by your manners, so that makes two of us."

She got up from the desk, pulled a key chain out of a hidden pocket in her perfectly tailored gown, and chose a tiny golden key from among the rest. She walked over to a tall mahogany cabinet against one wall and opened it to reveal row upon row of glimmering white and gold etherograph cylinders, all neatly catalogued with labels made out in a graceful feminine hand that Sacha was quite sure must be hers.

Sacha gasped at the sight of so many etherograph cylinders in one place. He wondered if his own recording was among them or if Morgaunt kept it somewhere else. Bella pulled a pasteboard box off the bottom shelf of the cabinet, brought it back to the desk, and unceremoniously dumped its contents out on the blotter.

There were some twenty or thirty cylinders there, all unlabeled and uncatalogued. And as Wolf watched, Bella began labeling the cylinders with little white tags that hung from loops of pale green string.

"There's been a cave-in on the new Harlem line of the subway," she said after she'd written out the first few labels. "There was an explosion that you must have heard as you were coming across the park. If you go to Lexington and Ninety-Second Street, you'll find Morgaunt there supervising the cleanup and trying to get the work back on track before they fall hopelessly behind schedule."

Wolf didn't acknowledge the information. Like Sacha, he was too busy staring at the etherograph recordings.

"The name Naftali Asher wouldn't happen to mean anything to you, would it?" he asked.

She wrote out another label and looked critically at her handiwork, tilting her beautiful dark head as if she were authenticating a questionable manuscript.

"Why do you let him use you like this, Bella?"

A sly smile curved her lips, but she didn't look up from the work. "Because he lets me use him right back."

Wolf made a rude sound.

"I don't trust you, Maximillian Wolf. I knew you weren't a man to be trusted the moment I first laid eyes on you. And when you think of what's happened to the people who *have* trusted you, can you really say I was wrong? Morgaunt has his faults, and Lord knows I've seen more of them than anyone else on God's green earth. But he's a builder, not a wrecker. He's built factories and businesses that employ thousands. And he's building something here, in this library, something of a scope and power you can't begin to appreciate." She gazed at Wolf across the desk as if he were an interesting taxonomical specimen. "You, on the other hand, are the kind of dangerous idealist who'd tear down the whole house because you don't happen to like the wallpaper in the dining room."

"I make mistakes, Bella, but I mean well."

"You mean well." Bella repeated Wolf's phrase as if it belonged to a foreign language. "Men always do the most terrible things after they say those words."

"And what is *Morgaunt* doing?" Wolf asked in a fierce and urgent voice. "For years I've watched the two of you travel from one end of the globe to the next, gathering the greatest library of black magic ever assembled in one place. Am I wrong to fear such power? Am I wrong to think that a man like Morgaunt poses a threat to the very idea of democracy?"

"Democracy!" Bella said, and her voice thrilled with a

disdain that Sacha felt all the way to his toes. "Do you know what 'democracy' means to me? It means the power of the lynch mob, nothing more and nothing less!"

"Perhaps, Bella," Wolf said quietly. "But Morgaunt's not the answer. He's not your friend. He's not anyone's friend."

"He's as good a friend as a woman like me can expect to have." Bella looked seriously at Wolf, as if she were revisiting some old judgment she'd made about him and confirming that she'd been right all along. "Goodbye, Max. It's been nice seeing you. Don't come again."

Suddenly Sacha found himself being propelled toward the door. Lily went with him, looking just as helpless and bewildered as Sacha felt. Wolf stayed behind just long enough to make it clear that he was leaving under his own steam, but he still looked harried and irritated when he joined them in the lobby.

CHAPTER ELEVEN

Death in the Pit

IT WAS ONLY a short walk from Morgaunt's mansion to the upper end of the still-unfinished Harlem subway line, and once they got there, it didn't take them long to find the site of the cave-in. All they had to do was follow the bright blare of the arc lights. The line ran a few blocks east of the Hudson River Line's train sheds and switching yards, through a neighborhood where slaughterhouses and tanneries were giving way to cheap apartments built on speculation.

When they reached the construction site, Sacha could only stare in amazement. It looked like a bomb had gone off. The entire block was clogged with fire wagons and rescue crews. A pall of dust hung thick in the air: the rubble of a dreadful explosion, still settling to earth long after the damage had been done and shading the white glare of the arc lights to a sooty gray. At the north end of the diggings gaped the black maw of the subway. And between them stretched the vast expanse of the open pit.

Sacha had seen subway construction sites sprouting all over the city in the past few years, but he was still shocked every time he realized just how deep they were. This pit went down and down and down, through cobblestones and gravel and dirt and bedrock. Water seeped from the walls and trickled down the cut face to fill stagnant sump ponds. Massive tree roots clawed out of the wounded earth, torn off in midair like severed fingers. Boulders the size of carthorses protruded from the walls as well—and some of them lay tumbled at the bottom. Sacha thought of what it would be like to be working in the pit when one of those behemoths calved from the wall and thundered down upon you, and he shuddered.

Between the putrid ponds and the fallen boulders, the ground was littered with piles of rock and bags of mortar. The pit diggers moving through this underworld were so covered in dust and grime that they seemed almost to be subterranean creatures themselves. Seeing them struggling through the muck so far below him made Sacha think for a moment of his grandfather's stories of the golem, a man made from river mud.

Wolf watched the ditch diggers intently for a few moments, but his face looked so impassive that Sacha thought his mind must be a thousand miles away. A half dozen engineers and foremen were gathered at one end of the platform talking over a set of blueprints, and after a moment, one of them broke away from the conference and walked over to ask Wolf if he needed help.

Wolf showed the man his badge and said he needed to speak to Morgaunt. The man's jaw hardened, and his eyes became wary at the sight of an Inquisitor's badge, but he bowed politely and pointed toward a jumble of hastily constructed wood-framed buildings halfway around the rim of the pit.

"Wait here," Wolf told the apprentices. "And don't wander around. It's not safe."

Lily waited until Wolf was out of sight and then started down the rickety wooden stairs into the pit.

"What are you doing?" Sacha asked, even though he knew already.

"Snooping!" Lily said cheerfully.

"Don't you remember what happened the last time you ignored Wolf like this?"

"Yep! We solved the mystery!"

"We did not—oh, I give up!" He made a face and stomped away from the edge of the pit so he wouldn't have to see Lily flouncing down the stairs. It would serve her right if Wolf came back and caught her disobeying him!

He couldn't resist for long, though. After fuming for half a minute, he stomped back to the stairs intending to follow her. He'd barely set foot on the top step, however, when half a dozen diggers surged up from the pit bottom carrying something long and heavy and wrapped in a dirty blanket. They pushed past Lily, huffing and panting, staggered up onto the sidewalk, and laid their burden down with a soft, heavy thud that gave Sacha a queer feeling in his stomach.

Sacha started for the stairs again, only to be stopped again by a voice he would have known instantly anywhere in the world.

"Why, Mr. Kessler! Don't tell me you're leaving already when I've gone to so much trouble to arrange a private chat with you."

Sacha turned around to see J. P. Morgaunt grinning at him.

"Wolf's looking for you," he told the Wall Street Wizard.

"No doubt he is. But that doesn't mean I'm looking for him." Morgaunt chuckled in a way that would have seemed good-natured and friendly in another man. "Frankly, Wolf and I have said all we have to say to each other. Those nuns ruined him for life. The meek shall inherit the earth, indeed! Does anyone ever stop to think what an unmitigated disaster *that* would be? The trains would never run on time again, and we'd all starve to death inside of a year. But I don't have to tell you that, Mr. Kessler. You may act meek and mild, but you're a lion where it matters." He rapped Sacha on the chest with a hand that, despite its elegant manicure and golden cufflinks, was as strong as any workman's. "And that pretty black-eyed sister of yours is a regular tiger!"

Sacha felt the blood draining from his face.

"Oh, yes, I know all about her," Morgaunt laughed. "And if you'll take my advice, you'll make sure she gets out of this strike nonsense before it's too late."

"Why can't you just give them what they want?" Sacha asked hopelessly.

Morgaunt's look was almost as pitying as the look Bekah had given Sacha when he asked her the same question. "Because it's cheaper to pay large young men of limited intelligence to beat them up until they go back to work. As an esteemed colleague of mine on Wall Street once pointed out, we can pay half the working class to shoot the other half." He winked cheerfully at Sacha. "And human nature being what it is, sometimes we don't even have to pay them."

Sacha would have liked to disagree, but, really, how could he? Morgaunt was right as usual. A lot more right—or so it seemed to Sacha—than all the people who pronounced pompous platitudes about the power of love, the nobility of humanity, and so forth.

Morgaunt started to speak again, but suddenly a soul-rending noise filled the air around them.

Someone had unwrapped the blanketed bundle, and it wasn't a bunch of wire or tools they'd carried up out of the bowels of the earth. It was a body—the body of a boy only a few years older than Sacha.

A woman came up the street at a run, outpacing the man who must have been sent to fetch her. Sacha guessed it was the boy's mother from the look of blank terror on her face. And he knew it for certain when she threw herself across the corpse and screamed again as if her very soul were being torn again from her.

The sound tore at Sacha like the shriek of a dying animal. And then, to his horror, she raised her tear-streaked face and began to claw at her cheeks. Sacha backed away instinctively, more terrified by the woman's wrenching grief than by the body itself.

Some of the bystanders grabbed the woman, pulling her off her son's body and tying rags on her hands to stop her from tearing at herself. But seeing her this way was almost worse. Only a moment ago, Sacha had seen her run up the street, a young mother in the prime of her life. But she stood up from her son's body an old woman, so bent and broken that anyone just coming upon the scene would have thought she was his grandmother.

"Look at her," Morgaunt said, shocking Sacha, who had almost forgotten his presence. "She's a creature out of prehistory, a ghost of the Stone Age. Do you know that when the English conquered western Ireland, there were tribes there who carried stone knives and barely knew how to make fire? What hope can there be of turning such savages into Americans?"

"They're still human beings," Sacha whispered raggedly.

"You spend too much time with that sentimentalist Wolf," Morgaunt scoffed. "He loves the Irish because they took him in when he was abandoned by a mother who was probably no better than she should have been. But a fox doesn't become a hound just because he moves into the kennel. The other cops know Wolf isn't really one of them. And they hate him for it . . . just as surely as they hate *you* for being a Jew."

"Are you trying to hire *this* half of the working class to shoot the other half?" Sacha snapped.

But Morgaunt just threw back his head and laughed. Sacha realized that Morgaunt hadn't really been trying to argue with him. He'd just been amusing himself by winding Sacha up. Sacha shook his head and turned away, determined not to give the man the satisfaction of knowing his taunts had struck home.

"Ah, but you shouldn't turn away from me," Morgaunt said. "And you shouldn't trust Wolf as you do. Men who think they're on the side of the angels are always dangerous. That's the difference between me and Wolf. I'm a businessman, a practical fellow who wants to see the world organized along sensible, orderly, profitable lines. And a good businessman knows the value of loyalty and the importance of rewarding it properly. Whereas Wolf is willing to sacrifice anything and betray anyone for his ideals, including you."

"I don't believe you," Sacha said stubbornly, even though he did . . . just a little.

Morgaunt's smile grew sad and understanding and almost gentle. "Of course you don't," he said. "They never do until it's too late."

And that was when Wolf and Lily found them.

Wolf gave Morgaunt a look that made Sacha suddenly suspect he'd purposely gone off and let the Wall Street Wizard corner him alone. He felt a hot rush of anger. Was Wolf testing him? Was he *trying* to throw Sacha in the way of temptation to see if he would agree to work for Morgaunt? Or could he just not be bothered to protect him from Morgaunt's jeers and mockery?

But Sacha's glare rolled off Wolf like water off a waxed coat.

As the two men moved away together down the platform, Sacha leaned on the railing and buried his aching head in his hands.

"What did Morgaunt say to you?" Lily asked.

"Nothing."

She frowned. "You don't look like it was nothing."

Sacha just closed his eyes and shook his head.

"Are you all right?" Lily asked. And when he didn't answer, she stood awkwardly beside him for a few moments before reaching out to pat him on the shoulder. It was a stiff gesture, as if it was something she'd never tried doing before and couldn't quite get the hang of. But oddly, it made him feel better.

CHAPTER TWELVE

A Dangerous Man

THE NEXT MORNING was Friday, the day of Sacha and Lily's lesson with Shen. Shen's lessons were the high point of their week. By now they'd been studying with her for the best part of a year. Lily was completely infatuated with their teacher, and truth to tell, Sacha had been bitten almost as badly with the kung fu bug.

During the first few months, Sacha had pulled muscles and tendons and ligaments that he didn't even know he had. And then the pulled muscles felt as if they'd developed pulled muscles of their own. He and Lily had shuffled around on legs they could barely raise off the ground with arms so sore they seemed to have stopped being regular parts of their bodies and turned into objects of the most refined torture.

But it had been worth it. Slowly, Shen had initiated them into the mysteries of something that Sacha was beginning to see as both a way of fighting and a kind of moving art. One by one, she had taught them the incredible movements—she called them forms—that they'd watched her students do that first day.

Sacha loved everything about the forms. He loved their names: Dragon, Snake, Tiger, Leopard, and Crane. He loved the way the different moves took on the spirit and character of each animal: the majestic, flowing power of the dragon; the slippery elusiveness of the snake; the power and agility of the tiger; the speed of the leopard; the perfect balance of the crane. They conjured up images of a beautiful land of tall mountains and pearl rivers and cedar trees—one that seemed to belong to an entirely different universe from dull and ordinary Hester Street.

And it wasn't just the forms of Shaolin kung fu that Shen taught them. She also told them stories of how the Shaolin monks had created kung fu in order to defend themselves against armed men without killing their opponents, and how they had traveled throughout China using their courage and their kung fu to protect the weak and prevent injustice. But the greatest masters, she told them, had gone beyond merely fighting—even in a noble cause—and had begun to seek spiritual wisdom as well as physical mastery. They had learned that kung fu was a means of preparing oneself to follow Wu Wei, the Path of No Action. And by following the Path of No Action, the greatest of them had gained such wisdom that they became Immortals.

Lily was convinced that Shen was an Immortal and

longed to ask her about it. And when Sacha pointed out that Shen always called herself a student too, Lily just scoffed at his objection.

"Shen a student? That's ridiculous! And anyway, I read about it in *The Seven Secret Sages of Shaolin*—or was it *Shaolin Sheriff*? Or—well, never mind where it was. One of those magazines. The point is, Immortals always say that kind of thing. Shen's just acting like a textbook kung fu master, with all this nonsense of being as ignorant as the beginningest student. I'm telling you, she's one of them!"

Lily regarded Shen with a kind of schoolgirl version of hero worship. Sacha made fun of her about it—but if he was honest with himself, he had to admit he had a pretty bad case of hero worship too. Plus, the more he thought about it, the more he liked the idea of learning kung fu instead of magic. Not just because it would have been nice to be able to wipe the mocking grin off Morgaunt's face yesterday, but also because it was obvious that Meyer Minsky and Magic, Inc., used guns and fists and brass knuckles alongside magic. And if Morgaunt was going to hire them to put down the Pentacle strike once it started, then someone was going to have to be ready to stand up and protect Bekah and all the other defenseless girls who were going to be on the picket line.

Sacha didn't know when that would be or what exactly the Inquisitors would be called upon to do. But he'd been hearing people muttering about the strike around Inquisitors Division for weeks. Mayor Mobbs had already announced that he was going to bring in the Inquisitors to "keep the peace" if Morgaunt and the IWW couldn't come to an agreement soon. Bekah and Uncle Mordechai insisted cynically that "keeping the peace" meant the police would turn a blind eye to the hexes of Minsky's starkers—while promptly arresting any striker who so much as muttered a protection spell. Still, for better or for worse, Sacha was going to be there when the strike broke out. And when it did, he was looking forward to using some of Shen's moves on the first starker who tried to go anywhere near his sister.

Today, however, Sacha had more than the strike on his mind. So, long before their lesson time, Sacha walked to the dusty apothecary's shop in Chinatown, stamping his feet and rubbing his hands against the cold that gripped the city.

Shen was washing the floor when he arrived, and he took up a brush and started to help her. For a while they just cleaned companionably together. Then Shen sat up, tossed her brush into the bucket of soapy water, and gave Sacha a look that made him flush to the roots of his hair.

"What?" he asked.

"Isn't that supposed to be my question?"

"Can't I come talk to you without you assuming I'm in some kind of trouble?"

"Based on past experience?" Shen grinned. "No."

"Maybe I just wanted to talk to you about baseball."

"Oh, yeah? Have you heard anything about that new pitcher the Yankees just picked up?"

"Who, the Italian guy? I don't think he was worth the money."

"Well, neither do I . . . as a pitcher." Shen leaned forward as if she were passing along a hot stock tip. "But you know what? I saw him at batting practice the other day. And he's a southpaw. I'm telling you, that short right-field wall at the Polo Grounds was made for this guy."

"That's not baseball," Sacha scoffed. "That's just a gimmick. Trust me, Shen, trying to turn that Bambino guy into a slugger is going to go down in history as the dumbest thing the Yankees ever did. And anyway, how were you at batting practice?"

"Oh." She waved her hand. "Old Shaolin trick. There's a way of making people you don't want to notice you just, well . . . not notice you. It's no big deal. I can teach it to you sometime. But only if you promise to use it selflessly for the betterment of baseball fandom."

She stood up, lifted the heavy bucket of water, and began walking toward the back of the practice hall. Sacha followed her. But when he started to say something else about the Yankees, she interrupted him.

"It's almost time for class, and Lily will be here in a minute. So why don't you tell me what you really came down here to talk about?"

Sacha bit his lip. He wanted to ask Shen about Wolf. But now that he was standing face-to-face with her, he couldn't bring himself to do it. Except for Wolf's confession that he'd gotten Shen's husband killed, neither Wolf nor Shen had ever said a word to Sacha about their history together. He knew that Wolf was in love with Shen; anyone could see that much. But though Lily was full of romantic fantasies about ill-starred lovers, Sacha wasn't so sure. He'd watched Shen very carefully, and he couldn't point to one word, one glance, one shade of a smile that had ever hinted Wolf meant more to her than any other student. And yet . . . and yet . . .

Haltingly and with many hesitations, he told her about his strange encounter with Morgaunt and his suspicion that Wolf had let him be cornered by the Wall Street Wizard.

"Maybe," Shen said calmly.

"But why?"

"You'd have to ask Wolf about that."

"Shen!"

"I'm not ducking your question. I don't understand Wolf. Sometimes I wonder if he understands himself. And he does have a perverse compulsion to, well, test people, for want of a better word. I sometimes think he's secretly convinced that everyone is going to betray him sooner or later, and he'd rather make them do it sooner and just get it over with. It doesn't have anything to do with you, so there's no point in taking it personally. He's only reckless for himself, never for other people. He'd lay down his life to save yours if it came to that." She made a wry face. "And then pick a silly fight with you and go off in a huff so he wouldn't have to endure your gratitude."

This sounded so much like Wolf that Sacha had to laugh.

"He's already trying to protect me," he told Shen. "Or help me protect myself. He wants me to learn magic."

"I know. He's been pestering me about it for months now. But I'm not so sure you're ready."

"What's *that* supposed to mean?" Sacha asked, feeling a little stung by Shen's words. After all, it was one thing for *him* to refuse to learn magic—and another thing entirely for Shen to say he wasn't up to it!

Shen just shrugged instead of answering. She picked up her bucket and staggered out the back door to the water pump. She dumped the slop water into the drain, opened the squeaky spigot, and scrubbed out the bucket. Then she set it against the pump to dry, upended at a precise angle. When she stood up, she was a bit red in the face from the exertion. Or at least Sacha hoped that was what it was, and not annoyance.

"I didn't mean to be rude," he apologized. "But—why not?"

"I thought you didn't want to learn magic," Shen said with the ghost of a smile on her lips.

"I don't, but—"

"But you still want me to tell you that you're ready to learn it."

Sacha flushed.

"I don't mean to make fun of you," Shen said. "The fact is, I don't know if you're ready or not. You are the only person who can answer that question. And if you're not sure, then you probably know what the answer is."

"How did Wolf know when he was ready?"

Suddenly Shen looked surprised and troubled. "What did he tell you about it?"

"Only that your husband was his first teacher. So I thought you'd know . . ."

Shen didn't speak for several moments. And when she did, her voice was carefully neutral and devoid of emotion. "Wolf didn't come to my husband to learn how to work magic," she said. "He came to learn how to *not* work magic."

"But why would he want to—"

"He burned a building down. And he wanted to make absolutely sure that he would never do such a thing again."

"Was it an accident?"

"Yes," she said without looking at him. "A very terrible accident."

"Did anyone die?" Sacha asked. But he knew the answer—indeed, he had known it from the moment Shen began speaking in that careful, quiet voice. "Is that why he became an Inquisitor? To stop things like that from happening again? Or—or because he felt guilty?"

"You really should talk to Wolf, Sacha. It's his story. He hasn't spoken to me about it for years, and he may think very differently now than he did back then. It wouldn't be right for me to put words into his mouth."

"So why are you telling me about it at all?"

"Because he should have told you. You need to understand how dangerous power is—all the ways it can turn on you, the foolish vanity of ever thinking you can control what a spell does once you've loosed it on the world."

"You think I don't know all that after what happened at Coney Island?"

"I'm not sure you know it *enough,* Sacha. And I'm sure Wolf doesn't. He's a good man. A very good man. Sometimes I think he's the best man I've ever known. But that doesn't mean he isn't dangerous."

"Is that why you won't work for him? Why you told him you wouldn't teach me and Lily the first time he brought us here? But then why did you change your mind, Shen? You looked at me so strangely that day. What did you see then? Were you—were you afraid *I* would be dangerous if you didn't teach me?"

Shen began to speak. Sacha hung on her words, hoping she would finally illuminate the landscape of darkness and confusion that he had struggled through ever since he'd begun his apprenticeship. But just then Lily's voice rang out in the chilly air.

"What are you two doing skulking around back here?" she cried, marching into the courtyard. "And when are we going to get started, anyway? We have to be uptown by eleven, remember?"

Shen seemed relieved by the interruption. She shrugged, smiled, and slipped past Sacha and back into the school. For the rest of their lesson, it seemed to Sacha that she avoided being alone with him, that she avoided his eyes, that she gave him no chance to ask again the questions that she had been so tantalizingly close to answering.

So that was it. Whatever Shen had been about to tell him would have to wait. And knowing Shen, by the time their next lesson rolled around, she'd probably have decided against telling him in the first place. Wolf had said Shen was a woman who didn't deal in easy answers—or any answers at all if she could help it. Sacha was starting to see his point.

CHAPTER THIRTEEN

Just Keep Your Mouth Shut and Look Magical

AFTER THEIR LESSON with Shen, Sacha and Lily spent the rest of the day following Wolf back to the same places they'd gone the first time they combed New York for a sign of Sam Schlosky—only this time Wolf had added the morgues to his list. Sacha had seen Wolf investigate serious crimes before, even magical murders. And he'd seen a hunger for justice in the man that verged on a lust for vengeance—and sometimes looked dangerously close to the destructiveness that Bella da Serpa had accused him of. But never had he seen Wolf so obviously frightened for a witness's safety. And as Wolf searched for Sam through the slums and shadows, Sacha couldn't help thinking that no other policeman in New York would spend this much time trying to protect a poor Jewish boy whose family couldn't even afford to pay tenement rent.

By the time Sacha finally stumbled back to Hester Street

that Friday night, the narrow streets of the tenement district were already engulfed in shadows. He knew he must be late for dinner. But he didn't know how late he was—or even remember what day of the week it was—until he stepped through the door of his apartment.

The quiet washed over him like water, and he realized that he had been hearing it all the way up the stairs, as if the whole building had stilled. No one was running a single sewing machine. Not in the Lehrers' backroom sweatshop, where tottering piles of half-finished piecework towered like black cloth haystacks. Not in the Goldsteins' sweatshop next door. Not upstairs at the Kusiks' or the Meyersons' or across the street or down the block. Not anywhere.

All the machines had stopped. And that could only mean one thing. Just like the vinegar-and-lemons smell of freshly scrubbed floors and the honey-wax smell of newly lit candles.

It was Friday night, *Shabbes.* The whole Lower East Side—or at least as much of the Lower East Side as still held to the old traditions—had laid down their weekday work, stepped out of the everyday world, and readied themselves to welcome the Sabbath into their homes as Jews had been doing since before the beginning of history.

Sacha walked through the Lehrers' back room into the kitchen. He couldn't be too late, he realized; his mother and sister weren't even home from work yet. But the Sabbath candles were already lit, twinkling in the window like two golden stars. And Grandpa Kessler was propped up in the feather bed as usual. And Mr. and Mrs. Lehrer had brought their chairs into the kitchen and were sitting around the table with Sacha's father and Uncle Mordechai.

The table was set, the soup was simmering on the stove, and the two loaves of challah lay on the table beneath their embroidered cloth. Mrs. Lehrer had seen to all that, making sure everything that could be done before Sacha's mother got home was done.

Uncle Mordechai was reading the *Alphabet City Alchemist,* as if to remind everyone that though he wasn't about to miss the best dinner of the week, he was still a stalwart atheist. But Mo and Mrs. Lehrer were bent over a prayer book, and Rabbi Kessler was reading a dusty tome of theoretical Kabbalah. Even Sacha's father had set aside his usual newspaper for something more serious.

Sacha hung his coat on the peg and started to go sit beside his grandfather on the feather bed. But then something drew him to the window and the darkening street below. He stood beside the candles, leaned his forehead against the cold glass, and cupped his hands around his eyes so that he could see beyond the reflection of the bright kitchen behind him. Outside, the city lay in darkness, but the horizon was still faintly flushed with the light of the day gone by. The sky shaded from the pink of sunset to a deep midnight blue, and a thin scattering of stars already glimmered in the heavens. The tenement rooftops lay black and jagged below them like the waves of a dark ocean. Yet here and there, glimmering out of the shadows, he could see the faint sparks of *Shabbes* candles in other windows. As he watched, another flame flickered into life, and another, and another, until all of Hester Street seemed to be reflecting back the stars of heaven.

The sight of those candles made his heart hurt. There was something indescribably sad in the thought of all those exhausted women staggering home from work, far too late to cook the Sabbath dinner, far too late to light the candles, and lighting them anyway. What kind of a gesture was that? What difference could a few lit candles make in all the inky darkness of the vast cruel city around them?

"When God's light first flowed forth into the cosmos," his grandfather said, coming up behind him so quietly that Sacha couldn't help starting guiltily, "it was so abundant that it filled the primordial universe to overflowing and shattered the vessels meant to contain it. And the divine sparks scattered, some of them remaining in Heaven and some of them falling deep into the shadows until they cooled and darkened and mingled with the husks of created things. And this is our task: to see the spark within the husk, to gather the light from the shattered vessels and raise it back up to God so that the world can be repaired again."

They stood side by side, staring out the window in silence.

"Do you have to work tomorrow?" his grandfather asked in a casual kind of voice that didn't fool either of them.

"No—well, not in the morning anyway."

"Good. You work too hard. And you should come to *shul* sometime. I talked to Mo about . . . what we talked about last week. And he thinks that would be the best thing for you."

Sacha sighed. He didn't want to go sit in *shul* for hours every weekend—let alone drag his exhausted body over there every night when he got home from work the way some of the rabbi's students did. And he didn't see how it could help him, either. Hadn't his grandfather as much as said that he and Mo didn't have any practical magic to teach him?

But before he could say any of this, Bekah and Mrs. Kessler got home.

"We need to talk to you," Bekah whispered when Sacha plopped into his usual place on the sagging feather bed between her and Grandpa Kessler.

"Who's we?" Sacha whispered.

"Shhh!" Bekah glanced nervously at their mother again. "Not here!" And then she jerked her head toward the ceiling.

Sacha would have liked to pretend he didn't understand the gesture, but of course he did. She was telling him to meet up with her at the Industrial Witches of the World headquarters on the seventh floor on Saturday night after *Shabbes* was over. He'd been avoiding Moishe all week in order to avoid getting roped into whatever ridiculous scheme the IWW leader had in mind. But if Bekah was determined to drag him into it too, then there was no hope of escaping.

Late Saturday evening, when *Shabbes* was good and over and he had used up his last excuse for staying away, Sacha reluctantly trudged upstairs. As he climbed the four flights of stairs that separated the Kesslers' apartment from the IWW headquarters, Sacha could hear the sounds of laughter and singing.

When he got closer, he realized someone was playing a guitar, too. But even that didn't prepare him for the spectacle that greeted him when he got there.

The main room was taken up by what seemed like an ocean of strikers. They were all gathered around a scruffy-looking young man with a guitar who was leading them in a rousing rendition of "Pie in the Sky." At first Sacha couldn't find Bekah in the crowd, but finally he caught sight of her perched next to Moishe on the windowsill.

Moishe had his arm around her—but one look at Bekah's face told Sacha that it would be worth his life to say anything about it.

"Come on outside where we can talk," Bekah shouted over the singing voices. And then she heaved the window open and stepped out onto the fire escape.

Sacha followed her, and Moishe followed him and closed the window behind them.

Moishe cleared his throat, sounding like a goose that was being strangled. "We need you to do us a favor, Sacha."

"I'm not spying on Wolf for you," Sacha snapped, remembering the last time Moishe had asked him for a favor, "so you can just forget about that!"

"No, no, nothing like that! This is a really little favor. We just need a few minutes of your time."

"What for?" Sacha asked suspiciously.

"Oh, nothing really. Just a social call."

"Who are we going to see?"

"Tomorrow morning. We'll pick you up at your house."

"Who are we going to see?"

"It's right nearby. It'll just take a minute. And you don't really have to do anything. Actually it would be better if you didn't do anything. Or say anything either. You just have to, you know, stand there."

"Who are we going to see?"

"It's on Essex Street." Moishe made the strangling goose sound in his throat again. "Um, at the candy store."

Sacha's mouth fell open.

"It's not like that," Bekah said when she saw his expression. "You don't have to talk to Meyer Minsky. We're going to do all the talking. Like Moishe says, you just have to stand there."

"You're going to the Essex Street Candy Store to talk to Meyer Minsky," Sacha finally managed to squeeze out. "Just you two."

"Not just us. The whole IWW central committee is coming."

"Oh, and who are they?"

Bekah listed the names of five other teenagers, none of whom outweighed Sacha by more than a few pounds.

"Have you completely lost your minds? Do you have any idea what Minsky and his starkers are going to do to you—that is, when they've finished busting a gut laughing?"

"Well, of course," Bekah said reasonably. "That's why we need you to come."

"See," Moishe said eagerly, "everyone knows you're

in the Inquisitors. So they'll think you can work powerful magic—"

"Even though we know you couldn't hex your way out of a paper bag," Bekah interrupted.

"Which means that you can serve as a force for peace by deterring all parties involved from resorting to violence," Moishe pointed out. "And what could be better than serving as a force for peace in the world?"

"Oh, I don't know," Sacha said sarcastically. "How about staying in *one* piece? Or maybe avoiding departing the world permanently, courtesy of Dopey Benny Fein?"

"Look, Sacha," Bekah said, "you have to help us. You just have to. Unless we want to see blood run in the streets, we have to get Meyer Minsky on our side before the strike starts. Otherwise Magic, Inc., is just going to rent its starkers out to the highest bidder. And that means J. P. Morgaunt. And if Magic, Inc., comes in to break up the strike, well, you know what that means."

Sacha did indeed know what that meant. Minsky was the most feared gangster in the Lower East Side, and he had made a fortune hiring out his thugs as strikebreakers. So if the IWW was going to win the strike, they needed to convince Minsky to fight on their side—or at least to stay out of the fight so they had a ghost of a chance against Morgaunt.

But there was still one big problem with Bekah's scheme.

"How am I supposed to protect you from Magic, Inc., when I can't work a spell to save my life?" Sacha asked.

"But they don't know you can't do magic," Bekah pointed out. "All they know is that you work for the Inquisitors."

"And that's supposed to prove something?"

"Well, sure. The Inquisitors cast hexes on people all the time."

"They do not!"

Bekah gave him another one of those looks—the ones she gave him when he'd just said something so stupid it wasn't even worth laughing at. "Oh, Sacha. Listen to yourself. Why do you think people become Inquisitors? Because they like using magic to push people around, and being an Inquisitor is a good way to do it legally."

"That's ridicul—"

"Oh, really? Then why is it that the Wobblies they arrest always seem to fall down stairs or trip and hit their heads on the curb by accident? And why is even Meyer Minsky afraid to spend a night in the Tombs?"

"Well, Inquisitor Wolf doesn't do anything like that!"

Bekah started to argue. But then a strange look came over her face. Not as if she disagreed with him, exactly. More like she was sorry for him.

"Sure, Sacha," she said.

"What?"

"Nothing."

"What?"

"Nothing. Really. I'm sure you're right. You're the one who works for him."

"Why are you talking to me like that all of a sudden?"

"Like what? I'm just talking."

"No, you're not. You're being . . . polite. In a totally not Kessler-like way. As if you think he's brainwashed me and you're not sure you can trust me anymore! How can you think that?"

"You said it, not me," Bekah said.

Sacha turned to Moishe. "Do you think that too?"

"Well, you know, Sacha . . ." Moishe wriggled like an underfed Houdini trying to squirm his way out of a straight-jacket.

"Fine! I'll go with you to the stupid candy store and stand around while you talk to the stupid starkers." Sacha cast a baleful glare at his sister. "When did you become so manipulative?"

"I'm not manipulative," Bekah said cheerfully. "People who are really manipulative never admit they are. Whereas I'm perfectly happy to admit it." She folded her arms across her chest and eyed Sacha down one side of her nose. "So. Can we count on you tomorrow morning?"

CHAPTER FOURTEEN

Minsky's Luck

THE NEXT DAY dawned bright and clear, with a kiss of warmth in the air that seemed to hold the promise of spring after all the long dreary months of winter. But Sacha didn't have eyes for the sunshine. He trudged off toward Essex Street, trailing behind Moishe, Bekah, and the rest of the strike committee like a condemned man walking down death row to his own execution.

The Essex Street Candy Store would have been a Lower East Side institution even if it weren't the headquarters of one of New York's most formidable magical street gangs. It stood across the street and just a few doors down from the famous pickle store. But while the chest-high barrels on the sidewalk outside the pickle store held pickled cucumbers and green beans and onions, the candy store's barrels held delicacies that all the kids on Hester Street dreamed of, drooled over, and saved their pennies for.

It was all indescribably delicious. And it was all sitting right out there on the street, just begging to be stolen. But no one ever stole so much as a gumball or a gobstopper from the Essex Street Candy Store. Because everyone from one end of Hester Street to the other had heard about what happened to the few sneak thieves foolish enough to steal from Meyer Minsky.

Gumdrops that turned into newts' tails. Gumballs that turned into eyeballs. Lemon fizzes that gave people shivering fits. Chewing gum that kept you chewing until your teeth chattered and you crawled back to Essex Street begging them to make it stop.

Whenever someone mentioned those rumors in front of Meyer Minsky, he insisted that it was all nonsense and anyone would tell you he wasn't the kind of guy who'd hex a child's candy. But even if only half of the stories were true, you'd have to be completely crazy to steal anything from those barrels. And however crazy you'd have to be on a normal day, you'd have to be twice as crazy today, when Dopey Benny himself was standing guard just inside the front door of the shop.

Dopey Benny looked even bigger in the candy store than he'd looked in the Café Metropole. His hulking shadow engulfed the cash register, the newspaper rack, and three entire bins of gumballs and lollipops. His arms looked like they'd been stuffed into his shirtsleeves like sausages into sausage casings and were straining mightily to get back out again. His bristly neck was so thick that Sacha wondered if he had to fasten his shirt collar with a boot hook.

"You kids oughta stay off the sugar," he said as they came into the shop. "It'll rot your teeth right outta your head."

"Um, yes, well," Moishe said with a gulp. And frankly, Sacha couldn't blame him.

"Take it from me." Benny grinned, showing teeth that would have looked petite on a carthorse. "Never touch duh stuff. And look. Never had a cavity yet."

Bekah cleared her throat at Moishe, who was still staring up at Benny's teeth. At first Sacha thought Moishe was just scared. But he'd learned over the last year that Moishe didn't scare nearly as easily as he looked like he ought to. And sure enough, he turned out to have something else on his mind.

"So tell me this, Benny. You guys break every other magical law in existence. How come you can't make candy that doesn't give people cavities?"

"Can we stick to the—" Bekah began.

"No, I really want to know," Moishe said. "It's something I always wondered about. I mean, what's stopping you? You'd make millions! You could give up your life of crime—that is, if you could get away with it."

But Benny just wagged his head sadly. "Oh, it's been tried," he told Moishe.

"And?" Moishe asked, completely enthralled. Sacha noticed that everyone else was hanging on Benny's words too.

"You don't wanna know. And I couldn't tell ya even if you did, because I promised I'd take the secret to the grave."

Benny nodded sagely. "Dat's what this job is all about. Trust. Trust and teamwork. After all, dere's no *I* in *magic.*"

"Well, actually—" Moishe began.

But Bekah had had enough. She stepped around the boys and craned her neck to stare the starker in the face. "That's all very interesting, Mr. Fein, and we'll take your dietary advice under consideration too. But right now we'd like to see Mr. Minsky."

"Who?" Benny asked. It was amazing, Sacha thought, how a guy who went around the neighborhood looking terminally confused most of the time could be so incredibly bad at pretending to look confused.

"Me-yer Min-sky," Bekah said, enunciating each syllable slowly and distinctly as if she suspected that Benny had suddenly become hard of hearing.

"I'm sorry, miss, I don't know nobody by the name of—"

"Oh, come on!" Bekah snapped. "We're not a bunch of uptown Inquisitors. We're from the neighborhood. And we know exactly what goes on in the back room of this candy store and who's responsible. And what's more, we know where your mothers live! Meyer's mother lived three blocks away on Orchard Street until he bought her a house in Brooklyn Heights last year. And Myrtle Fein lives two flights up from us in the fifth floor left-hand flat at number eighteen Hester Street, where she spends every Saturday afternoon gossiping with my mother—"

"Oh!" Benny said as if he'd been suddenly struck by divine revelation. "Dat's where I know you from!"

"Yes, yes," Bekah said impatiently. "I'm the one whose brother works for the Inquisitors. And we've brought him with us today, and he's a very dangerous man, so I strongly advise you not to trifle with us!"

"Uh—hi, Benny," Sacha said, ruining the effect somewhat.

"How's life treatin' ya?" Benny asked comfortably. "Your boss ever figure out who toasted the Klezmer King?"

"Er—not yet."

"Benny!" Bekah interrupted. "Can we please go in and see Meyer now?"

"He's not here, miss," Benny intoned dutifully.

"Then why is his car parked across the street exactly where it's parked every morning?"

Benny followed her pointing finger, and sure enough, there was Minsky's car, glistening in the wintry morning sunlight. But Benny still wasn't ready to give up the fight.

"Well, not every morning," he began in a quibbling sort of voice.

"You're right," Bekah snapped. "He didn't come down here for eight months last time he got sent up to Sing Sing."

Benny's face sagged mournfully. "Now, why'd you gotta go and bring that up? Just because a fella asked you—"

"She won't do it again," Moishe interrupted. "And if you don't mind, Mr. Fein, perhaps you could just go back and tell Mr. Minsky that the central committee for the Industrial Witches of the World is here to see him about the Pentacle strike?"

"Who, you?" Suddenly Dopey Benny's look of droopy-eyed mystification was completely genuine. He looked around the circle of Wobblies, and his mouth opened wider with every new face he saw. "Youze just a buncha kids!"

Moishe suppressed a sigh. "Who do you think works at Pentacle, Benny?"

"Oh, right . . . Well, but if there's a strike and all, well, I mean, the cops'll come. Maybe even the Inquisitors. And"—he leaned forward confidentially with a look on his face that was disturbingly reminiscent of Sacha's mother—"you could get in trouble."

Sacha tried to smother a laugh and only succeeded in turning it into a strangled sort of sneeze.

Dopey Benny's mournful eyes turned upon Sacha. "Sounds like you got the hay fever," he commiserated. "It's a bad year for hay fever. I got it somethin' awful."

"Oh, jeepers!" Minsky called from the back room. "Just give up and send them in, Benny!"

Benny heaved a relieved sigh, followed them into Minsky's inner sanctum, closed the door behind them, and leaned against it with his massive arms crossed over his chest.

Minsky was lounging in a leather-upholstered armchair, pointy-toed shoes crossed on a massive oak desk that would have looked more at home in J. P. Morgaunt's library than the back room of a candy store. As the strike committee filed in, he began casually tossing his buffalo head nickel and catching it on the back of his left hand. "So what do you want from me?" he asked when he'd tossed five heads in a row.

Moishe and Bekah took it by turns to explain the situation.

"I don't take sides unless I'm paid to," Minsky said when they'd finished. "Picking sides is bad business."

"We're not asking you to take sides," Moishe replied. "We're just asking you to stay out of the fight."

"Staying out is taking sides," Minsky pointed out.

"Then take sides," Bekah exploded. "Or are you too scared to?"

Minsky's eyes settled on Bekah with a look of blank astonishment. "Are you calling me yellow?" he asked in a voice that made Sacha's skin crawl. "And before you answer that question, maybe I should mention what happened to the last guy who called me yellow."

Bekah met Minsky's stare without flinching, though she did jump a little when he tossed the buffalo head nickel onto the desk, where it spun and clattered, and finally landed ominously tails up.

Benny shuffled nervously at the door. "Don't be too hard on her, boss, she's just a—"

"Just a what?" Meyer Minsky asked in his soft, smooth voice. "Just a kid? I don't think so, Benny. I don't think they're just kids at all."

He stood and walked over to Bekah, put one perfectly manicured finger under her chin, lifted her face up until they were practically nose to nose, and stared at her. And then he walked along the line of teenagers, staring them in the eye one after another until he got to Moishe.

Moishe stared Minsky back in the face without flinching—which was more than most gangsters in New York could manage to do. The stare lasted for almost a full minute, and by the end of it, the two of them were standing toe to toe and Moishe was practically cross-eyed.

"You actually think you're going to beat J. P. Morgaunt," Minsky said at last. "You really do. In fact, you think you're going to change the whole damn world, don't you?"

Moishe's eyes were watering with the effort of not blinking. He looked like he'd forgotten to breathe, and Sacha started to worry that he was going to pass out. But finally he spoke. "Someone has to change the world," he said. "Might as well be us."

For a moment, Minsky didn't move. And then he stepped back, laughing. "You hear that, Benny? These kids are gonna change the world! Whaddaya think of that?"

Dopey Benny still stood against the door with his arms crossed, staring down at the strikers from under half-closed eyelids. "I think you kids should go back to woik," he said finally. "It'd be more healthier for you."

"That's the most cowardly thing I've ever heard!" Bekah snapped. "You ought to be ashamed of yourself, Benny!"

"Well—but—I—"

Minsky chuckled at Benny's discomfiture, and Bekah whirled on him and even lifted a finger as if she planned to shake it at the gangster while she scolded him. Then she remembered who she was talking to and gulped audibly.

"You were saying?" Minsky asked in a quiet purr.

For a moment, Sacha thought Bekah was going to back down—but he should have known his sister better. "I was about to say that no gentleman would take money to beat up girls," she told Minsky with a contemptuous curl on her soft lips. "But it's obvious that you aren't a gentleman. And it's just as obvious that you're too afraid of Morgaunt to turn down his money and do what's right!"

"Boss," Benny said frantically, "she's just a little goil! She don't mean it! Don't—don't—"

"I won't hold your harsh words against you," Minsky told Bekah, "because I can see that you are following your conscience, just as a good Jewish girl should do. And as the Bible tells us, *a woman of valor is worth the price of rubies*. But to the men who have come here with you—and I give them the compliment of treating even the youngest among them as men, since they're setting out to get their heads bashed in and leave their blood on the streets—to the men among you, I say this: think twice before you insult me as this girl has just done. This fight is between you and Morgaunt. You've told me that you think it's my duty as a Jew to support you—"

"Your duty as a man!" Bekah interjected.

"Careful, Miss Kessler," Minsky said with a sly smile. "When a girl can't stop scolding a fellow, he's liable to start thinking she's sweet on him."

That shut Bekah up—in fact she turned pale and buttoned her coat up to the throat and didn't say another word.

Minsky went on with his warning. "You boys want me to come into the fight on your side, if I understand you aright.

Maybe I will, and maybe I won't. But I'll say this now: if any *man* among you insults me the way this young lady just did, I'll come in against you. I've never started a fight in my life, but I've never walked away from a fight either. Nor ever lost one. And I don't intend to lose one, not short of dying. So don't make an enemy of me if you plan to keep living in this town."

"So does that mean you'll help us?" Moishe asked, in a voice as calm and steady as if he hadn't just heard the most fearsome gangster in New York threaten to kill him.

Minsky looked Moishe's skinny frame up and down, his blue eyes pausing at the skinny neck and the bony wrists poking out of the boy's shirtsleeves. A ghost of a smile drifted across his lips. Finally he said, "I'll think about it."

"Thank you, Mr. Minsky," Moishe said. "You're doing the right thing. I really believe you are. You won't regret this."

Minsky's smile sharpened into a wry grin. "Kid," he said, "I already regret it!"

"You were pretty tough in there," Sacha told Moishe as they were walking home from the candy store.

Moishe looked surprised at the compliment, as if people didn't compliment him often enough for him to be used to the idea. "You did okay yourself," he answered. He slowed down, and they fell behind the others. Then he started to speak, hesitated, and started again. "I, uh . . . I've been wanting to talk to you about something. Privately."

Sacha waited.

"A certain person we both know has mentioned to me that he might be willing to meet with you."

Sacha's heart pounded. "You mean S—"

"Shhh!"

"Oh. Right. Sorry."

"Anyway, this person. We'll call him our Mutual Friend. Our MF, for short—"

"Thank God you know where he is!" Sacha interrupted. "Wolf is terrified of what's going to happen if anyone else finds him first. You have to tell him to come in and give himself up. It'll be much safer than—"

"As I was saying," Moishe broke in, "our MF would like to talk to you. But he's only willing to see you on one condition."

"Fine! Anything! Just as long as he—"

"You come alone. No cops."

"But what about Wol—"

"No cops. Period. And that means especially no Inquisitors."

"I can't do that, Moishe. I can't lie to Wolf."

"Well, then you can't talk to Sam," Moishe snapped—and then clapped his hand over his own mouth when he realized that he'd forgotten the secret code himself.

"Oh, come on, Moishe. This is crazy! Listen to yourself! Do you hear what you sound like? I know there are some bad cops out there—"

"And some bad Inquisitors."

"Okay, and some bad Inquisitors, too," Sacha said. "But you can trust Wolf."

Moishe swung around to glare fiercely at him. "Oh? And how do you know? In fact, what do you know about anything except what your precious Inquisitor Wolf tells you?"

"Moishe—"

"Oh, right, I forgot. You have inside information from the lovely Miss Astral, too. Do you know what her father is? Do you know what he does for a living? He's the slickest Wall Street Wizard of them all!"

"I've never even met Lily's father. Really. I couldn't care less about him. And I don't think that Lily is some sort of secret spy for the oligarchy. Seriously, Moishe, she's not that good a liar."

Moishe shrugged eloquently.

They walked along in silence for another half a block until Sacha finally relented.

"Okay!" he said. "I'll come talk to him. Where is he?"

"Can't tell you. I'll pick you up at your house tomorrow night after the meeting of the central strike committee. Alone."

"Okay. When?"

"I can't tell you."

"Moishe!"

"Okay, okay! Tomorrow night. And you'd better be alone!"

"Can't you convince Sam to trust Wolf? There are worse

things than getting arrested, you know. Wolf thinks coming in voluntarily would be a lot safer."

"Well, Sam doesn't. He thinks he's up against something that even Wolf can't protect him from."

"Some*thing*?" Sacha asked with a sinking feeling in the pit of his stomach. "What's that supposed to mean?"

"I don't know," Moishe whispered. "But Sam says you're the only one he'll trust."

Sacha struggled for a moment. But it was no good. "I can't do it," he said. "I can't go meet him without at least telling Wolf about it first. I've caused too much trouble that way before now."

Moishe licked his lips nervously and glanced around to make sure no one else was listening. "Sam said you might refuse. And he said to tell you this if you did: you have to come, because you're in even worse trouble than he is."

"What? That's crazy!"

"Well, it's what he said. And he said that if you asked why, I should tell you this: *your own mother's life might be at stake.*"

CHAPTER FIFTEEN

War Council at the Witch's Brew

THE NEXT MORNING, Inquisitor Wolf led his two apprentices to the Witch's Brew, the Hell's Kitchen saloon that he normally sent them scurrying out to every morning for his steaming growler full of mud-thick coffee.

Sullivan, the mountainous bartender, greeted Wolf like a long-lost brother. Sacha knew Wolf had grown up in a Catholic orphanage in the worst section of Hell's Kitchen, so he supposed he shouldn't have been surprised. But somehow he was. And he was even more surprised a few minutes later when Philip Payton sauntered casually into the saloon and sat down at their table, despite the fact that he was still officially on vacation.

"What's *he* doing here?" muttered a skinny fellow at the bar. "I didn't pay good money to drink with—"

"Yer right about that," Sullivan interrupted with a glare that made the man gulp. "In fact, I don't recall you paying me any money at all this month. And young Mr. Payton here pays nice and regular."

Payton gave Sullivan a small nod of thanks, and to Sacha's amazement the mountain of a man actually smiled at him. "An' how's your mother doin', Philip?" the bartender asked. "I haven't seen her round the neighborhood lately."

"No," Payton said. He paused and cleared his throat awkwardly. For the first time since Sacha had known Payton, the older boy looked at a loss for words. "We're a bit busy lately." Payton cleared his throat again. "We're thinking about moving."

"Not out of the neighborhood, I hope?"

"Actually, yes."

"Ah." Sullivan frowned at Payton and seemed to be choosing his next words carefully. "Not because of the recent unpleasantness? I'm sure that won't happen again."

Payton looked Sullivan square in the eye. "My father's not."

"Ah," Sullivan repeated.

Sacha glanced at Lily questioningly, but she just shook her head as if to say she had no more idea what Payton and Sullivan were talking about than he did.

An awkward silence fell. When Payton spoke into it, he sounded less sure of himself than he usually did. "My father thinks we need a neighborhood of our own. And there are others who think the same. They're looking to move to Harlem."

Sullivan suddenly became very busy cleaning the gleaming taps at the bar—even though it didn't look to Sacha like they needed cleaning at all. "I can't fault a man for doing what he thinks is needed to keep his family safe," he said at last. "And do I hear lots of people are moving up there, now that the subway's going to run north of the park. So what's the rent runnin' in Harlem these days?"

"I . . . uh . . . actually, they're looking to buy a building."

"Well, now!" Sullivan rocked back on his heels in surprise. "It's a fine thing to own a piece of God's green earth, and there's no denying that. Though I still say the day your da moves out, it'll be a sad loss for the neighborhood." He glared at the lone drinker who had complained about Payton. "I'd much rather have respectable colored folk for neighbors than a pack of drunken scofflaws who've got nothing better to do on a Saturday night than throw bricks through people's windows!"

Sullivan delivered these last words in a bellow that made the man leap from his chair in terror. As he hurriedly excused himself and scurried out the door onto Forty-Third Street, Sacha glanced at Inquisitor Wolf. But as usual, there was no way of telling what was going on behind the inscrutable expression and the smudged glasses.

"By the way, Philip," Sullivan said as the doors squeaked back and forth on their hinges in the wake of the man's hasty exit. "You wouldn't happen to have seen Paddy Doyle lately, would you?"

"No," Payton said flatly. "I haven't."

"Pity," Sullivan said, still in that careful voice. "You used to be such good friends. But then boys do grow apart sometimes as they turn into men and find their way in life."

"I suppose so," Payton said stiffly.

Wolf leaned forward and cleared his throat to get Payton's attention, but Sullivan wasn't finished yet. "Still, I do hope you'll find the time to drop by and see Mrs. Doyle before you move," the bartender said.

Payton's face softened slightly. "I'll try."

"I hope so. She always was fond of you. And her own boys all turned out so wild. No father around to keep them in line—and all of 'em far too handsome for their own good, if you ask me. It's a scientific fact that no handsome Irishman ever did a lick of work in his life. My wife can tell you all about it. She read a book once where one o' those doctors who measures the bumps on people's heads proved it mathematically." Sullivan grinned, showing a mouthful of peg-like teeth stained brown by decades of strong coffee. "Me, on the other hand, I'm plain as a post. That's why I've risen so high in the world!"

Payton chuckled at the joke—if it was a joke, which Sacha wasn't entirely sure of—and then came over and sat down at the table across from Inquisitor Wolf.

"All right," Wolf said, ticking items off on his fingers. "What do we know so far? One, Naftali Asher and his wife arrived in America dead broke four years ago. Two, Asher was a perfectly ordinary klezmer player, but possibly—if we believe Kid Klezmer's claims about the hate spell—a powerful magician. Three, Asher couldn't find work playing music, but he did find work at Pentacle—"

"If only we could crack the Pentacle connection," Payton interrupted, "I'm sure the whole story would fall into place."

"I think so too," Wolf said. "But that's going to have to wait until we find Sam Schlosky."

Sacha felt a sudden terrible pang of guilt. Maybe he was doing the wrong thing again. Maybe he should just tell Wolf about Moishe's offer to help him meet with Sam. But no, Moishe had said Sam wouldn't trust anyone but Sacha. Once he had heard what Sam had to say, then he could decide whether to tell Wolf about it or not. After all, he was only going to meet Sam and listen to his story. What harm could come of listening?

"In any case," Wolf went on, "we do know this much: one month Asher is sick and broke, and a few months later, he's the toast of the Bowery and the most famous klezmer player in New York. And he's playing songs that come straight from Edison's etherograph recordings. So the big question is, who gave Naftali Asher that music?"

At that moment a tall, lean shadow fell over the table and Sacha looked up to see Paddy Doyle himself staring down at them. The boy studiously ignored Inquisitor Wolf, Sacha, and even his ex-best friend, Philip Payton. Instead his snapping blue eyes and his rakish smile were all for Lily.

"Well, if it isn't lovely Miss Lily, the Fifth Avenue slugger," he said, playing up his Irish brogue for comic effect while still managing to sound annoyingly suave and debonair. "And how are you this fine mornin'?"

"Quite well, thank you," Lily replied, for all the world as if she were talking to one of her mother's high-society friends instead of a Hell's Kitchen Hexer.

"And have ye heard how the Yanks battled Boston last night?"

"Only that we won."

"We did indeed." His smile broadened into a wicked grin. "'Twas a shinin' victory, with grand pitchin' on both sides. And when O'Malley hit the winnin' run, he slid into home spikes first and practically took off the pitcher's kneecaps."

"Was there blood everywhere?" Lily asked with ghoulish glee.

"Aye, and gore aplenty. It was a glorious sight to see!"

"You were there?"

"Snuck in over the back fence."

"I wish I were a boy!" Lily sighed. "I'd sneak into the games in a minute. But as it is, I couldn't even go if I bought a ticket. My mother doesn't approve of young ladies attending professional sporting events."

"That's a pity," Paddy said casually. "I'm sure I would have had much more fun with you than with the young lady I did take. She had no appreciation for the fine art of pitchin'. Kept wantin' me to stop watchin' the game and kiss her." His eyes widened in a look of mock dismay. "Can you imagine such a thing?"

Judging by the look on Lily's face, Sacha was pretty sure she already was imagining it. "Don't you have anything better to do than pester Miss Astral?" he snapped.

He took great care to pronounce Lily's last name very clearly so there would be no mistaking it. Paddy grew pale when he heard it, and Sacha thought he even looked a little sick to his stomach.

"Good afternoon, Inquisitor Wolf, Mr. Payton, Mr. Kessler." Paddy cleared his throat and gave Lily a final regretful glance. "And, er, Miss Astral."

"So," Wolf asked Payton when the saloon's front door had swung closed behind Paddy, "what have you found out?"

"Well," Payton said, "I managed to confirm most of Kid Klezmer's story. Naftali Asher did work at Pentacle before he got famous. And he certainly was broke. I even found the pawnshop where he tried to pawn his clarinet to make the rent one month. But then, listen to this. The pawnshop owner said that the clarinet was only there for one night. Asher came back the next day to get it. He paid cash. And he said he'd gotten a new job and wasn't going to have to worry about money ever again and he was about to become the greatest klezmer player that ever lived."

"So that matches up with the wife's story," Lily said. "He must have gotten his first theater booking."

"No," Payton corrected. "That's exactly my point. This was two months before anyone hired him to play the clarinet. Two months before he ever had a concert, he already had a job and a paycheck. And he was already telling people that he was going to be the most famous klezmer player in New York."

Everyone stared at Payton.

"I don't get it," Sacha said finally. "Who hired him?"

"Maybe J. P. Morgaunt?"

"But why would Morgaunt hire a washed-up klezmer player who had to sew shirts in a magical sweatshop for a living?"

"He must have had something Morgaunt wanted. Enough to pay him good money for it. Enough to let him turn Edison's etherograph recordings into klezmer songs."

"But what could a poor sweatshop worker like Naftali Asher possibly have that Morgaunt would want so much?" Lily asked.

"I don't know," Payton answered with a determined look on his handsome face. "But I plan to find out."

CHAPTER SIXTEEN

Sam's Secret

THAT EVENING SACHA got back to his apartment early and fidgeted his way through dinner, jumping up like a sprinter at the starting gun every time a door opened or a stair creaked anywhere in the whole building.

When Moishe finally arrived, Sacha made some excuse to his parents about going upstairs to the IWW headquarters to talk to a friend and followed the older boy toward the door.

"You won't want your coat," Moishe said when Sacha started to grab it off the peg. "It'll just get in your way where we're going."

Moishe led him out of the apartment. And then, to Sacha's amazement, instead of heading downstairs toward the street, he started climbing the stairs. Moishe led him past the IWW headquarters, up a final ladder-steep flight of stairs, and out onto the rooftop.

"He's on the roof?" Sacha asked incredulously. But Moishe just smiled enigmatically and trotted off across the rooftop. Sacha followed him into the maze of tenement rooftops, scrambling over cornices and jumping across alleyways. It was hard to keep track of where they were, but Sacha was pretty sure Moishe was heading toward Allen Street. And when he heard the roar of the Elevated far below them, like the sound of a swift river floating up from a deep-cut canyon, he was sure of it.

Still, knowing more or less where you were was one thing. Knowing how to get down without breaking your neck was another. So when Moishe knelt over a grimy skylight and pried it open, Sacha was relieved to be leaving the world of birds and returning to the world of people.

Moishe looked around carefully, dropped into the empty stairwell, and helped Sacha down after him. Then he beckoned to Sacha and set off down the stairs, as surefooted as a cat in the shadows.

Sacha followed him down one flight, two flights, three flights . . . and soon realized that Moishe had dragged him across several blocks of rooftops only to head straight to a distant basement.

Sacha hated the tenement basements. They were places of vice and terror, either home to stale beer dives and whiskey joints or realms of mold and must and shadows.

This basement was the moldy, musty kind. He could tell that right away. And worse still, it wasn't even a full basement; just a sort of earthen cave underneath the building where you had to crouch and scramble to get anywhere. There was no light, either.

But there was sound. There were sounds Sacha didn't like and couldn't make sense of. And they were getting louder. At first he thought he was hearing running water. But then the ripple became a thrumming, and the thrumming became a flutter, and the flutter became a throaty, gurgling whisper that made his blood run cold and his heart grow faint with terror.

Moishe scurried through one dark, damp chamber and into another, and Sacha followed him. At first he ran his hands along the walls to keep his bearings, but then the bricks became so damp and slimy that he decided he'd rather get lost than touch them. And anyway, it was clear where Moishe was headed: to the whispering room.

Then Moishe opened the door, and a stray shaft of moonlight shot through the barred window in the room beyond. Sacha saw a billowing, rustling, gray ocean of feathers stretching out under the low ceiling—and he almost laughed out loud.

It was Mrs. Mogulesko's goose flock. He'd known she kept them in basements, moving around all the time to stay one step ahead of the health authorities. But he'd never understood just how many geese Mrs. Mogulesko had—or just how much a flock of brooding geese could sound like whispers in the shadows when your nerves were stretched taut and you had dark thoughts in mind.

The geese must have thought that the boys were Mrs. Mogulesko arriving to feed them. As the door opened, they surged forward, clucking and pecking and looking for dinner. Moishe pushed Sacha into the room, shooed the geese away from the door, and slammed it shut just in time to stop a few bold adventurers from making a break for freedom. Then he looked around, searching for something.

It was brighter in here than in the rest of the basement. A few barred windows looked out on a grimy airshaft on one side and an empty alley on the other. Sacha followed Moishe's gaze, peering out over the heaving sea of geese, and saw a framework of wooden planks set up against the back wall to form a rough sort of shelf. Perched on the shelf, hunched over pathetically like a scrawny baby bird who'd fallen out of his nest and couldn't figure out how to get back, was Sam Schlosky.

"Well," Moishe said, wading through the geese to Sam's hiding place, "here he is. Alone, just like you asked me to bring him. So you might as well tell him what you told me."

But Sam still wasn't ready to tell Sacha whatever Moishe had brought him to hear. Instead he peered down at them nervously, picking at the sleeve of his coat and rocking back and forth on the shelf as if he were thinking about hopping to the ground and running away.

"How do I know I can trust you?" he asked Sacha. "How do I know you won't just go and tell that Inquisitor of yours everything?"

"Maybe I should tell him," Sacha said. "Maybe he can protect you from whoever you're hiding from."

"He can't," Sam said in a hollow voice.

"Who are you afraid of?"

"The same thing you're afraid of," Sam whispered. "The watcher in the shadows."

"Whoever it is, Wolf can protect you from it."

"No, he can't," Sam whispered.

"Tell him what you told me," Moishe urged. "Tell him about the deal Naftali Asher struck with Morgaunt."

"Naftali got his songs," Sam said. "And Morgaunt got shirtwaists."

At first Sacha didn't understand.

"Don't you see?" Moishe exclaimed. "Asher was the scabbalist! Sam's the anonymous source that told the papers about it!"

"But I haven't told anyone the whole story," Sam said.

"What do you mean?" Sacha asked, his heart thumping in his chest. "And why are you telling me? What do I have to do with it?"

"Don't *you* know?" Sam peered down at Sacha from his rickety shelf. He seemed to be leaning toward him and shrinking from him at the same time. "I thought the new scabbalist was your—"

But before Sam could say the name, the door to the basement flew open with a *crack* like lightning striking.

"Hands up!" shouted a loud voice. "And don't even think about using magic! It's the Inquisitors!"

Suddenly the air was thick with feathers and magic. Spell-flinging Inquisitors burst into the room in a sea of blue

uniforms. Sam jumped down from his shelf and ran crouching toward the rear of the basement, where the meager light from the window grates turned to blackest shadow. Moishe grabbed Sacha's arm and began dragging him along after Sam, frantically casting hexes behind him as he ran. Moishe wasn't a particularly powerful magician—Sacha could tell at a glance that he was only using little everyday spells. But what power he had, he used cleverly. He was doing something to the geese, throwing them into an angry panic so that they rose up in a wave, beating their wings and slashing at the pursuing Inquisitors.

Still, it was no good. The Inquisitors were stronger than Moishe. The geese scattered before them. A pair of burly detectives slipped through the flock first, and were instantly on the boys' heels. Sam stumbled and then sank to the ground under the power of some hex that Sacha didn't even recognize. Then Sacha felt something grabbing at his own ankles. He tripped. Moishe's hand slipped out of his grasp. A nightstick slammed down on Sacha's head—and he sank into warm, velvety darkness with the outraged shrieks of Mrs. Mogulesko's geese whistling in his ears.

CHAPTER SEVENTEEN

Minsky's Bargain

WHEN WOLF SHOWED up to bail Sacha out of the Tombs the next morning, he was white with fury. He barely spoke as they went through the long process of filling out the paperwork and retrieving the goose-soiled tatters of Sacha's clothing.

Something told Sacha that Wolf must have had to call in huge favors and pull strings all over town to get him out. But on the other hand, he had discovered something important, hadn't he?

"Listen," he began. "I'm really sorry about this, but Sam told me something importa—"

"Shhh!" Wolf hissed. "The walls have ears here!"

Sacha kept his mouth shut until they were out on the street. And only then did it occur to him to wonder where Sam was.

He looked back at the horrible building they had just escaped from. Its real name, carved right across the façade for anyone to read, was the Hall of Justice. But now he understood why they called it the Tombs. And he prayed he'd never have to set foot in the place again for as long as he lived.

Sam was in there right now, Sacha realized, and probably being given the third degree this very minute. From the look on Wolf's face, he must be sure Sam had already confessed to Naftali Asher's murder—or that he would have confessed long before they could pull enough strings to get him out.

"Aren't we going to get Sam out?" he asked Wolf.

"No."

"Aren't you even going to try?"

"And what do you think I've been doing for the last two weeks?" Wolf asked in a voice as hard and cold as river ice. "If Sam dies in the Tombs, it won't be my fault, it'll be yours!"

Sacha froze, horrified by Wolf's words. But Wolf wasn't even looking at him anymore. He had turned on his heel already and stalked off down Mulberry Street.

"Wait!" Sacha cried.

But either Wolf didn't hear him, or he didn't want to hear him. He stepped off the curb to cross the busy street without even looking back, and the last Sacha saw of him was his black coattails vanishing behind a passing omnibus.

Maybe it was because he was still stinging from Wolf's angry words. Or maybe it was because he felt guilty. But as Sacha watched Wolf stride away, an idea began to take shape in his mind that was either brave or crazy or both.

Before he could have time for second thoughts—or time to lose his nerve—he marched off down Mulberry Street, made his way back across the Bowery, elbowed his way through the midday shopping crowds on Hester Street, turned up Essex, and marched straight into Meyer Minsky's candy store.

Dopey Benny and two of Meyer's most fearsome starkers were lounging around the candy counter flicking wads of used chewing gum at the stamped tin ceiling and laying bets about whether they would stick or not.

"Hey, kid," Benny asked in his adenoidal drawl, "how's your sistuh?"

"Oh—uh—fine. Is Meyer here?"

"Nope." Benny flicked a wad of gum at the ceiling and squinted critically at it while it stuck for a moment, then peeled off and fell to the floor with a soft smacking sound. "Is your sistuh about to get buried?"

"What?" Sacha yelped.

"You know. Buried. Ban and wife, for bettuh or worse."

"Do you mean *married?* No! And anyway, it's none of your business!"

"Okay, okay," Benny said in a wounded tone. "I don't see why you gotta be sharp wid a guy for askin' a perfectly dormal question!"

"Okay. Sorry, Benny. Just . . . don't talk about my sister. Okay?"

"See what I mean?" Benny asked mournfully. "Why would you wanna go and say a thing like that to a fella?"

The other starker's piece of gum thwacked against the ceiling and stuck. But when Benny tried to repeat the performance, he failed again.

"It's your spit, Benny," one of the other two gangsters pointed out helpfully. "That's the problem. It ain't like normal spit."

"And what's that supposed to mean?" Benny asked ominously.

"I dunno. It's . . . not sticky or something. Maybe it's a sinus thing."

"You got something to say about my sinuses," Benny sniffled, "you can say it to my face."

"Hey, guys! Take it outside!" said the third gangster.

"Maybe we will," growled Benny, the pent-up magic suddenly flaring and spitting around him. "Fists or hexes?"

"Either way's fine by me," said the smaller gangster. But Sacha noticed that he was already edging nervously away from Benny.

Sacha sighed, defeated, and began to trudge back out of the candy store. But Benny's voice called him back: "Hey, wait a minute. Come back in half an hour. No promises, but I'll tell Meyer you wanna talk to him."

When Sacha returned, the three starkers were still there. But instead of flicking gum at the ceiling, they were staring covetously at the long sleek motorcar that idled at the curb like a luxury ocean liner floating at harbor. Sacha eyed the car as he walked by and couldn't help noticing that it glimmered with more than just wax polish. There was a curious, flimmery sort of sheen to it. Not exactly an aura, but a rainbow-hued glimmer, like the colors that flow over an oil slick just as the rain starts to wash it off the pavement.

Meyer Minsky was a man who didn't leave much to chance. His car was armored with both bulletproof glass and bulletproof magic.

Minsky was sitting at the same desk, flipping the same buffalo head nickel. "You want me to find the Klezmer Killer?" he asked incredulously when Sacha made his carefully rehearsed speech.

"Sam Schlosky's innocent," Sacha pleaded.

"And why should I care about Sam Schlosky? No offense, kid, I'm just askin'."

"Well, er . . ."

Minsky flipped the coin again and slapped his hand down on top of it before Sacha could see whether he'd thrown heads again. Sacha noticed the gangster wore several large rings on his well-manicured fingers. One of them was twisted into the shape of a snake's head with eyes of onyx that winked and glittered at him.

"I'm waiting," Minsky said quietly.

Sacha took a desperate gamble, praying it wouldn't come back to bite him like the sly, winking serpent wrapped around Minsky's little finger. "Whoever killed Naftali Asher, that's who framed Sam Schlosky. And whoever framed him, that's who sent the watcher in the shadows to kill your people."

Minsky stared hard at Sacha for long enough to make the breath freeze in his lungs. His feet felt rooted to the spot, but he couldn't tell if it was magic that was holding him there or sheer physical terror of the man.

"And who do you think that might be?" Minsky asked.

Sacha swallowed nervously. "J. P. Morgaunt."

Minsky's eyebrows rose. "Aha. Now we're getting to it. Are you sure you came here on your own? Or is Wolf still trying to drag me into his fight with Morgaunt?"

"No! I swear he doesn't even know I'm here! I just want to help Sam!"

"Is that so?" Meyer said dangerously.

"Yes!"

"Heads or tails? And you better think damn carefully about your answer if you want to walk out of here instead of getting carried out."

Minsky's hand was still clapped over the coin on the desk. Sacha tried to swallow, but all the spit seemed to have dried up in his mouth, and his tongue felt like cardboard.

"Tails," he whispered.

Oh, God. What on earth had made him say tails? Minsky had just flipped heads forty times in a row. And now, on a life-or-death throw, he called tails?

Minsky didn't look down at the coin when he raised his hand. He just kept watching Sacha, reading the throw by the look on his face.

Tails.

"Son of a gun," Minsky murmured.

"See?" Sacha said. "I'm not lying."

"Maybe you are, maybe you aren't," Minsky snapped. "And maybe the nickel's trying to double-cross me. I took it out of Jimmy the Gimp's pocket the day he died, and I'm never quite sure if it remembers that I'm the one who shivved him—not that I'm admitting anything officially!"

Sacha eyed the nickel in alarm, then looked up to find Minsky still watching him.

"Okay. I'll help you," Minsky said at last.

Sacha went limp with relief.

"I'll help you. But this is a big favor you're asking for. And that means I'm going to expect a big favor back from you someday."

"What kind of favor?" Sacha asked suspiciously.

"Can't really say. Who knows what I'll need and when I'll need it? I might not call this favor in for years and years. Not until you're a big grownup Inquisitor yourself, just like my old friend Max."

Sacha shuddered. "I won't do anything illegal."

"Oh, really?" Minsky sounded almost amused now. "And why would that be?"

"Because I don't want to be that kind of cop."

But Minsky just laughed. "No one wants to be that kind of cop, kid. But somehow that's the kind of a cop they all turn into."

"Not Wolf," Sacha said—though he wasn't sure whether he believed it or just wanted to believe it.

"That," Minsky said, "has yet to be determined."

"Not Wolf," Sacha insisted. "And not me."

Meyer slashed his hand down on the table in a sharp, cutting gesture. Sacha jumped at the impact but forced himself to remain still. He and Meyer stared across the desk at each other, and all he could think was that talking to Meyer Minsky was like being a lion tamer in the circus: you blink, you die.

Then Meyer laughed. "I'll give you one thing," he said. "You got nerve. I'll tell you what. I'll do this favor for you. And when the day comes that I ask you for a favor in return, I promise you this: it won't be a crooked favor. When I show up on your doorstep, you'll know that I'm in the right, and the cops are in the wrong. So that way, when you risk a train ride up the river for me—because it will be that kind of favor, or what would be the point of asking you?—at least you'll have the moral satisfaction of knowing that you're putting yourself on the line for an innocent man."

Sacha stared at Minsky, speechless. He couldn't think of a word to say in reply to this decree. And he was pretty sure that it wouldn't make a difference what he said. Minsky wasn't bargaining with him; he was just telling him how it was going to be.

"So where does that leave us now?" he finally managed to choke out.

"It leaves us friends." Minsky stood up, brushed an invisible speck of lint off of his beautifully tailored trousers, thrust his lucky coin back into his trouser pocket, and strode out of the room without even glancing at Sacha. But his voice drifted back as he swept toward his magic-plated limousine. "You're all right, kid. You're all right until I say you're not."

A few days later, Dopey Benny knocked on the door of the Kesslers' apartment after dinner.

"Meyer wants to see you," he told Sacha.

Sacha and his family exchanged shocked and nervous glances—but luckily Benny was too busy staring at Bekah to notice.

"Now?" Sacha asked.

"Dat's what he says, kid."

"Isn't it a little late for that, Benny?" Sacha's father asked.

"Oh, hello, Mr. Kessler," Benny said, politely removing his hat and looking a little sheepish about having forgotten it. There was something about Sacha's father, quiet as he was, that kept even the roughest boys in the neighborhood on their best behavior—and Benny Fein was no exception. "I'm sorry it's so late, but Meyer really needs to talk to him." Benny waggled his eyebrows and dropped his voice to a portentous whisper. "*Inquisitor* business."

Sacha's father glanced questioningly at him, and Sacha shrugged slightly.

"Okay, Benny. Walk him home yourself when he's done, though. Will you?"

"I solemnly promise, Mr. Kessler!"

And they were off.

When they reached the Essex Street Candy Store, its

storefront was already dark and shuttered. But Sacha could see a sliver of light shining from the back room, and sure enough, Minsky was waiting for him there—this time with Kid Klezmer in tow.

"I asked the Kid to come along 'cause I thought he ought to hear this too," Meyer explained.

Sacha waited, but Meyer didn't speak. And after a moment, he realized that both Minsky and Kid Klezmer were waiting for a fourth man to speak—a man so silent and unobtrusive that Sacha hadn't even realized he was in the room with them.

"Tell him what you saw, Nebbs," Minsky prompted.

"What I saw on the tracks?" the little gray man asked.

"No, at the opera," Minsky cracked. "Don't be a putz, Nebbs!"

The little gray man turned to Sacha with a solemn wink. "Meyer thinks he's a funny guy."

"No, Nebbs," Minsky said, "I am a funny guy. You've just got no sense of 'umor."

Suddenly Sacha realized who the little man was, and he stared in open fascination. Nebbs was short for *nebbish:* nobody. And this wasn't just a *nebbish* sitting in the chair across the table from Sacha. It was *the* Nebbish, the legendary mastermind of the formidable Magic, Inc., intelligence-gathering arm. The man who was famous all over town for not being famous, who was known far and wide for being unknowable, who wouldn't stand out in a crowd of one, and who made a room feel emptier just by walking into it.

Sacha peered at him, racking his brain to remember whether he'd ever seen the man before. But he just couldn't be sure.

And, really, wasn't that the point?

"So I was over near Astral Place a few weeks ago," the Nebbish said, "not too far from Pentacle Shirtwaist Factory, and I saw something that made me stop and look twice. And what do you think it was?"

"I don't know," Sacha said when it became clear that the Nebbish was waiting for him to say something.

"The Klezmer King, that's what. But he was skulking along like he didn't want anyone to know he was the Klezmer King, if you get the picture. So, 'Nebbish,' I sez to myself, 'that's a man who'd pay good money not to be noticed right now. And when you see a guy who'd pay good money not to be noticed, you know he's about to do something some other guy'd pay good money to know about.' So what do I do? I follow him. And where does he go? Straight to the Astral Place subway station. And what does he do?"

The Nebbish pantomimed a man walking down a flight of stairs.

"So he went into the subway?" Sacha asked.

"Yeah," the Nebbish said. "And then some. He walks out onto the platform, looks around like he wants to make extra sure no one's watching him—which no one but me is—and walks straight to the end of the platform and jumps down onto the tracks and keeps walking."

He looked at Sacha expectantly.

"So what did you do?" Sacha prompted.

"What do you think I did? I followed him!"

"And?"

"Well, once I get off the platform, I can see that he hasn't gone far. Just to the edge of the light, so no one who's up on the platform can see him. And he's just standing there waiting, like he's got an appointment or something. And after a minute, sure enough, someone shows up."

"Get a load of this," Meyer said. "You're gonna love it."

Sacha didn't think he was going to love it at all, but he waited as calmly as he could while the Nebbish cleared his throat and went on with his tale.

"This other individual, I never saw his face, you understand? He came out of the tunnel, but he stayed in the shadows so I couldn't get a look at him. I bet even Asher couldn't see his face. It was like he set the meet-up that way on purpose. But I'll tell you what—I heard his voice. And that was enough for me. I'd know that voice anywhere. It was the watcher in the shadows."

The four of them stared at each other.

"What did it say to Asher?" Sacha asked at last.

"I couldn't tell. But I heard what Asher said to it. And it wasn't nice."

"We know about that already," Sacha said. "He was doing some job for them, and he was trying to quit it."

The Nebbish shrugged, tilting his balding head to one side. "Maybe you know more than I do, but that's not what I heard him talking about. From what I heard, he wasn't talking about quitting. He was talking about killing. He was telling them that Sam Schlosky was onto them, and he didn't have the nerve to keep the secret, and they'd better kill Sam fast before he squealed to the Inquisitors."

Sacha's head spun, and his stomach clenched in fear. He felt as if the entire case had suddenly shifted underfoot, with victim becoming killer and suspect becoming victim. Suddenly Rosie's film of Naftali Asher's death took on a whole new meaning. The answer had been in front of them all along. They just hadn't seen it. Or rather they hadn't *heard* it.

They'd all assumed that Asher had shouted "No! Sam!" at the very end because he'd thought Sam had caused the accident—or because he hoped Sam would save him. But what if those final words meant something completely different? What if Asher had called out Sam's name not as a cry for help, but as a cry of protest? What if he'd thought that *Sam* was supposed to die instead of him—and had realized only with his dying breath that he'd been double-crossed?

If that was true, then Sam Schlosky was in even worse danger than Wolf feared he was.

CHAPTER EIGHTEEN

Night Doings

SACHA WAS HALFWAY to Hell's Kitchen before he realized that Inquisitor Wolf would be long gone by this time of night.

No matter, he told himself. Someone at the Inquisitors Division would be able to find Wolf for him. For something this important, they'd tell him where Wolf lived. This was an emergency, after all.

But when he asked the booking sergeant for Wolf's address, the man just laughed in his face. Sacha couldn't tell whether he was afraid of waking up Wolf or just wanted to cause trouble, but it hardly mattered. Sacha wandered around the Inquisitors Division for a few more minutes, hoping he'd stumble on someone who could help him and trying to work up the nerve to imagine going down to Chinatown to roust Shen out of bed in the middle of the night and ask her if she knew where to find Maximillian Wolf. He could think of about five different ways *that* conversation might go—and he didn't have the nerve to face any of them.

Finally he set out in search of the only other person he could think of who might know where Wolf lived.

It was long past closing time at the Witch's Brew, but there were still a few late-night drinkers hunched around the bar and lounging at the tables. And to Sacha's immense relief, Sullivan was still there too. The big man was in his shirtsleeves, clearing glasses, turning up the chairs on the tables, and getting ready to mop the floor with a steaming bucket of vinegar and scalding hot water.

Sacha tugged at the door, but it was locked already. He pounded until Sullivan lumbered over to peer through the glass into the darkness.

"What in the name of Pete are you doin' out so late?" Sullivan asked when he saw who was standing on the sidewalk.

"Wolf!" Sacha gasped. "I have to—find—emergency—"

"Slow down a minute," Sullivan told him. "Catch yer breath, and let's make sense of this, shall we?"

"I need to find Inquisitor Wolf!" Sacha said when he had caught his breath.

Sullivan's eyebrows rose in surprise. "Sorry, lad, I'd like to help you, but I don't think I can," he said.

"But—don't you know where he lives?"

"Used to. But that was a long time ago."

Sacha could have cried in frustration. "Can't anyone help me? It's an emergency!"

"Ah. Well, that puts a different face on the problem. Can't Payton roust him out for ya?"

"But I don't know where he lives either!" Sacha cried.

"I think I'd better go with you," Sullivan said. "I hardly like the thought of you wandering around Hell's Kitchen alone at this hour of the night. Or better yet, I'll send someone."

He turned to the drinkers at the back table and hollered, "Hey, Paddy! I need a favor!"

Sacha glanced toward the table just in time to see Paddy Doyle's sleek blond head turn to look at them. "What can I do for you?" Paddy asked with his usual happy-go-lucky charm.

"Take Sacha here over to fetch Philip Payton."

Paddy's brow darkened, and his voice turned sullen. "Ask someone else."

"It's you I'm askin', Paddy." Sullivan's voice suddenly had a dangerous edge to it, and Paddy must have heard it just as clearly as Sacha did. The next instant, Paddy was standing at Sacha's side looking nervous and chastened and quite a bit younger than usual.

"The boy's got an important message," Sullivan said simply. "I'm thinkin' it's a matter of life and death, or his own mother wouldn't let her little chick be strayin' from the nest so late. So you'll get him to Payton's house safely. Or is that too much trouble for you, my boy?"

"No trouble at all, Sullivan. I'll take care of it."

And then they were off.

Paddy Doyle led Sacha through a maze of back streets

and alleyways that made his head spin. He practically had to run to keep up. And by the time they began climbing Pepper Hill just to the north of the Hell's Kitchen neighborhood, Sacha's legs were shaking and his breath was rasping in his throat.

Finally they popped out of a mews full of livery stables and onto a quiet residential street lined with low brick houses. Most of the houses were neat and well-kept behind their wrought-iron low garden walls, but Sacha noticed that the front windows of a few of them had been hastily boarded up, and glittering shards of broken glass littered their garden walkways.

Paddy turned up one of the garden walks, trotted up the short flight of steps to the front door, and pounded on it until a light went on in an upstairs window.

"Who is it?" a man's voice called down from the second story.

"Paddy Doyle."

There was a long silence, and then footsteps inside the house, and then another silence. Finally the door opened.

The minute Sacha saw the man in the doorway, he knew he must be Philip Payton's father. He was an older, heavier, more solid-looking version of Payton. But the firm-set mouth and chin were the same. And so was the cool, measuring gaze coming through his round-rimmed spectacles.

"Hello, Paddy. It's been quite a while since I've had the pleasure of speaking to you."

Paddy shifted uncomfortably on the doorstep.

"Can I do anything for you?" Mr. Payton asked.

"I just brought someone to see Philip, that's all. He says it's an emergency."

"Are you from the Inquisitors Division?" Mr. Payton asked Sacha.

Sacha was still trying to catch his breath, but he managed to nod.

"Well, come in, then, both of you. I'll go wake Philip up."

"Not me," Paddy said hastily, then slipped away into the darkness.

Mr. Payton looked after Paddy for a moment without commenting. Then he led Sacha into the house. Sacha peered around curiously, trying to see as much of the place as he could in the dim moonlight filtering through the lace curtains. They were in a tidy front hall, with a dining room on one side and a sitting room on the other. He could see a spinet piano in the front room, with sheet music open on it, and a child-sized violin and bow crossed atop the piano's lid as if some children of the house had been practicing before bedtime. A flurry of movement drew his eyes to the top of the stairs just in time to see two little girls in bare feet and white nightgowns being shooed back into the shadows by an older girl.

And then Payton was coming down the stairs two steps at a time, pulling on his coat. Payton listened to Sacha's story in silence. Then he grabbed his hat and set off into the night with Sacha behind him.

Sacha hadn't thought much about where Wolf lived.

But even if he had, the nondescript boarding house Payton eventually led him to would have been about the last place he would have imagined. Payton had to pound on the front door for a full five minutes before the landlady limped down the creaking stairs to let them in.

She knew Payton—or at least she knew him well enough to bring them upstairs to knock on the door of Wolf's room. But she wouldn't let them in, no matter how they pleaded. And when they asked where Wolf might have gone, all she could do was shrug and say she didn't know.

Back on the sidewalk, Payton hesitated for a moment—and then he turned his steps downtown toward the Tombs.

They got there just as the first faint light of dawn was starting to color the sky over the East River. Payton stopped across the street from the grim building and looked at Sacha, his handsome face torn between frustration and anger.

"You'd better go in alone," he said.

Sacha started to argue, but the look on Payton's face stopped him short.

"Just go," Payton said. "Tell them Wolf sent you down to get Sam Schlosky out."

"But they wouldn't release him for Wolf this morning! They'll never do it for *me!*"

"Maybe not. But it's still better than doing nothing."

Sacha took a last long look at the Tombs. And then he squared his shoulders and marched up the trash-littered steps and went inside.

Wolf was already there waiting for him.

But when Sacha ran to him and began to spill out everything that had happened, Wolf just put a hand out to silence him.

"Never mind that," he said gently. And from the sound of his voice, Sacha knew suddenly that something terrible had happened.

"Aren't they going to let Sam out?" he whispered with a terrible sinking feeling in the pit of his stomach.

"It's too late for that," Wolf said. "He died last night."

CHAPTER NINETEEN

Where All True Magic Comes From

SACHA BARELY remembered stumbling out onto the sidewalk, or shaking off Payton when he tried to ask what was wrong. He fled down Mulberry Street and lost himself in the ramshackle alleyways of Little Italy with no thought in mind but to get as far away from the Tombs as he could. By the time he began to come to his senses again, he was deep in the heart of Chinatown. And almost without realizing where he was going, he found his steps turning toward the little apothecary's shop and the secret courtyard that led to Shen's door.

Shen was scrubbing the stone floor in the practice hall. By now Sacha was familiar enough with this ritual that he went over to the sink without a word, picked up a rag, got down on his knees, and began scrubbing shoulder to shoulder with her.

For perhaps a quarter of an hour, they scrubbed side by side in silence. Then Shen finished cleaning the last great stone square, stood up, and wrung her scrub rag out over the bucket. The water dropped into the pail as clean and clear as water trickling from a mountain spring. Obviously the floor was now clean enough even for Shen.

"Now, tell me," she said pleasantly. "What is it that brings you here so early?"

Sacha wrung his own scrub rag out over the bucket, struggling to put words to the questions seething in his mind. Haltingly, he told her everything that had happened since he had followed Moishe to Sam Schlosky's secret hiding place.

"If only I hadn't gone to meet him!" Guilt twisted his stomach. "The Inquisitors would never have found him if I hadn't led them there!"

"That's possible," Shen admitted.

"And then I just stood there like a lump while Moishe tried to fight them off!" The memory of it made him so hot with shame he could barely stand thinking about it. "None of this would have happened if I knew how to use magic! Wolf told me to learn! But I wouldn't listen. And now look!"

"You couldn't have done anything against police weapons, even if you'd started learning magic the first day you came to work for Wolf," Shen said gently. "It takes years to develop that kind of power."

"So then why can every housewife on Hester Street do magic? And every Hell's Kitchen Hexer over the age of twelve? I mean, come on, Benny Fein can work magic! And he hasn't got the brains God gave a turnip!"

"Memorizing spells isn't the same as mastering the deep

wellsprings of magic," Shen pointed out. "The more power a magician has, the more dangerous it is for him to use it."

Sacha jumped to his feet and flung his rag into the bucket, sending a great gout of water splattering across the stone floor. "I hate magic!" he spat. "I hate everything about it! What has it ever brought anyone but misery?"

"You don't mean that," Shen said gently. "Why don't you tell me what's really eating at you?"

And slowly, stumblingly, Sacha began to confess the fear that was growing inside him: the fear that his dybbuk was back and that Morgaunt still held some secret power over it. And the deeper fear—that he would be swallowed by his own shadow and would become nothing more than Morgaunt's creature.

"If all this is true," Shen said at last, "then your grandfather is right. No mere spellmongering will help you."

"Then what will?"

"There are many kinds of magic, Sacha. There's back-alley spellmongering—what the everyday people of the world do—and then there is true Magery. True Mages can be people with formidable powers but no formal training to teach them the right way to use their power. Or they can be people like the great Warrior-Mages of China—men and women who understand that every act of true magic changes the balance of the universe. A knowledgeable Mage is a great power for good. But the other kind leave a tangled wake of chaos behind them . . . even when they don't go seriously wrong."

"You sound like my grandfather," Sacha said. "He says

the mark of a true Kabbalist is that he doesn't use his power at all."

"Your grandfather's a wise man," Shen said. "The more powerful the Mage, the greater the danger that his magic could disrupt the natural harmony of the world. That is why all great Mages in every corner of the world face the one great choice sooner or later: either to stray into Necromancy or to follow the Path of No Action."

"But I'm not a great magician," Sacha said dispiritedly. "All I can do is see *other* people do magic. And what does that amount to but a silly parlor trick?"

Shen smiled her quiet smile—and a fragrant white flurry of jasmine petals drifted down from the rafters, blanketing the courtyard in the silent out-of-time peacefulness of winter's first snowfall.

Sacha looked at the fragrant drifts. Then he looked at Shen. Magic glimmered around her like starlight. Shen's magic looked just like her smile: kind, gentle, a little sad . . . and very wise. And the oddest thing about it was that, though it was clearly magic—and powerful magic at that—it wasn't doing anything. It was just there. Calm and self-contained, and with a deeply rooted serenity that had more than a little of the hard-won wisdom of experience in it.

"Don't belittle your gift," she told him. "You may not know how to work magic yet—at least not what you think of now as magic. But when you see someone's magic, you see his heart, because that is where all true magic comes from. For the rest of your life, no Mage will be able to work his craft in front of you without opening up the most secret book of his soul for you to read. And knowing who the people around you really are—for good or for bad—is a gift given only to a very few."

"But how does that help me stop the dybbuk?" he asked desperately.

"It doesn't," Shen said. "I'm going to be honest with you, Sacha. I don't know that you *can* stop it."

"Then you can't help me?" Sacha whispered.

"On the contrary. I can help you a great deal. But I don't think raising false hopes is helpful, so I'm not going to do that." She got up, brushing her hands on her pant legs. "Come on, let me walk you home."

When Sacha left Shen on the sidewalk outside his front stoop and climbed the stairs to his own apartment, Dopey Benny was standing in the kitchen again. Sacha was starting to wonder if Benny was going to grow roots there.

"Meyer wants to see you right now," Benny said. So Sacha sighed in exhaustion and trailed after him to the candy store.

When he got there, Minsky was sitting at his desk in the golden pool of lamplight. And the Nebbish was hovering in the shadows behind him.

But this wasn't the same Nebbs Sacha had met the evening before. His back was bowed, the light had gone out of his eyes, and the skin of his face looked as dry and withered as a year-old apple. He looked as if something had sucked the marrow out of his bones and turned him into an old man overnight.

"Tell him, Nebbs," Meyer said in a voice that made Sacha want to turn around and run straight home and lock the door behind him. "Tell him what you told me. Don't leave out a word of it."

Nebbs sat gathering his thoughts for a long time, as if just bringing his tale to mind were a deathly struggle. And then he began.

"After you told us about the Schlosky kid, Meyer started wondering if it wouldn't be a good idea for someone to go down to the Tombs and keep an eye on him. You know, to make sure he didn't have an unfortunate accident while he was in the lockup. So I got myself run in for—well, never mind what for—let's just say it's easier to get into the Tombs than out of them.

"Anyway, I get down there right before they bring dinner around, and there's little Schlosky, just like you said, looking only slightly the worse for wear. Not that I got to see much of him, because the cops pulled him outta the tank right after dinner and took him upstairs for a little talk. Anyway, he comes back downstairs round about dark, looking a little more worse for wear than he did when he left. And that's when things really start to get strange. 'Cause they don't put him back in the fish tank with the rest of us. They take him down to the last cell on the row. And they give him the whole cell, all to himself. Or at least we thought he was alone at first. But then the whispering started."

Minsky moved slightly in his chair, and Sacha looked over and saw the gangster staring hard at him.

"At first we thought it was the kid talking to hisself," Nebbs went on. "But then he started talking too, and we could hear there was two people in the cell."

"Did—" Sacha had to stop and swallow. "Did you see the other one?"

"Not then. Can't even rightly say I heard him. Just a kind of slithering whispering sound. Hardly a voice at all. But whatever it was, you could tell it was talking to the kid, 'cause he started answering back. Telling it to stop. Saying he'd do anything. Begging it to leave him alone. It went on all night, and I tell you it was the worst thing I ever heard in my life. And in the morning—right there where there'd been nothing but air and shadows the night before? There were two boys in a cell that only started out with one. Sam, dead as a doornail. And the other one, looking like the goddamn cat who ate the canary."

"But there must have been two boys the night before," Sacha protested. "You must have missed the other one."

"I know what I saw," Nebbs said. "And I know what I didn't see. And I'm telling you: there was one boy there at sunset and two at sunrise."

Minsky was still staring hard at Sacha, his fist clenched around his lucky nickel and his expression unreadable. "Tell him about the flies, Nebbs."

"Oh, yeah," Nebbs said. "That's the kicker. I never been in the Tombs when the place wasn't crawling with flies. Even in the middle of winter, they're never really gone. But last night, all that time that the whisperer was driving Sam Schlosky dead crazy? There wasn't a single fly in sight."

"And what happened in the morning?" Sacha whispered.

"The other boy just walked outta there, easy as you please. You woulda thought there wasn't a locked door or a binding spell in the place."

"Did you—did you see his face?"

"I thought you might want to know about that," Minsky said in a soft and dangerous voice. "Go ahead and tell him, Nebbs."

The Nebbish stared at Sacha. Then he turned to Minsky and raised a trembling hand to point at Sacha before answering. "Just like I told you, boss. It was him."

CHAPTER TWENTY

Sparks and Husks

SACHA STARED at Minsky, but the gangster suddenly seemed as far away as the stars and the moon. Sacha felt the same sinking dread he'd felt when his dybbuk had stalked him through the streets last summer. He seemed to be looking up at the ordinary world from the bottom of a well, trapped so far below the living realm of warmth and laughter and sunlight that no one up there could possibly reach him.

Minsky spoke, but Sacha barely heard the words. When he didn't answer, the gangster leaned forward, grabbed Sacha's shoulders, and shook him roughly.

"I said, is this some kind of sick joke?"

"No," Sacha whispered.

"Then how the hell do you plan to explain it to me?"

"I can't."

"That's the best you got?" Minsky was furious. "Not good enough! Not even close to good enough!"

"It wasn't me!" Sacha cried. "It was a dybbuk! Someone set a dybbuk on me!"

"Who?"

"Morgaunt!"

"Not possible! Only a Kabbalist can summon a dybbuk!"

"He has a machine that can do it."

"There's no machine can do that," Minsky growled.

"There is! Edison made it for him!"

Minsky looked dumbfounded. "Wait a minute. Are you talking about the etherograph?"

He let go suddenly, and Sacha sat rubbing his arms and trying to catch his breath. Meanwhile the gangster had risen to pace around the little room.

"They got an etherograph in the Tombs that they're hooking people up to, you know that?"

Sacha nodded. "Wolf says they're putting them in all the police stations."

"Well, he's right. They are. And they've been dragging my boys in for months now, one after another, on nothing, no-count, nonsense charges, and hooking 'em up to those things. And not just my boys either. They've been going after every gang in New York. It's like they're trying to hook every wise guy in town up to those damn machines of theirs."

"Then they've got recordings of all them. Morgaunt has a cabinet in his library. He has hundreds of them. Thousands, maybe."

"Does that mean he can make dybbuks of all of 'em?"

"Maybe." Sacha shuddered at the idea of a gangster army of dybbuks. "I don't know."

"And how was the Klezmer King mixed up in all this?"

Sacha hesitated, not sure how much of the case to reveal to Minsky.

"You better not be holding out on me," Minsky said in a silky, threatening murmur.

"I'm not, I'm not! I just—we don't really know all that much. We think Morgaunt gave Asher some etherograph recordings. That's where his new songs came from. And it seems like he must have agreed to make shirts for Morgaunt in return."

"Make shirts?" Minsky scoffed. "Morgaunt's got an army of people to make shirts for him! Why would he want to hire Asher?"

"Well, Asher seems to have been an unusually powerful magician. And Morgaunt wanted to stock up shirts in preparation for the Pentacle strike, so—"

"Oh!" Minsky said as understanding dawned on him. "Asher was the scabbalist!"

"Yes. Or we think so, anyway. But then he tried to go back on the deal, and that's when Morgaunt killed him."

"And hired a new scabbalist to replace him. I get it. Okay, so that explains the Klezmer King. And I guess it explains Schlosky. But how are *you* mixed up in this?"

"I don't know that, either." Sacha shivered. "I just know that Morgaunt . . . he thinks I'm a Mage, or will be someday. And . . . and he wants me to work for him."

"And is that what you want?" Minsky asked, ever so softly.

But all Sacha could do in answer was shake his head no, no, no, no, no.

Minsky stared at Sacha for a long time after that, his arms folded across his chest, his eyes hooded and unreadable.

"I don't know if I believe you or not," he said at last. "And I'll tell you this, too: when I had Benny bring you in, I didn't plan to let you walk out of here alive. But now . . . now I've got a bunch of guys I need to talk to all over town." Minsky chuckled grimly. "I think it's time to call a meeting of all the gangs. You kids got a magicworkers' union? Well, maybe we need to take a leaf from your book and start a gangsters' union before J. P. Morgaunt steamrolls right over us and gets a monopoly over all the black magic in town."

God help us all, Sacha thought. *I think I've just set loose a magical gang war.*

Minsky strode to the door and yanked it open. "Go home, kid. And stay out of trouble. I'm not reeling you in yet, but I got my eye on you. And I'm feeling real nervous about the whole situation, in case you hadn't noticed. So if I were you, I wouldn't do anything to make me more nervous than I already am."

Instead of heading for home, Sacha ran toward Canal Street and his grandfather's little storefront *shul,* searching instinctively for the only person he still believed could save him. He dashed inside, slammed the door shut behind him, and turned to peer out the window into the dark streets that suddenly seemed unfamiliar and full of unspeakable dangers.

"It's back, isn't it?" said a quiet voice behind him.

Sacha whirled around, heart hammering in his chest.

But it was only Mo Lehrer, who was sweeping out the rabbi's *shul.*

"Where's my grandfather?"

Mo nodded toward the back room just as Rabbi Kessler shuffled out, waving an open book at Mo and grinning from ear to ear. "So listen to this, Mo! Here's how Rabbi Halberstam answers your question. And what's more, he quotes Rashi, Rabbi Akiva, and Ramban, all of whom he completely disagrees with. And you know what? I completely disagree with all of them—and him too!" Rabbi Kessler chuckled in gleeful anticipation. "So roll up your sleeves, Mo. We've got our work cut out for us!"

Then he saw Sacha and stopped in his tracks.

"It killed a boy," Sacha said raggedly. "Moishe's brother. He was barely older than I am."

"Oh, Sacha. I'm so sorry this has come upon you."

"Please, Grandpa! You have to help me stop this!"

"I can't."

"Because of some stupid rule—"

"No. Not because of some stupid rule, Sacha. I can't teach you how to stop it because *I don't know how.*"

Sacha wanted to weep. Some part of him had still believed, right up until this moment, that his grandfather would know how to save him from the dybbuk. But now he could see in his grandfather's eyes that there was no hope of that.

"Then what use is all this?" he asked bitterly, waving a hand at the dusty little storefront *shul,* which suddenly looked poorer and more dilapidated than ever to him. "How can you claim to teach people something you can't even do yourself?"

"Sacha," Mo said gently, "people don't come here to *do* magic. They come here to *understand* it. And *that* is of great use. What is the meaning of the most secret name of God, Sacha? *I Am That I Am.* There is nothing in all Creation that is more powerful—more truly powerful—than seeing what *is.*"

"Great! And how is 'seeing what *is*' going to save my life?"

Rabbi Kessler sighed. "I don't know," he said—and Sacha saw tears shining in his tired old eyes. "But it's all I have to give you."

They stared at each other for what seemed like an eternity, Mo standing forgotten beside them. When Rabbi Kessler finally spoke again, all he said was, "Get me a glass of water."

Sacha stared at his grandfather in disbelief. But Rabbi Kessler just smiled—and when his grandfather smiled like that, Sacha knew better than to argue. So he took his grandfather's ever-present water glass from the table and looked around until he saw the water bucket—kept in the corner with a cloth over the top, just as it was at home. And then he dipped the glass into the cold water and brought it up full again.

"Now hold it up to the window and tell me what you see in it."

"Water," Sacha muttered.

"And what else? Hold it up higher, so the light shines through it."

Sacha held the glass up at arm's length so that the sunlight streamed through it. And he saw . . . dust. Thousands, maybe millions of tiny dust motes swirling in the sunlight. They looked dull and lifeless in the shadows, but they shone like fallen stars where the sunlight struck them.

"Remember the story of creation, Sacha? God poured forth His infinite light into the cosmos, but the vessels made to receive that light were too weak to hold it. So they broke, and the sparks of creation fell to earth and were buried in the husks of our mortal bodies. That glass is your body, and the water is your soul. When you dip your little glass of water from the bucket, you're born. And when you pour it back into the bucket, you die. And between those moments, the water in the glass doesn't remember that it was once united with the water in the bucket. Just as the water in the bucket doesn't know that it is of one essence with all the water of all the world's oceans. But the sparks remember, Sacha. The sparks remember."

Sacha watched the sparks rise and fall in a swirling dance like the flight of dust motes in a shaft of sunlight.

"We live in a broken world," Rabbi Kessler murmured. "The breaking began at the very dawn of creation, and every wicked thing that people do makes the world more broken and the path of return longer and steeper. But still, even in the most broken soul, there are sparks of the divine that yearn to return to their source and be made whole again. They seek a vessel, a husk—a body through which to make that journey. That is what the divine sparks within your dybbuk seek in you, Sacha." He saw Sacha's look of surprise. "Yes, Sacha, even as all that is twisted and fallen in the dybbuk seeks to destroy you, there is still a spark of the divine within it, a remnant of a living soul that desperately yearns to return to its creator. And yet you would set out to destroy this soul-double of yours. You would have me teach you some spell that would banish your shadow to the outer darkness while letting you go free in the sunlight. That cannot be. You might as well ask me to shatter this glass and catch the water in my hands before it hits the floor."

"Then what hope is there for either of us?"

"The same hope all souls have. Dybbuks aren't golems. They aren't creations of man, made from straw and river mud. They are a breath of God, just as we are. And every year, when God opens the Books of Life and Death, their souls hang in the balance just as ours do. As long as that is so, the path of return is still open to them. The climb out of the darkness may be long and hard, but it still begins with one step."

"You want me to make a *dybbuk* take *teshuvah*?" Sacha asked incredulously, almost unable to force his mind around the idea. "How am I supposed to do *that?*"

"I don't know," Rabbi Kessler said quietly. "But I do know this: there's no spell that will do it for you."

Sacha was just drawing breath to ask another question when he heard a rush of voices and a roar of running feet in the street outside. He went to the door and saw a crowd surging down Canal Street.

Sacha grabbed one of the runners and held him back long enough to ask what had happened.

"The strike's on!" the boy cried. "The workers at Pentacle are going to walk out tomorrow morning, and word is half the other factories in town may go on strike with them!"

CHAPTER TWENTY-ONE

Strike!

SACHA RAN BACK to his house first, thinking that the best place to find out what was really happening would be the IWW offices. When he got there, he found Bekah manning the translation desk: a rickety card table with a sign tacked onto it that read TRANSLATIONS in every language Sacha spoke and several that he didn't. On either side of the translation table were identical tables, one labeled REGISTRATION and the other COMPLAINTS.

"I just ran all the way from Greene," panted a girl who couldn't have been more than twelve. "We need help! The police are arresting people for illegal assembly!"

"That's nothing," said a girl who was holding a bloody rag to her face. "We just got beat up by starkers right in front of a cop. He said, 'I ain't here to look out for you lot, I'm here to look out for Mr. Morgaunt!'"

"Complaints to the left!" Bekah cried, waving them away as if she'd heard it all before. "If you don't need translators, then get out of the way and let the girls who need 'em come through! Italian, anyone? We've got three Italian speakers ready to go here!"

From every corner of the room, requests flew at her—faster than Sacha could imagine anyone, even the super-efficient Bekah, fielding them:

"*Oy, veh!* And where were the Italian speakers yesterday when we needed them?"

"Today we need Russian!"

"Russian? Who needs Russian? I need Litvaks! Are there any Litvaks in here? Anyone here even know what the heck a Litvak is?"

"And I need—excuse me, dearie, what language is that you're speakin'?—Well, gracious me, I don't even know what I need! A mind reader, maybe!"

Sacha was still gawping around open-mouthed when a police messenger dashed up the stairs from his own apartment.

"Is Sacha Kessler up here?" the boy shouted. "I need Sacha Kessler, and I need him now! All Inquisitors are to report to duty immediately!"

Forty minutes later, Sacha slammed into the lobby of the Inquisitors Division, sweaty and out of breath after a mad sprint from the nearest subway station. He caught sight of Lily and Payton first, since they stood out in their street clothes surrounded by a milling throng of navy blue uniforms. A moment later he saw a sight as intimidating as any he ever wanted to see in life: Inquisitor Wolf in full uniform.

He looked like he had grown six inches. And his spectacles flashed menacingly from beneath the shadow of his peaked Inquisitor's cap.

"I need to talk to you!" Sacha gasped as soon as he managed to push through the crowd to Wolf's side.

"Not here."

"But I have tell you about Sam—"

"Not here."

Sacha started to argue, but before he could speak, Commissioner Keegan climbed onto the booking desk and called for silence.

"Men!" he cried. "The moment has come! This is our hour of trial! The strike starts tomorrow morning, and we will be ready for it. Expect hard work in the days ahead. We are at the front lines of the fight for Freedom, Prosperity, and the American Way. There is a conspiracy of foreign magical elements afoot. These people hate us for one reason and one reason alone: because we are free. And it is your great task and mine to defend America's freedom!"

He glanced around the room and raised a warning finger. "Of course, this does not mean that we take sides in the coming conflict. No, we are on the side of all those who share our great American values and are willing to cooperate with the forces of law and order. Remember that, men, for there will be those who seek to discredit and malign us. Be disciplined, be courteous—but above all, be firm! We are the last bulwark against a flood of foreign magic that threatens to engulf this great nation. We must stand firm—and yet we must stand also for the rule of law. Remember that, men, and you will not dishonor your uniform!"

And that was it. Commissioner Keegan jumped down from the booking desk. The navy-and-silver-uniformed throng began to move. And the next thing Sacha knew, they were all loading into the paddy wagons.

"Are we going to the strike?" Sacha asked Lily when he managed to squirm and elbow his way over to her.

"I don't think so. Or not yet, anyway. I think we're going to guard Penn Station."

Twenty minutes later, they were indeed at Penn Station, milling about with a horde of other confused and agitated Inquisitors and searching all the incoming night trains for IWW reinforcements. This duty lasted for the rest of the night, until Sacha was yawning and stumbling with exhaustion. But at seven thirty the next morning, something suddenly changed. A messenger arrived from headquarters, and a wave of excited whispers swept through the ranks. The first morning train from Philadelphia was bringing in a carful of private detectives from the Pinkerton agency fresh off a mining strike in West Virginia. At first the rumors said there would be twenty of them. Then the number rose to forty, fifty, seventy. But one fact stood firm amidst the swirling tide of rumors: the Inquisitors were going to provide the Pinkertons with a protective escort to the strike site.

Sacha gasped at the unfairness of this, but Lily just

shrugged and asked him what he'd expected. And when Wolf overheard him, he gave Sacha a look that all but froze the words in his mouth.

Fair or unfair, at seven twenty sharp, they were on platform eight waiting for the Pinkertons. Sacha wasn't quite sure what he expected to see when the train finally pulled into the station and the doors slid open. But whatever he'd imagined, the actual reality of the Pinkertons was beyond his wildest dreams.

They looked like an exhibit from Buffalo Bill's Wild West Show. And they sounded like—well, the few genuine commuters on the train cringed onto the platform looking as if their ears were about to explode. The Pinkertons seemed to have a running competition to see who could swear the loudest and grow the most exotically styled facial hair. Sideburns battled for elbowroom with waxed handlebar mustaches as sharp and shining as Hessian bayonets, beards and goatees of every length and profile, and even bushy, drooping Pancho Villa mustachios.

And that wasn't the only running competition between the Pinkertons. As they thrust the porters aside and marched off the train, even the most casual observer couldn't have failed to note the alarming collection of weaponry they had brought with them. The contingent of Inquisitors awaiting them on the platform had been sent to provide a police escort to the strike zone. But one sight of the arriving Pinkertons left Sacha thinking that it was the *police* who needed protection from *them.*

Still, they got the Pinkertons loaded into the paddy wagons and trundled down to Pentacle just in time to see the first skirmishes break out between the strikers and the factory guards. As they climbed out and began lining up across the street from the factory, Sacha looked around, trying to make sense of the scene. The wide street in front of Pentacle's gates looked like a military encampment on the night before a great battle. The morning sun glinted off streetcar tracks and soldiers' bayonets. The cobblestones stretched away toward the factory gates like waves rippling on a black lake. And on the opposite sidewalk, between the police and militia lines and the silent factory gates, he could see a roiling mob of Pinkertons and thugs—the strikebreakers.

Sacha felt torn between eagerness to see the strike for himself and terror that his sister or Moishe would see him with the police and think he was helping the strikebreakers.

"What's going on?" he asked nervously. "What are we supposed to do here?"

"Whatever we're told to do," Wolf answered shortly.

"But this isn't our job," Sacha protested. "We're Inquisitors, not strikebreakers!"

"Tell that to Commissioner Keegan."

Word passed along the lines that Morgaunt had decided to lock down the factory at noon and kick the strikers out before they could call their strike. And then another rumor swept along the lines: the strikers would walk out themselves at ten.

As the hour drew nearer, the streets around Pentacle got

quieter and quieter. Passersby seemed to be steering away from the area with the same instinct that makes horses run away from an approaching storm. Even the streetcars and omnibuses stopped coming by on their scheduled rounds; Commissioner Keegan had shut them down, Sacha found out later, as part of his security cordon around the strike.

When two o'clock finally arrived, the streets were so silent that they could hear the church bells at Trinity striking the hour a full mile away.

A minute passed. And then another, and another.

Nothing happened. No one came out of Pentacle or any of the other factories and office buildings in the surrounding streets.

"Cowards!" a trooper scoffed a few feet to Sacha's left. "It was all just wild talk. They don't dare strike with us here."

"Well, boys," said the squad captain, "I'll bet a silver dollar we'll all be home for dinner!"

And then it happened.

The first sign was a low murmur, like the distant rumble of a passing freight train. It began faintly, but it soon grew louder. It rose and swelled until it seemed to Sacha that a mighty river was rushing toward them between the steel buildings and would sweep them all away like a flash flood ripping through a desert canyon.

Suddenly, every door up and down the street was filled with workers. Tailors with their mending kits. Office girls in crisp skirts and shirtwaists. Brawny young pressers. They were all walking off the job together. They were doing it in an orderly, quiet, serious, peaceful manner. But they were walking off the job just the same.

And suddenly Sacha understood what it was that Commissioner Keegan had sent his men here to do:

Nothing.

Nothing at all.

As the first rank of striking workers appeared, the strikebreakers set on them like a pack of wild dogs, ripping hats off girls' heads, tearing at their hair and clothes, knocking people down and dragging them along the cobblestones.

The strikers fled into the street, but the militia was waiting for them with bayonets at the ready, forcing them to stumble back onto the sidewalk. Some of the girls tried to fight back—and were promptly arrested for disturbing the peace. But most of them were too young and small to stand up to the grown men attacking them. Soon the shrieks of girls were rising above the crowd, and the gutter was flowing with blood, and the dark cobblestones were littered with a white confetti of torn hats and scarves and ribbons.

And all the while, the police just stood by with their hands in their pockets as if none of it had anything to do with them.

Sacha started forward, with no thought in his mind other than coming to the aid of these poor defenseless girls. But a hard hand on his chest stopped him short.

He turned, outraged—and found himself face-to-face with Inquisitor Wolf.

"You want to get yourself arrested too?" Wolf asked him in a low, urgent voice. "Just what do you think that's going to accomplish?"

"I don't care!" Sacha shouted. "This is wrong!"

"And you think a useless symbolic gesture is going to make things right?"

"Two wrongs don't make a right!" Sacha retorted. But even as he said the words, he knew they sounded childish.

He was just about to give up and step back into the line next to Wolf when he saw something that stopped his heart cold: Bekah, standing in the door of the factory, looking out at the struggling mob on the sidewalk.

For an instant, her eyes lifted to the line of police on the opposite pavement, and Sacha could have sworn she recognized him. Then she calmly took off her new hat and hung it up on one of the iron spikes of the factory gate, as if she figured it would have a better chance of staying in one piece there than it would on her head. Sacha saw that she had cut her hair short, like the other IWW girls, so that her boyish curls would give the Pinkertons less to grab hold of. And then he saw her take one deep, determined breath and step into the crowd.

After that, it was hard for Sacha to remember quite what he'd done—other than yell "I quit!" and call Wolf a lying hypocrite.

The police and militia weren't expecting anyone to break through their cordon from the police side. They mostly moved aside for Sacha, probably figuring he was carrying a message for the Pinkertons. Before he himself quite knew what he was planning, he had crossed the street and was elbowing toward the line of strikers.

He caught sight of Bekah a few yards away. She was arm in arm with several other girls, and they were all trying to make a united front and push past the Pinkertons to safety. For a moment, it seemed they would make it. But then a huge Pinkerton agent stepped in front of them, fists raised and brass knuckles flashing.

Sacha gave a bloodcurdling yell, raised his hands in front of him just as he'd done in Shen's practice hall, and sprang forward in his best version of Golden Leopard Speeds Through Jungle. The Pinkerton must have just seen Sacha out of the corner of his eye; he froze in the very act of bashing the brass knuckles down on Bekah's head and spun to face Sacha. When he saw who his assailant was, he laughed.

"Shows what you know!" Sacha growled, and slid in under the man's right hook with a Green Dragon Shoots Pearl that even Shen would have declared satisfactory.

The Pinkerton punched thin air, stumbled, and almost went to his knees.

Emboldened, Sacha drew an attack with the Dragon's Chi Spreads Across the Water.

The man's eyes widened—perhaps because Sacha appeared to be leaving himself wide open to attack, or perhaps just at the sight of a skinny thirteen-year-old swaying back

STRIKE
STRIKE

and forth in front of him while howling and gesturing like a deranged banshee.

His brawny arm reared back, the brass knuckles flashing like rings, and swept down in a vicious arc toward Sacha's head.

And then everything went black.

CHAPTER TWENTY-TWO

Mordechai Gets a Job . . . and Bekah Gets a Proposition

WHEN SACHA CAME to, he was lying in the family's single big feather bed at home with his mother bending over him. He raised himself up on his elbows with some difficulty and looked around. Bekah was there—and she seemed to be in one piece, though her hat was missing and her hair disheveled. But the house was in chaos.

"Who did this to you?" Mrs. Kessler cried as soon as she saw that Sacha was conscious.

"The Pinkertons."

"But I thought you were working for the police!"

"Not anymore, he's not," Bekah said ominously. but Sacha threw her a pleading look that made her stop before she said anything else.

"And where was the great Inquisitor Wolf while you were getting beat up by grown men?" Mrs. Kessler demanded angrily. "I have half a mind to tell him what I think of a man who leaves his own apprentice to be rescued by a mere girl!"

"Listen," Sacha said. "Can we just not talk about it until I feel better? Please?"

He must have looked even worse than he felt, because Mrs. Kessler gave a silent nod and began gently removing his bloody clothes. Within a very few minutes, she had poured him into a hot bath, wrapped him with warm towels, pressed cold compresses to his nose, and funneled several cups of steaming chicken soup into him. And then—at long last—he managed to crawl into bed. He was asleep before she had finished tucking him in.

Sacha did his best to think about all his problems over the next few days. But every time he thought of poor Sam Schlosky and his own grandfather's insistence that no one else could help him stop the dybbuk, the only solution Sacha could come up with was to stay in bed for the rest of his life. As it was, he could barely lift himself off the pillow without his head spinning and his ears ringing. His mother wouldn't hear of his getting up—and for once, he didn't have the energy to argue with her.

Meanwhile, the strike was going like gangbusters. The front gate of the Pentacle Shirtwaist Factory became the site of a daily running brawl between the Pinkertons and the shirtwaist girls. Most of the girls, like Bekah, had cut their hair short to keep the Pinkertons from grabbing it, and when a contingent of girls from Vassar came down by train to join the picket line, they all bobbed their hair too. Soon the new "Pentacle bob" was sweeping the nation. No one was quite sure how it had happened, but the undeniable fact of the matter was that the strike had become *fashionable.* Mayor Mobbs announced that the police would maintain public order at any cost, and called up the state militia—whose members gave a boost to the local economy by immediately getting fleeced in every establishment up and down the Bowery. The staircase of the Kesslers' apartment building turned into a public thoroughfare, with crowds of strikers trooping up and down at all hours as the IWW headquarters expanded into two neighboring apartments and soon threatened to overflow even its new larger quarters. And still, the strike wore on.

All too soon, Sacha's parents began to worry about money. They tried not to mention it in front of the children, but Sacha and Bekah had both been poor long enough to know what those whispered late-night conversations meant.

There were only two bright spots in the general gloom. First, Sacha's mother really did seem to have found a fall-back job at the "other" shirtwaist factory, even if it was on the night shift. Second—and this was the truly amazing development—Uncle Mordechai finally got a job.

He came home early from the Metropole one night specifically to announce that he was determined to sell the labor of his arm to the capitalist machine if that was what it took to keep the family together.

"I'm perfectly happy to mooch when the mooching's good," he said, "but a man has to know when to bow to reality and stop standing on principle. The time has come for me to put family ahead of morality and sacrifice my youthful ideals to the wicked world!"

Having delivered this thrilling speech, he threw himself into his chair in an elegant attitude and began combing through the want ads—a task that turned out to be so exhausting that he retreated to the Metropole half an hour later "just for a little refreshment of the spirit."

He came back so refreshed that he could barely contain himself.

"You'll never believe what happened to me just now!" he cried. "The goyim say God helps those who help themselves, and they must be right, because I think I just landed a peach of a job. No, no, never fear! It's not a real job. Nothing so shocking! No, this is something where I could make good money and still be able to hold my head up as a respectable revolutionary. I'm going to be a lady's escort."

"A what?" Mrs. Kessler squawked. "Mordechai! You wouldn't! And even if you would, don't you dare talk about it in front of the children!"

"No, no, it's not what you're thinking. It's really quite innocent and aboveboard. You see, I ran into Nathan Feldman down at the Metropole—"

"Nathan Feldman!" Mrs. Kessler cried. "His mother told me he was an usher in a Broadway theater!"

"He just told his mother that because he had to explain why he bought a brand-new top hat and tails last month from Bloomingdale Brothers. According to Nathan, it turns out that there are all sorts of occasions upon which ladies wish to be able to produce a well-turned-out young man whom they can claim is their beau or fiancé. So Nathan—and I can assure you with perfect modesty that he isn't half as handsome or charming as I am—rents himself out by the hour for soirées, balls, weddings, and so forth. There's nothing immoral going on, unless you think there's something wrong with dancing the foxtrot at a debutante's ball under the gimlet eyes of a squadron of matronly chaperones. It's not that these young ladies want to actually be his inamoratas. They just want to be able to point to him and claim that they are.

"Nathan's made such a success of it that he's styled himself Prince Nachmaninov, rented a spectacular apartment on Central Park West, and has spent the last month working on an exclusive contract with a society matron who employs him to pose as an eligible bachelor. She's got a daughter coming out this year, and genuine eligible bachelors are in such short supply that she considers it prudent to whip up the appearance of some competition in order to appeal to their sporting instincts. Now tell me, wouldn't I make a bang-up eligible bachelor? Doesn't that sound like just the ticket for me?"

Mrs. Kessler snorted. "It sounds like just the ticket for getting your head kicked in by a jealous boyfriend."

"Not to mention outraged fathers," Mr. Kessler added

in a tone that suggested he thought the outraged fathers had the right of it.

"Not at all!" Mordechai assured them blithely. "No jealous boyfriends involved. Let alone outraged fathers. In fact, quite the reverse. You see, that's the genius of Nathan's concept. It's the parents who actually hire us. And for me, Nathan has something truly brilliant in mind. You see, rich people don't think of marriage the way we do. For them it's a business proposition. A uniting of bank accounts, not individuals. But young girls have such romantic notions. And Nathan offers parents a safe way to disabuse their daughters of such notions. The crux of Nathan's brilliant plan is this: I am to pose as Count Vogelonsky, a wealthy Russian nobleman. I shall woo these girls—discreetly, you understand, not in any way that might compromise their reputations. And then, when they declare their tender feelings for me, I shall confess to them that I am not Count Vogelonsky, but merely an impoverished Anarcho-Wiccanist revolutionary posing as Vogelonsky."

"Basically," Mr. Kessler translated, "you're going to lie to them."

"Where's the lie?" Mordechai asked virtuously. "I *am* an Anarcho-Wiccanist—though of course I abhor violence on aesthetic grounds and thus consider myself more of a visionary progressive than an outright revolutionary. And I'm most certainly impoverished."

"I know you're not going to listen to me," Mr. Kessler said in a resigned tone. "But really, Mordechai, as your older brother and someone who feels obligated to protect you from your own lunacy—can I say what an absolutely terrible idea I think this is?"

Mordechai gave his older brother an affectionate look. "Why, Danny. I'm touched. I really am."

"Then you'll take my advice and call this crazy scheme off?"

"No," Mordechai said cheerfully. "But it's nice to know you care."

"But what about these girls?" Bekah asked incredulously. "What are *they* supposed to do after you tell them you're a penniless revolutionary?"

"Why, they'll throw me over, become disillusioned with love and romance, and settle for the eligible bachelors their parents have already chosen for them."

Mrs. Kessler just rolled her eyes and threw up her hands, but Bekah wasn't about to be put off so easily. "And what if one of the poor girls really does fall in love with you?" she asked. "What if she still wants to marry you after she finds out you're a penniless revolutionary?"

Mordechai looked thunderstruck by this idea, as if the possibility had never even crossed his mind. "Why, then," he said at last, "I suppose I'd have to marry her."

Soon Mrs. Kessler bustled off with a bowl of soup for a sick neighbor, and Sacha's father settled in with the evening papers. Sacha would have liked to read the papers too, but he couldn't keep his mind on anything. So instead he just sank into the dull, brooding, worrying state that was fast becoming normal for him.

He was startled out of his brown study by a heavy knock at the door.

"I'll get it!" he said quickly, and slunk off through the Lehrers' room, certain that Wolf would be waiting on the other side of it with an official pink slip from the Inquisitors Division.

But when he finally screwed up his courage to open the door, it wasn't Wolf who waited in the hallway. It was Dopey Benny Fein.

Benny cast a furtive look around the stairwell, as if he was worried that his mother was going to come downstairs and catch him. Then he ducked inside, slammed the door behind him . . . and just stood there, wringing his hat in his huge hands and looking like a bull in a china shop.

"Can I help you?" Sacha asked.

But Benny was too busy peering over his shoulder into the apartment to answer. When he'd inspected every corner of the Lehrers' room, the gangster began inching his way toward the kitchen, still looking around and over the Lehrers' piles of piecework as if he expected someone to jump out from behind the clothes at any minute.

"Are you looking for someone?" asked Sacha. But he might as well have asked the wall, for all the attention Benny paid him.

Danny and Mordechai Kessler looked up in surprise when Benny lumbered in.

"Hello, Benny," Sacha's father said. He was one of the few people in the neighborhood who still talked to Benny like a normal person and hadn't gradually become more and more frightened of him as he changed from Mrs. Fein's overgrown but slightly slow-witted son into Meyer Minsky's most fearsome starker.

"Uh . . . hello, Mr. Kessler," Benny said politely. And then he nodded to Mordechai—who nodded back somewhat stiffly and suddenly became extremely interested in his newspaper.

"Pull up a chair," Mr. Kessler said. "And have a slice of cake while you're at it. You always used to love Ruthie's bundt cakes."

But Benny had other things besides cake on his mind. He was craning his neck again to peer into every corner. Pretty soon he was going to either have to give up hunting for whatever he was hunting for or start opening cupboards and pawing through canned goods to find it.

"Are you looking for someone?" Mr. Kessler asked.

"No, sir! I—uh—erm." Benny turned desperately to Sacha. "Can I talk to youze for a minute?"

"Uh . . . sure, Benny."

"In private!" Benny said in a whisper loud enough to carry to the next block.

Sacha followed Benny into the other room and listened with growing confusion while Benny launched into a long, rambling explanation of his personal finances and job prospects with Magic, Inc. At first it sounded like Benny was applying for membership in some elite country club that he was sure would never accept him. But gradually he realized that Benny was applying for membership in the Kessler family—as his brother-in-law!

"Wait a minute. You want to *marry* Bekah?" Sacha felt as if he'd set off to cross the street, after carefully looking both ways for traffic—and run smack into the side of an omnibus.

"Yeah," Benny said, his adenoidal voice sinking to a worshipful whisper. "I came down here to talk to your father aboud it but, well . . . to tell ya the truth, I always was kinda scared of him."

Sacha glanced toward the kitchen to see if his father had heard any of this. Mr. Kessler was still sitting at the kitchen table reading the business pages—or at least pretending to read them. But behind the newspaper, he was shaking with laughter. Mordechai, meanwhile, was practically in tears—and as soon as he caught Sacha's eye, he began to perform an elaborate pantomime of eating his section of the newspaper.

Sacha didn't think either of them was taking the situation nearly seriously enough.

"Dat's why I want *you* to talk to him," Benny explained.

"Now?"

"Well, soon. And in the meantime, maybe you could walk out with me and Bekah. You know, to keep tings respectable. 'Cause she's a respectable goil. And I respect that."

Behind their newspapers, Sacha's father and uncle collapsed in simultaneous coughing fits.

"Whaddaya say we just walk around the block a couple times when she gets home? Dat okay wid you?"

Thankfully, Sacha was saved from having to say what he thought of this plan by Bekah herself.

"I really do think we're making progress," she said as she breezed through the door, already unwinding her scarf and unpinning her hat from her short curls. "Today I actually got one of the Pinkertons to accept a pamphlet from me. Just like Moishe says, it's all a matter of appealing to the best side of people. After all, the Pinkertons aren't capitalists or propertarians. They're just people. Who knows? Maybe the Pinkerton I talked to today has a mother who works magic—"

"My mother does magic," Benny said. "Her matzo ball soup"—he flicked a kiss off his fingers into midair—"supernatural!"

"Oh," Bekah said. "Hello, Mr. Fein. What are you doing here?"

Benny twisted his hat in his thick fingers as if it were one of Mrs. Mogulesko's kosher geese. "I—uh—fine weather we're having, ain't it?"

"Not really." Bekah said. She frowned at him for a moment, then walked to the stove and stood before it, rubbing the warmth back into her hands.

"I would like to go for a walk with you, Miss Kessler," Benny said, blushing furiously. "Also, I would like to take you home to meet my mother."

"But I already know your mother," Bekah said reasonably. "She lives right upstairs. Are you all right, Mordechai? You sound like you're coming down with a cough."

"No, no, carry on!" Mordechai said in a strangled voice. Sacha could see him kicking his older brother under the table.

"What on earth is going on here?" Bekah asked the room at large. When nobody answered, she turned to Benny and said, "Listen, Benny, I don't have time to visit your mother tonight. I need to go upstairs and help out at the IWW. But if you'd like to help too, that would be lovely."

"Oh—er—well, I don't know if Meyer would—"

Bekah put her hands on her hips and leaned back to stare the gangster in the face. "Does Meyer Minsky run your life, Benny? You're a grown man! Don't you do *anything* without his permission? If you want my opinion, you starkers ought to go on strike too one of these days!"

And with that, Bekah marched out of the apartment and up the stairs toward the IWW headquarters. Benny stood staring after her for a moment with a slightly dizzy expression on his face. Then he gave a fatalistic shrug and followed her.

When she came back downstairs, though, Bekah was alone.

"I have to talk to you," she told Sacha.

"Don't look at me! I have nothing whatsoever to say about your love life!"

"Forget that," Bekah said. "This is serious."

The look on her face was enough to wipe the grin off

Sacha's lips. He followed her out onto the landing and eased the door closed behind them so they could be sure Mrs. Lehrer wouldn't hear them.

"What?" he asked.

But Bekah wasn't ready to tell him. She paced in a tight circle on the landing, and then fidgeted with her dress. Then finally, she came out with it.

"What do you know about Mama's other job?"

"The night job?"

"Yeah. The one she got when she left Pentacle."

"Nothing. It's just a sewing job, right? Same thing she always does."

"But not at the same place. In fact, we still don't even know where she's working, do we?"

"I thought you knew," Sacha said uncomfortably.

But Bekah shook her head.

"So what? Why are you suddenly all worked up about it?"

"Because," Bekah said, lowering her voice, "one of the girls upstairs has been working on the night cleanup crew at Pentacle. As a spy, see? We've got girls going in on the cleaning crews to make sure they're not bringing in scabs at night. And she just told me she saw our mother there last night."

"That's impossible!"

"She seemed pretty sure about it."

"So . . . what are you saying?"

Bekah glanced over her shoulder as if she were afraid that someone might have come down from the IWW headquarters to spy on them. "I'm not saying anything," she whispered urgently. "I'm just . . . scared."

"Of what?" Sacha asked impatiently.

"Think about it, Sacha! Connect the dots! The strikers have Pentacle locked down tighter than a bank vault, but Morgaunt still keeps shipping shirtwaists to all the uptown department stores. Everyone's convinced Morgaunt has a scabbalist working for him. The only question is who."

"Wait a minute. You're telling me you think our mother is the scabbalist? That's the craziest thing I ever heard!"

"Hello! Wake up, Sacha! Her father was only the most famous wonderworker in all of Russia! Don't you think she could have inherited a little of his talent?"

"She's *not* the scabbalist!"

"Why not?"

"Because—well, she's just not."

"What makes you so sure?"

"Because her family's the most important thing in the world to her," he blurted out. "And if you found out she was doing that, it would rip our family apart!"

But Bekah just shook her head.

"That's crazy," he insisted. "You know it is. Mama would do anything for us!"

He stared at Bekah, horrified by what he had just said—and horrified by the look on Bekah's face.

"That's exactly my point," Bekah said.

CHAPTER TWENTY-THREE

Lily Rides the Subway

THE NEXT MORNING, Sacha heard the sound he'd been fearing all along: the firm *rat-a-tat-tat* of a stranger knocking at the door.

By sheer good luck, it was Saturday morning. His father and grandfather were at temple. Mordechai was at the People's Theater, and Bekah was off God knew where. Only Sacha and his mother were at home.

Mrs. Kessler went to the door, looking apprehensive and mystified. After all, no one who lived in the Hester Street tenements bothered to knock before coming in to visit, and no one who didn't live there wanted to visit at all.

While his mother opened the door, Sacha burrowed into the pillows and pulled the blankets up around his neck. He felt like a coward, but he couldn't help it. He knew exactly what he would see when the door opened: Maximillian Wolf in all his Inquisitorial glory, come—at best—to make Sacha's sacking official, or—at worst—to cart him off to jail for public disorderliness and disobeying orders. But when the door swung open, it wasn't Wolf who was standing in the hall. It was Lily Astral.

"Close your mouth," Lily told him smugly. "You look like a carp in a Chinatown fish shop!"

She stepped through the door, sidled carefully around the edge of the room between the cookstove and the kitchen table, and sat down in the chair that Sacha's mother hurried to pull out for her.

Mordechai had long ago broken the chair by leaning back on two legs and putting his feet on the table, so it squeaked and wobbled ominously even under Lily's skinny frame. But Mrs. Kessler just flapped her dish towel nonchalantly and said, "Never mind that, dear, the chair'll be fine. You can't weigh more than a plucked chicken!"

"How did you get here?" Sacha asked. It wasn't the most brilliant question, but there were so many jostling around in his brain that he didn't seem to have much control over which one got to his mouth first.

"By subway!" Lily sounded utterly delighted with herself. "Marvelous things! I had no idea! Have you ever ridden on one? Why didn't you tell me about them? Anyway, that's not the point. You gave me a real runaround, Sacha Kessler! When I realized that the house near Gramercy Park was all a put-on, I thought you really had me. By the way, you might want to avoid that neighborhood for a while—that housemaid's a regular Tartar! Anyway, Wolf was about as much help as a dime-store Indian. And Shen . . . well, have you ever noticed how hard it is to find the Young Ladies' Dancing and Deportment Academy when Shen doesn't want to talk to you? But then I thought, hey, why not go straight to the top?"

"Oh, my God," Sacha muttered weakly. "You asked Teddy Roosevelt to find me?"

"Nope. Though now that you mention it, I think maybe I ought to write to him about you. I asked Meyer Minsky. Why are you looking like that? As soon as I realized you'd tricked me, I put two and two together and realized that you must live in the tenements. So I—"

"Tell your friend to have some cheesecake!" Sacha's mother urged, sliding a glowing golden wedge of her famous cake across the table toward Lily.

"Mama!" Sacha protested. "That slice is the size of Alaska! And hasn't anyone ever told you it's polite to *ask* before you shove food in people's faces?"

"Ask, shmask! Who needs to ask? Just look at her, poor thing. She's obviously starving!"

"I'm sure she's not starving," Sacha said in what he hoped was a squelching voice.

"Well, I'm sure she is. I can practically see her ribs through her coat! Ask her if she wants sour cream on top of it. Sour cream really puts the fat on a girl's hips! And boys like to see a little wobble in a girl's walk—"

"Mother!"

But Lily was happily oblivious. "What did you call this?" she asked around a huge mouthful of cake. "I could eat it forever! It must have about nine hundred eggs in it!"

"Only twelve," Mrs. Kessler confessed, somewhat regretfully. "Another slice you vant? Mit sour cream you vant?"

"I've never had sour cream on a cake before," Lily said, as if Mrs. Kessler had just revealed a whole wonderful new universe of culinary possibilities to her.

"Anyway," Lily told Sacha while Mrs. Kessler was fetching the sour cream. "Like I was saying, I figured out for myself that the secret you were hiding from me was that you lived down in the tenements. It was the only thing that made sense of all the little details that didn't quite add up now that I thought about them. And who runs the tenements? Meyer Minsky! I wasn't exactly sure where that candy store was, of course. But I *could* find my way back to the Café Metropole. And luckily, once I was there, I ran into that nice Count Vogelonsky—"

"Who?"

"Oh, I forgot," Lily said brightly. "I haven't seen you since then! Remember that nice man we ran into when Wolf took us to talk to Meyer Minsky?"

Sacha ground his teeth but somehow managed to nod more or less calmly.

"Well, I met him again just the other night, because he came to a fancy dress ball at my mother's house. And I was right about him after all; he *is* a Russian nobleman. His name is Count Vogelonsky, and he's best friends with Prince Nachmaninov."

"Nach-*what?*"

"Nachmaninov. *N-A-C-H*—well, anyway, that's not the

point. The point is *he* knows everyone and goes to all the best parties and lives in the Dakota. So when I ran into his friend again at the Café Metropole, I knew I could trust him to help me."

"You have got to be kidding me!"

"Sacha, you're shouting. And I really can't explain anything to you if you insist on interrupting me like this. Anyway, Count Vogelonsky escorted me to Essex Street—he's *such* a *perfect* gentleman, Sacha, you really could learn a thing or two from him—and Meyer told me where you live, and here I am!"

"And what happened to Count Vogelonsky?" Sacha asked sarcastically.

"He thought it would be indelicate to intrude upon a conversation between friends."

"I bet he did!"

"You don't have to look so jealous," Lily said tartly. "My mother *does* have her heart set on marrying me to a title, but I think she'd prefer an English lord. Those Russian exiles can be a little flighty. And besides, father says they make very unsound investments. Land is really the only safe place to put your money these days, what with all the investment bubbles and penny stock hexes."

"Look, Lily. This is really . . . really . . . well, I appreciate your trying to help, that's all. But it's no use. Wolf will never give me my job back after what I did."

"I don't know about that," Lily said stoutly. "But I do know he won't give it back to you if you don't ask for it!"

"It's not that simple!" Sacha protested. Suddenly he was angry at her. "What do you know about my life? My family is full of Kabbalists and magicworkers—including the magicworkers those Pinkertons were beating up the other day! I'd be a worm if I didn't stand up for my own sister when grown men are ganging up on her—and a liar if I told Wolf I'd never disobey him again!"

"I understand how you feel, Sacha."

"You don't understand a thing about me!" Sacha snapped. "You're a stuck-up little rich girl who's never had to worry for a second about money or magic or—or—anything!"

"I thought we were friends—"

"Well, think again! I don't need your pity!"

"It's not pity!" she retorted. "And *you're* the one who doesn't understand anything!"

Suddenly Sacha heard a suspicious quiver in her voice. Had it just begun, or had it been there all along?

"It's being friends. Or at least I thought that's what we were."

Suddenly Sacha looked—really looked—at Lily. What he saw surprised him. When they first met, he had thought she was just a spoiled little rich girl, paper thin, with no personality beyond the blond hair and blue eyes and prissy dresses. But over time, they'd become almost friends. Now a guilty little voice whispered to him that he had been the one holding back from real friendship all along. He had kept secrets from her because he hadn't trusted her—even though she had long ago earned that trust. And he had been held back not by her pride, but by his own . . . well, what else could he call it but snobbery?

The girl staring at him now had nothing to do with the Lily Astral he'd been so sure would despise him if she knew how poor he was. Her eyes weren't even blue. They were green—and not the bright, brilliant, bewitching green of Mrs. Astral's eyes, but a changeable ocean color that moved from green to blue to gray with every shift of her mercurial moods.

And right now, they were a soft, sad, hurt-looking rain gray.

"I'm sorry," he said. "I didn't mean to be nasty."

"Yes, you did." She sniffled slightly. "But I forgive you. I'm noble that way. Plus, we don't have any time to waste if you want to go back uptown and apologize to Wolf before he hires another apprentice."

"Oh, Lily! Even you can't be naive enough to think I still have a job to go back to!"

"Of course you do. You just have to—"

"And anyway, I quit. I said I quit, and I meant it."

"Quitting is yellow!" Lily said vehemently.

"Quitting is—oh, never mind, Lily. Look, I just can't go back, all right? I'll be happy if Wolf just leaves it at that instead of, well, I don't know, arresting me, or making me give back all the money they've paid me."

But Lily wasn't having any of it. "If you quit," she said, assuming a posture that reminded Sacha eerily of Teddy Roosevelt, "you'll be letting the J. P. Morgaunts of the world win. You'll be giving up on the chance to make things better, to make your life better, to make the world better. You'll be yellow. And you won't be my friend anymore. So get up, get dressed, and get your job back. I'll be waiting for you outside. You have five minutes."

She marched past Sacha's astonished mother, opened the door, and turned around for a parting shot:

"And don't make me come back!"

After that, there was really nothing to do but shrug and follow orders.

CHAPTER TWENTY-FOUR

Is There Room in New York for an Honest Inquisitor?

WHEN SACHA and Lily walked into the office, Wolf was talking to Payton—and the two of them clammed up as if they'd been talking about something they didn't want Sacha to hear.

"Your resignation is on Payton's desk," Wolf said with a vague wave of his hand. "You can just sign it and get started packing your things. No need for formalities."

Sacha felt completely crushed. He wasn't sure he wanted the job back, but it was humiliating to feel that Wolf didn't even care enough to ask. If Lily hadn't been blocking the way out, he would have left right then and there. But she cleared her throat meaningfully and gave him a shove in the ribs, propelling him into Wolf's office.

"What is it?" Wolf asked, sounding annoyed by the interruption.

"I—uh—I—can I talk to you?"

"Certainly. Have a seat."

And then, as if it had all been choreographed in advance, Payton slipped out of the office, closing the door behind him, and Wolf and Sacha were alone.

"Well?" Wolf said. "What is it?"

And that was the moment when Sacha realized what he should have realized sometime during the long trip uptown: that he had absolutely nothing to say to Wolf.

He began to stumble through a halfhearted apology, but Wolf cut him off.

"Forget about it," he said. "Water under the bridge, as Shen would say."

Sacha waited for a moment, but Wolf didn't go on. Apparently this was all he intended to say on the subject.

"So . . . can I come back?"

"Do you *want* to?"

"I—I don't know."

"Well, that's honest, at least. Though I'm not sure honesty bodes well for your career in the New York City Police Department."

"You don't think there's room in New York for an honest Inquisitor?"

"Not much," Wolf confessed. Then he grinned. "But you're just a skinny little thing. Maybe if you keep really quiet, no one will notice you."

"Thanks," Sacha drawled. "That's encouraging."

And that was it: he had his job back. Not that there was much time for celebrating.

Wolf's smile faded. "So what did you want to tell me about Sam Schlosky?"

Sacha told Wolf about the Nebbish and his awful story. When he was done, Wolf called Payton and Lily into the office and made him repeat the whole thing.

"What do you think, Payton?" Wolf asked when Sacha finally fell silent again.

"I think we ought to get a warrant to search Pentacle."

"That would mean rousting out one of the two honest judges in New York in the middle of his dinner. *And* calling in every favor I have coming to me," Wolf pointed out.

"I know. But whoever the new scabbalist is, he's in just as much danger as Naftali Asher ever was."

Three hours later, they were at the Pentacle factory with a search warrant. The Pinkerton at the front door began to protest that he'd have to call management before he let them in, but Wolf just looked mildly at him—and he retreated into his little office, murmuring confusedly.

"We'd better not waste any time," Wolf said. "I don't know how long that will hold him for."

For the next hour, they searched Pentacle from top to bottom. The more Sacha saw of the place, the less he liked the idea of his mother and sister working there. Whenever he'd heard Bekah or his mother talk about going off to "the factory," he'd imagined an efficient, scientific, industrial kind of place. He'd thought it would be planned and orderly and full of large, impressive machines. Instead it was like a gigantic version of the Lehrers' room, with more sewing machines and more steam irons and more teetering, slithering piles of unfinished clothes blocking off what little light came through the dirty windows. It was bad enough to think of his mother slaving away at those sewing machines from dawn to dark six days a week. But the idea of Bekah, seventeen years old and facing a lifetime in this place?

They searched between the rows of abandoned sewing machines. With every new workroom they moved through, Sacha felt a strange uneasiness settle over him. There was something creepy about walking through a shut-down factory. He could feel the absence of the noise and bustle that should be going on all around him. He could feel that they were alone in a place meant to contain hundreds of people. He could almost see the dust settling on the stacked bolts of cloth and the rust eating away at the idle machinery.

Meanwhile, they found nothing. The place was as echoingly empty as a mausoleum. Then, finally, Payton opened an unmarked door that led to a steep, narrow flight of wooden stairs—and they heard the distant but unmistakable hum of a sewing machine.

As they crept up the stairs, the sound of the sewing machine grew so much louder that they stopped worrying about the noise of their own footfalls; no one could hear footsteps over that racket. They reached the top of the stairs and stepped onto the landing. Warm yellow light spilled out of an open doorway. The rattle and hum of the sewing machine was almost deafening now—but over it Sacha could just make out the sound of a woman's voice. Whoever the lone seamstress was, she was singing while she worked.

Wolf and Payton slipped across the landing, with Sacha and Lily close behind them. Then Sacha watched as Wolf cautiously opened the door into the attic beyond. The look on Wolf's face told him immediately that their search was over. And when he peered around the edge of the half-open door himself, he knew that they had found the scabbalist—and that his life would never be the same again.

This attic was just as large and cavernous as the workrooms they had seen on the floors below. But its windows had all been carefully painted over to keep anyone from being able to see that there was another workshop up here. The floor of the room was covered with a thick layer of dust, as if no one had walked across it in a very long time. A single trail of footprints led through the dust to a modern steam-powered sewing machine at which a lone seamstress sat sewing.

She was finishing a shirtwaist in a perfectly normal, nonmagical way, holding the basted seams taut as she carefully sewed over them with good strong stitches. But there was nothing nonmagical about the glowing, pulsating aura around her—or about what was going on behind her. Hundreds of shirts hung in midair, squeezed into the workshop shoulder to shoulder, like rush-hour subway passengers. Bolts of cloth shuttled back and forth overhead. Bobbins scuttled around like nimble white spiders. Meanwhile, the shirts echoed every gesture the lone seamstress made, sewing

themselves together out of thin air as obediently as if they were pupils in a magical sewing class.

Extraordinary as all this was, Sacha barely noticed it.

He was too busy noticing that the woman sitting at the sewing machine was his mother.

Mrs. Kessler looked up and stopped sewing as they came in. The shirts stopped too, looking like surprised ghosts.

"Oh, dear," she said, looking like schmaltz wouldn't melt in her mouth. "I hope this won't be a problem for you at work, Sacha."

CHAPTER TWENTY-FIVE

The Scabbalist Unmasked

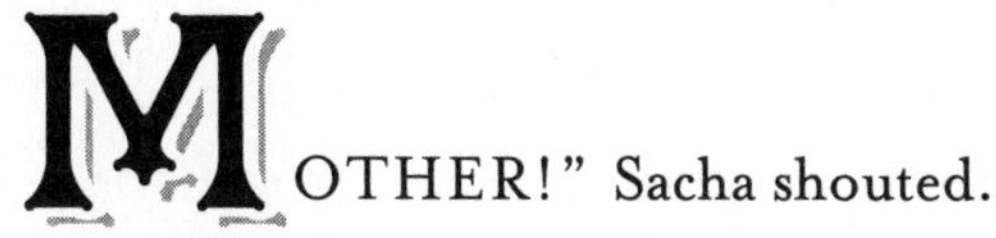

MOTHER!" Sacha shouted.

"What?"

"Mother!"

"So what?" She shrugged, and spoke in Yiddish. "Everyone has to make a living."

"But—but—"

Wolf cleared his throat. "If you don't mind—"

But by this time, neither Sacha nor his mother were paying any attention to him.

"I only did it for you and Bekah," Mrs. Kessler pleaded. "I wanted to give you a chance in life! I wanted to give you the things I never had!"

"Does Father know about this? Or have you been lying to him just like you lied to me and Bekah?"

"It's not lying. I just didn't want to embarrass the menfolk. They take magic so seriously. And anyway, this isn't real magic." She waved her hand vaguely in the air above the sewing machine as if to suggest that all this—the vast room, the towering bolts of cloth, the shirtwaists now draped all over the place in limp attitudes like puppets whose strings had been cut—were just some strange delusion that had nothing to do with magic at all. "It's just—doing what a mother has to do."

"If you don't mind—" Wolf said again.

"Excuse me!" Sacha snapped. "In case you didn't notice, I'm talking to my mother!"

"And you'll be talking to her boss, too, if we don't get out of here pretty soon!" Payton pointed out.

Sacha's eyes followed his pointing finger to the mirror hanging above the door. It was small and dusty and far too high on the wall for any human being to see his reflection in it. But it commanded an excellent view of the whole room from corner to corner. It didn't take magic to see that there was only one reason for it to be there.

"We need to go now!" Payton said.

Sacha reached over to grab his mother's arm and help her up—and suddenly she was awash in magic.

Bright fire played across her familiar features, making her face seem as if it belonged to a stranger. Sacha had sensed the aura that hung about her before this. But as she had been working strong spells when they came in, he had assumed it was her own magic. Now that he really looked at it, he knew no spell of hers could have had that cold, steel-sharp flame inside it.

Only one person he'd ever met worked magic that looked like that.

"What spell did he put you under?" Wolf asked, thrusting Sacha aside and shaking Mrs. Kessler roughly, as if he were afraid her mind would slip away from them. "There's no time to waste! I can't save you if you don't tell me what spell he used!"

She started to speak, but the words died before they reached her lips. She opened her mouth again—and again no words emerged. Now Sacha could see the magic flickering around her like fire.

She swallowed painfully, as if something sharp were stuck in her throat. The magic was stronger now, hotter. It rippled and writhed around her like the heat waves that twisted the air over the fires that hoboes lit in open oil drums on cold winter nights. Suddenly she seemed to find a flaw in the terrible spell that bound her—not enough to get free of it, but a crack just wide enough to squeeze a few words through before it slammed shut.

"I did it for you, Sacha!" Her throat sounded like it was on fire, and she was coughing now—a terrible, racking cough that sounded like the death rattle of a consumption victim.

Then, somehow, she gathered the strength to keep speaking. "He took my memory away. But he came back in dreams, whispering, whispering about the wicked things he'd do to you and Bekah if I didn't do his bidding."

His mother clutched at her throat as if hot coals were burning her. The magic rippled in the air like an open flame. Sacha could actually feel the heat pulsing from his mother.

And he could smell a thick burning smell, too—but surely he had to be imagining that?

"I can't break the spell," Wolf said roughly. "He still has a hold over you. He's using your own strength to fight me. What hold does he have over you?"

"Save my Sacha!" his mother shrieked. "He has his soul! Ah, that poor child in the pit, how can I abandon him?"

And suddenly, with a dizzying double sight, Sacha knew what she was telling them. He heard the voice of cold iron mocking and tormenting him.

His mother had seen the dybbuk. That was the hold Morgaunt had over her. And with a mother's heart, she had seen what Sacha hadn't been willing to hear when his grandfather explained it to him: that he and the dybbuk were one, and that he could no more live without his shadow than his shadow could live without him.

Then she seized her throat with both hands and her eyes rolled into the back of her head as she crumpled to the floor, insensible.

Sacha leaped forward to catch her as she fell—her skin was so hot that touching it felt like putting his hand to a stove. He screamed and almost dropped her. And then Wolf and Payton were beside him, their hands wrapped in rags plucked from the pile beside the sewing machine.

As they laid his mother down, Sacha heard a sound like the muffled tinkling of leaden bells. A handful of brilliant gemstones fell from Mrs. Kessler's mouth and spilled across onto the dusty floor. At first Sacha thought they were diamonds. But then the diamonds began to smoke and sizzle. As the steam rose off them, they turned from white to orange to the angry red of smoldering coals, hot enough to scorch and pit the wooden floorboards.

Wolf nudged the coals with one foot, and they scorched the leather toe of his boot, too.

"May your words turn to flaming coals in your throat," he murmured, as if he were reciting an old curse to himself. And then a sudden grin flashed across his face as he saw what Ruthie had done. "But she coated the coals with ice, didn't she? Imagine coming up with that! Clever woman!"

Wolf's smile faded quickly, though, replaced by an anxious scowl that grew more worried with every passing moment.

The flames forked and flickered around Sacha's mother like snakes' tongues. Then another sort of magic began to mingle with the flames—a cold, wintry kind of magic, as calm and hushed as a New York side street the morning after a fresh fall of snow had blanketed the city.

The two magics seemed to battle each other—heat against cold, molten steel against ice water. But it was no use. The fire was winning. Sacha could see it in his mother's flushed cheek and hear it in her agonized breathing.

"Get your grandfather!" Wolf ordered. "Now! Run!"

Sacha and Lily arrived at the *shul* on Canal Street just as Rabbi Kessler was settling in for a nice argument with a few of his favorite students.

"Wonderful, wonderful!" Grandpa Kessler cried, as he caught sight of Sacha. "We just needed one more to make a minyan, and here you are!"

But then he saw the look on Sacha's face.

They had made it almost all the way back to the factory when Sacha heard a familiar purring sound—and turned around to see the Astral family limousine behind them. Mo and Rabbi Kessler watched open-mouthed as the long, sleek automobile coasted to a stop beside them. And their mouths opened even wider when the back door swung outward to reveal Maleficia Astral, swathed in snow-white lace and looking as if she had dressed especially for the role of angelic rescuer.

"Oh, thank God!" Lily cried. And somehow, before Sacha could decide what he thought about this new development, Lily was dragging him into the familiar car beside her.

Mo and Rabbi Kessler got in beside them—Mo apologizing profusely for treading on Mrs. Astral's dress. Mrs. Astral said a quiet word to the impassive chauffeur. And then they were off.

"Well, this is exciting!" Mrs. Astral said. "He told me you would be here, and I dashed right off to find you!"

"Who told you?" Lily asked, suddenly looking a little squeamish. "Inquisitor Wolf? Did he call you on the telephone? Where'd he find one?"

"Hush, dear," Mrs. Astral said in that absent-minded tone of voice she always seemed to use when she spoke to her only daughter. "Let the men talk."

And then she turned to Sacha.

"Sacha," Lily whispered, tugging at his sleeve, "I'm not sure—"

But it was too late. Sacha had been dubious about getting in the car in the first place—he was always dubious about Mrs. Astral when she wasn't right there in front of him. But now that she was talking to him and gazing into his eyes and smiling sympathetically at him, he could think no evil of her. So he told her everything, the words tumbling out in a great rush.

"Oh, how terrible for you!" she exclaimed.

"Can't you ask the driver to go faster?" Sacha pleaded. "We have to get to Pentacle!"

"Don't worry about that, dear. It's all taken care of. We've come up with a much better plan."

"Who?" Lily asked. "Wolf? Or—" She burst into a violent coughing fit before she could finish her question.

Not that it made any difference. Because by that time, they had all realized that they weren't going to Pentacle at all. They were heading uptown. And the driver must have been going very fast indeed, because a few minutes later, they squealed around the corner of the Gothic arch of Morgaunt's Fifth Avenue mansion.

Bella da Serpa met them at the door. She looked surprised to see them. But after the briefest of hesitations, she shrugged and led them into the dark and empty library.

A moment later, Morgaunt arrived. He took one look around the library, grasped the situation, and exploded in fury.

"What are they doing here?" he asked Maleficia Astral, his eyes blazing. "How could you be such a fool?"

"But—you told me—" Lily's mother protested, suddenly sounding like a chastened child and not the first lady of New York high society.

"No one will ask questions about a bunch of poor Jews, but how are we going to explain the death of John Jacob Astral's daughter?"

"I can take care of her," Lily's mother said, showing a chilling lack of concern that Morgaunt had just suggested murdering her own daughter. "Just a simple memory hex—"

But Morgaunt cut her off with an angry gesture. "No, this has all gone terribly wrong. It's time to cut our losses and move on."

Mrs. Astral tried to say something, but Morgaunt just turned to Bella da Serpa and began speaking to her as if they were the only two people in the room.

"Call my private subway car," he told the librarian. "We're going on a little ride with Miss Astral." He turned a cold eye on Sacha. "And as for this one, I have a piece of unfinished business with him that I should have dealt with long ago."

CHAPTER TWENTY-SIX

The Rabbi's Bargain

SACHA LOOKED AT Lily, who was taking this all in with eyes the size of dinner plates, but Morgaunt was already turning his attention to Sacha. "I had a more subtle game in mind for you," Morgaunt told him, "but I'm afraid this has forced my hand." He glanced at Mo Lehrer and Rabbi Kessler. "Too bad about the old men, though. There's really no reason for them to be involved."

"Now, wait just a minute!" Mo Lehrer stepped forward, thrusting out his chest in a pitiful gesture of defiance. "If Sacha's involved, we're involved!"

"Oh, really?" Morgaunt drawled. "And what does that mean? That you'll pray to your pathetic God while I kill the boy right in front of you?"

"You wouldn't dare!" Mo pointed to Rabbi Kessler. "That's the greatest Kabbalist in New York!"

But Morgaunt just threw back his head and laughed.

Then he turned his steely gaze on Sacha. "Come here, boy. I want you to meet someone."

Sacha felt his feet moving, carrying him forward toward Morgaunt's beckoning finger. He tried to stop them, but they seemed to belong to someone else, someone who wanted to go to Morgaunt, who wanted to obey him, to follow him—

"Stop!" cried a voice that he barely recognized. It was Mo Lehrer—but a Mo Lehrer that Sacha had never seen before. He faced Morgaunt across the floor like David taking on a modern-day Goliath. As Sacha watched in amazed disbelief, Mo raised his hand to cast a spell at Morgaunt.

"No," Rabbi Kessler said in a voice that carried across the great hall despite its quietness. "Not that way. Not his way."

"But, Rabbi—"

Grandpa Kessler shook his head mournfully. "Listen to your heart, old friend. Use the name of God to fight him, and you become no better than he is."

Mo began to protest, but then he sighed and shrank into himself and admitted defeat without another word.

Morgaunt smiled coldly. Then he flicked a finger at Sacha and a circle of flame burst up around him, trapping him inside.

"I wouldn't do that if I were you," Rabbi Kessler said.

"Or what?" Morgaunt taunted.

Rabbi Kessler said nothing.

"I thought as much," Morgaunt said scornfully. "What's the point of having power when you don't have the guts to use it?"

Sacha wanted his grandfather to argue—to do something, at least—but he just bowed his head.

Then Morgaunt began to chant, if you could call it chanting. It was more like a droning muttering, really. As if Morgaunt couldn't even be bothered to say the spells in a proper voice. As if he was toying with forces that would overpower ordinary mortals, but that he couldn't even be bothered to be frightened of. Magic was a tool to Morgaunt, Sacha realized. He used it, but he despised it. Just like he despised all the nameless workers who wore themselves out in his factories.

Morgaunt droned on. The ring of flames smoked and crackled and threw off a sickly greenish light. Sacha grew dizzy. He shook his head, trying to clear his brain. He was seeing double. Was there a shadow between him and the flames, or was there another person standing in the circle beside him? He wasn't seeing double at all, he realized suddenly. The shadows flickering across his eyes weren't an echo of the library, but the image of a completely different place.

It was a pit, dark except for a faint shaft of light from far above. And there was someone in the pit. It was a child—a boy no older than Sacha himself. He was crumpled up against the wall with his face hidden so that all Sacha could see of him was a mop of dark curls and a pale strip of neck above tattered clothing.

Sacha's heart wrung with pity. He didn't have to see the boy's face. Just one look at the shivering body in its pathetic rags was enough to know that he was looking at a prisoner who had abandoned all hope of rescue.

He bent over the boy. Without thinking, he reached out to touch him, to console and comfort him. And then the boy turned to face him.

Ice flowed through Sacha's veins, stripping away his warmth, his strength, his very will to live. The face looking up at him was his face. And the eyes—black, bottomless, hopeless—were the eyes of his dybbuk. As he looked into the dybbuk's eyes, he could sense its thoughts and memories. He saw the preceding months stretching out in his mind's eye as if he himself had lived them, as if the flashes of memory were his own and not the dybbuk's. He saw Morgaunt seducing Naftali Asher with the etherograph's eerie music, giving the musician his heart's deepest desire even as he plotted to use Asher to bring down the IWW. He saw his mother as Morgaunt cast the spell of forgetting on her. He saw the dybbuk sabotaging Asher's electric tuxedo and understood at last the double game Morgaunt had played—murdering Asher and hiring Sacha's own mother in his place so that Wolf could only solve the case by destroying his own apprentice. And finally Sacha caught the haziest glimpse, limited by the dybbuk's own confusion, of Morgaunt's larger plan to wrest magical power from Minsky and the city's other gang lords.

Then the darkness swirled sickeningly, and he was standing once again in Morgaunt's library, the dybbuk beside him—and both of them trapped in the circle.

"What are you waiting for?" Morgaunt asked the dybbuk. He strode to the mahogany cabinet and wrenched its doors open. Inside, Edison's etherograph cylinders glimmered white and gold in the firelight. Morgaunt plucked a cylinder from the cabinet and held it out so that the dybbuk could see it. From the way the dybbuk was looking back and forth between the cylinder and Sacha, he could guess exactly whose soul was imprinted on the fragile golden foil.

"Kill him, and it's yours," Morgaunt told the dybbuk.

"I wouldn't do that," Rabbi Kessler said again, but this time, Morgaunt didn't even bother to look at him.

Suddenly a wave of angry defiance swept through Sacha's body. He was dead already—that much was obvious. But he'd be damned if he was going to go down without a fight.

He lunged at Morgaunt, but as he reached the edge of the circle, the line on the floor exploded into a wall of fire. He staggered back, and in that instant, the dybbuk was upon him. He fought it any way he could, grabbing and tearing at its ragged clothes, even though he could barely get hold of the creature itself.

Sacha heard his grandfather outside the circle telling him to stop, but he ignored him. Worse, he felt angry at him for not standing up to Morgaunt. What was the use of quietly talking to a man who was hell-bent on committing murder? What was the use of standing by and doing nothing while Morgaunt did evil?

But the more Sacha fought the dybbuk, the more he felt himself slipping under its power. He grew weaker, and the dybbuk grew stronger. Moment by moment, he became less certain of what he was fighting for. Moment by moment, it became harder to remember that he was Sacha, easier to think of himself as the shadow and the dybbuk as the real boy.

Finally, Grandpa Kessler stepped forward, crossing the line of flames as though they were nothing more than a pattern woven into Morgaunt's Persian carpet.

As he crossed into the circle, he changed. His bent back straightened, and his shabby clothes shone with an inner fire. He became awesome and terrible. He stepped in between Sacha and the dybbuk like an avenging angel. The dybbuk quailed before him.

And then, as Sacha watched, frozen in horror, his grandfather stepped forward, opened his arms wide, and gave himself over to the creature. Suddenly the avenging angel was gone. There was only an old man, frail and small.

"Come to me," he told the dybbuk. "Come and be at peace."

The dybbuk wavered for a moment, then stepped into the circle of the old man's arms.

Sacha had seen the dybbuk attack before. He had seen it grow strong on Antonio's hatred and hunger for revenge. He had seen it prey on Lily's secret loneliness, a loneliness he understood all too well when he heard the way her mother spoke about her to Morgaunt. But what the dybbuk drew from Rabbi Kessler's soul was completely different. It wasn't hate and sorrow, but warmth and love and life itself.

For a moment—just for a moment—it seemed that it would be enough to fill the howling emptiness inside the dybbuk. But it wasn't. Rabbi Kessler might as well have tried to fill an ocean with his little glass of water. The dybbuk's hunger grew. The old man wavered and faded. And still the swallowing darkness rose around them.

"No!" Sacha screamed.

It was too late.

His grandfather was gone, and he was alone in the circle with the dybbuk.

"Kill him!" Morgaunt bellowed.

The creature bore down on him, stronger than ever now that it had devoured yet another life. Sacha retreated to the edge of the circle. He felt the flames licking at his back. He could see Lily on the other side of the circle, writhing desperately in Bella da Serpa's arms. And then he saw Lily raise one foot and stomp with all her might on the librarian's pointy-toed shoe.

Bella shrieked, and Lily wriggled out of her grasp, dashed forward, and trampled on the flames until she had cleared a path out of the circle for him.

Now Sacha was free to leave—but so was the dybbuk.

Sacha dashed to the break in the flames, but the dybbuk got there first. For a moment, it wavered at the opening, unable to decide whether to escape or to attack Sacha.

"Kill him!" Morgaunt shouted.

He brandished the etherograph cylinder over his head, urging the dybbuk on, taunting it with its long-coveted treasure. The dybbuk turned to watch. And then, instead of attacking Sacha, it flung itself on Morgaunt like a cornered tiger, slashed viciously at his face, and ripped the cylinder from his hand.

The dybbuk fled across the entrance hall, its bare feet pattering like rain on the polished marble. Sacha raced after it. He wanted to stay by his grandfather's body, but something stronger than grief had taken hold of him. The dybbuk couldn't be allowed to escape into the teeming city and prey on its defenseless millions.

He could hear Bella da Serpa's high-heeled shoes skittering across the marble close behind him, and he hoped fervently that Lily and Mo were coming too.

At the far end of the hall, the dybbuk ducked into a dark doorway. Sacha followed—and almost fell straight down a long flight of stairs. Down it curved, far deeper than any basement, deep into the earth below the mansion. What could the dybbuk possibly want down here? Was it going back to the pit Morgaunt had pulled it out of?

A smell wafted up from the darkness below—and just as Sacha recognized it, the stairs dumped him out into a place he had heard rumors of but never seen before: J. P. Morgaunt's private subway station.

The dybbuk was just in front of him, racing alongside the tracks. The platform narrowed to a slender walkway above the tracks. There was nowhere to go but forward. If he reached out, he might just be able to grab the dybbuk. What he would do then, he had no idea. But he did know that he couldn't afford to let the dybbuk escape.

Closer . . . closer . . . he almost had him.

Sacha leaped forward. But the dybbuk leaped too—right off the platform onto the tracks.

The third rail glinted menacingly in the shadows. He heard a popping crackle as the dybbuk crossed over it, but nothing happened. Either the dybbuk had just barely brushed the electrified rail or it was immune to electricity.

Sacha gathered his nerve and jumped. He landed with a wrenching stumble and almost fell face-down across the third rail himself. Somehow he kept his feet and kept on running—but it was no good. The dybbuk was far ahead.

Going, going, gone . . . until it was lost in the inky darkness, a shadow melting into deeper shadow.

Sacha pulled up, limping, and hobbled back toward the station. He could see Lily and Bella da Serpa standing at the edge of the platform, where they had stopped when they saw him give up the chase. They peered anxiously into the shadows while they waited for him to reach them. Or at least Lily looked anxious. He couldn't tell what Bella da Serpa was feeling, and before he had made it back to the station, she slipped away.

"Are you all right?" Lily asked.

"Yes," he gasped. But he hardly knew what he was saying; all he could think of was his grandfather's limp body lying upstairs in the library.

By the time they climbed the stairs, there were police swarming over the whole house. Sacha expected to be arrested any moment, but then he saw Wolf coming out of the library supporting a haggard-looking Mr. Lehrer.

"My grandfather—" Sacha began, knowing what the

answer would be but hoping against all logic and reason that he would be wrong.

"I'm sorry, Sacha." Wolf turned a worried gaze on him. He seemed to be waiting for Sacha to fall apart. But Sacha only felt numb and disoriented, as if he were moving through a dream that made no sense to him.

"Your mother's fine," Wolf said. "I got her to your house, and your father and sister are taking care of her."

Sacha felt a wave of relief sweep through him—the only emotion he could identify in the swirling fog that had filled his mind since he'd watched his grandfather die. The relief didn't quite take away the terrible image of that death. But it did remind him that things could have been worse—much, much worse.

"Who called the police?" Lily asked.

"They're here to help Mr. Morgaunt." Wolf's voice was suspiciously bland. "It seems that the one of the servants panicked when the dybbuk attacked Morgaunt and ran to the nearest call box to report a magical assassination."

"Is Morgaunt dead?" Sacha asked, feeling a wild surge of emotion that he didn't want to put a name to.

"No. But he'll carry those scars for the rest of his life."

"Good!" Lily said with savage satisfaction. "And at least since someone called the police in, they won't be able to just cover the whole thing up this time!"

Wolf smiled bitterly. "I wouldn't count on that."

CHAPTER TWENTY-SEVEN

The Elijah Cup

THE NEXT WEEKS crept by excruciatingly slowly. Every morning, all Sacha could see around the breakfast table was the fact that his grandfather wasn't there. Every night, the feather bed felt emptier than it should be. It felt like there was an aching hole in the family on Hester Street that would never be healed over. And worst of all, he could see the rest of his family constantly trying not to talk about it—and trying not to blame him for it.

He couldn't stop blaming himself, though. He couldn't stop going over all the decisions he had made that led up to that terrifying night at Morgaunt's mansion, thinking of everything he could have done differently. Still, time passed, and life gradually began to return to normal. According to the newspapers, Morgaunt lay at death's door for weeks. Whoever was managing Pentacle in his absence must not have been as tough as he was, because they abandoned the fight, shipped the Pinkertons out of town, and handed the IWW what amounted to an almost total victory. Everyone at Pentacle went back to work—everyone, that is, except Sacha's sister. A few weeks after his grandfather died, Sacha finally confronted his father about the apprentice's pay that was accumulating in the bank for his "education."

"I'm never going to use that money," he told his father. "And Bekah *could* use it. She's the one who ought to be going to school, not me."

"No!" his father snapped. "You're saving that money for college, and that's that!"

He sounded uncharacteristically stern, but Sacha had known he would. There were few things that mattered more to him than Sacha's education.

"No, I'm not," he insisted. "And I want Bekah to have the money."

"You're not old enough to make that decision!"

"I've already made it!"

"Then you'll unmake it, young man!" But then, before Sacha could get out the hotheaded answer that was on the tip of his tongue, Mr. Kessler laughed. "How can I suddenly sound so much like *my* father?" he asked.

"I don't know," Sacha said. "I never heard him sound that way."

"That's because he knew better by then," Danny Kessler said ruefully. "And I should know better too. You truly want to give Bekah that money?" he asked in a softer voice. "You've really thought about what you're giving up?"

"I'm not giving up anything that matters as much to me as going to school matters to her."

"Well, you're earning a man's wages, so I guess it's time I started trusting you to make a man's decisions. But don't start thinking you know better than your *mother* about anything! I can tell you right now that's not going to get you anywhere!"

So Bekah stopped working and started going to school full-time. Meanwhile, the cold and snow relinquished their grip on the city, and the skies turned blue again, and every day spring seemed closer, until suddenly—without Sacha even quite noticing that April had arrived—it was Passover.

Passover might not have been the most important holiday of the year, but it marked the arrival of spring every year, and somehow it always felt to Sacha like it brought with it the promise of a fresh start and new possibilities. And it was the one holiday that no one on the Lower East Side complained about, not even the most stalwart atheists or the most flaming Anarcho-Wiccanist revolutionaries. Mordechai would be home soon. And Moishe was already here, sitting on the old feather bed beside Bekah as her unacknowledged (at least by her) boyfriend. Even Bekah, who wouldn't be caught dead in synagogue on any other holiday, didn't think taking a stand against bourgeois convention meant you couldn't enjoy Passover.

And it wasn't just the Kessler family gathered around the table this year, either. Sacha's mother had taken the unprecedented step of inviting Lily Astral to the feast. And then, to everyone's amazement, she had issued an invitation to Inquisitor Wolf as well.

"He saved my life, after all," she said when Sacha tried to protest that this might be a bit too familiar. "That makes him my friend too. Besides, he's an orphan. And it's a *mitzvah* to feed orphans on Passover."

Sacha could have pointed out that Wolf was a grownup with a job and a salary, not a starving waif in need of sustenance. But why bother? Wolf was coming, and there wasn't a thing Sacha could do about it. And the funny part of it was that, as soon as he saw the Inquisitor's lanky frame folded into one of the wobbling chairs around the old kitchen table, he didn't want to do anything about it. His mother had been right; Wolf did belong there that night. If nothing else because having him and Lily around the table made Grandpa Kessler's spot on the feather bed seem less gapingly empty than it had for the past month and a half.

At the last possible moment—with his usual unerring instinct for the exact moment when all the work was done and there was nothing left to do but eat—Uncle Mordechai swept through the door with flowers for the table and flowery apologies for Mrs. Kessler.

He caught sight of Lily Astral, half raised his hand in greeting, and then eyed her with a vague look of confusion on his handsome features.

"Have we met somewhere before?" he asked doubtfully.

But Lily didn't seem to have any doubt at all about it. She

gasped out loud and jumped from her chair as if it had just caught fire.

"Count Vogelonsky!" she cried, curtseying—or at least Sacha thought that was what she was trying to do. "I never imagined I'd see you here!"

"Er, yes," Mordechai said, glancing apprehensively at his sister-in-law. Once he had made sure that Mrs. Kessler was busy with the food, he swept elegantly across the floor—or as elegantly as he could, given the need to sidle around the kitchen table without burning his pants on the stove—and leaned over to kiss the back of Lily's outstretched hand. "*Enchanté,* I'm sure."

Unfortunately, however, he had bumped into Mrs. Kessler while trying to get around the stove. She had turned around just in time to catch sight of the hand kissing and was now staring hard at him with her own hands balled into fists on her hips.

"Mordechai Kessler," she said in a tone of voice that Sacha had long ago learned meant it was time to duck for cover, "what on earth do you think you're doing?"

"Nothing, nothing!" Mordechai assured her. "Just welcoming our fair guest to our humble abode—"

"Do I look like an onion?" Ruthie Kessler demanded. "Do you think I grow upside down with my eyes closed and my head in the ground?"

"Er, um—"

"This is all part of that appalling scheme you and Nathan

Feldman cooked up to break the hearts of poor defenseless young women for money, isn't it?"

"No, Ruthie, no! You don't understand—"

"Oh, I understand. And I've got a good mind to make sure Nathan's mother understands too."

"That, my dear woman, would be extremely unfortunate."

"Extremely unfortunate for you, you mean!"

"So just who are you anyway?" Lily asked doubtfully. "Is your real name Count Vladimir Vogelonsky or Mordechai Kessler?"

"Ha ha! Mordechai Kessler indeed!" Mordechai gave Lily his most charming grin. "That's just a little joke my friends are having with me—"

"Mordechai!" Sacha's father growled.

"All right, all right!" Mordechai cried. And then he gave up the fight and confessed everything.

Lily seemed completely overwhelmed by Mordechai's confession. She kept opening and closing her mouth, trying to speak, and looking back and forth between Mordechai and Sacha as if she thought *he* was somehow involved in the charade.

"Close your mouth," Sacha told her with a smug sense of satisfaction, "You look like a carp in a Chinatown fish shop."

Meanwhile, Mrs. Lehrer had been bustling around the room putting the finishing touches on things. Finally, everything was ready. The rickety kitchen table was splendid under Mrs. Lehrer's grandmother's snow-white lace tablecloth.

They had laid out the Passover dishes and silver. The lamb shank glistened and steamed on the Passover platter. The *afikoman* snuggled in its cloth. Everything was in its place. All was ready. And everyone who should be there was there. Except for the one person who would never be there again.

Sacha felt a lump rising in his throat, but before he had time to think about it, his father got to his feet. Mr. Kessler looked around the table. The rest of the family stared back at him, as silent and white as if they were ghosts themselves. Sacha looked at his mother and saw unshed tears glistening in her eyes. Suddenly he was struck by a thought almost too appalling to put into words. Was his father going to cry? He'd never seen his father cry in his life, and he wasn't sure he could stand it.

Mr. Kessler coughed and looked off into the distance for a long moment. But when he finally spoke, his voice was clear and steady.

"My father always said it was a sin to be unhappy on the Sabbath," he told them. "So I don't even want to think about what he'd have to say to anyone who dared to be sad on Passover."

And then he began leading the Seder as naturally and comfortably as if he did it every year. It took the rest of the family a few moments to catch up with him. But they managed it—mostly because it was plain from Mr. Kessler's face that he expected them to.

Wolf and Lily seemed surprisingly at home around the

Kesslers' kitchen table. Wolf went along with the Passover festivities as if he'd been at a hundred Seders before—which, for all Sacha knew, he had been. And Lily was happily eating everything in sight, asking his mother what went into the *haroset,* and displaying a ghoulish fascination with the ten plagues.

Still, Sacha wondered how strange this three-thousand-year-old story of slavery and deliverance must seem to them. And when his father began to tell the story of the Israelites' escape from Egypt, he felt a sharp twinge of guilt about one face that was missing from around the table: Philip Payton's. He had asked Philip at the same time he'd asked Wolf and Lily. But perhaps he'd asked him awkwardly; he often felt awkward around Payton. Whatever the reason, Payton had refused the invitation. Now, listening to his father tell the Passover story, Sacha thought of Wolf's other, unofficial apprentice—for, after all, hadn't Wolf once said that Payton would have been an apprentice but for the color of his skin? What did Payton think about that? Would he even keep working for Wolf when his family moved to Harlem? And would they find what they were looking for there? Somehow Sacha doubted it—and he seemed to hear an echo of Bella da Serpa's mocking voice telling Wolf that democracy was nothing more than a lynch mob.

Sacha glanced at Lily. Maybe Payton had talked to her about it; she'd always seemed to get along with him much better than Sacha did. He was pretty sure that Payton told her all kinds of things he wouldn't dream of talking to Sacha about. And then Sacha intercepted a knowing look between Bekah and Moishe—and decided he'd better not even look in Lily's direction anymore, lest anybody get the wrong idea.

And then, all too soon, the last word of the ancient tale was spoken. Sacha and Bekah took up the traditional children's chorus ("Can we eat yet?"), and their father pretended to be shocked and appalled by their lack of manners, as always.

But just as they were all about to tuck into the copious main course of Mrs. Kessler's magnificent Passover dinner, there came a thunderous knocking on the front door that could only mean one thing.

"I, uh, was having Passover dinner with my mother upstairs," Benny Fein said, lumbering through the door that Mo Lehrer had jumped up to open for him, "and, uh, I tought I'd come up and say a Happy Passover to youze all," Benny said. But while he spoke, his eyes were roving round the room, searching for Bekah. And when he finally found her sitting next to Moishe on the feather bed, a black scowl settled over his face.

"Why don't you pull up a chair and join us, Benny?" Mr. Kessler suggested when it became painfully clear that nothing short of an earthquake would get Benny out of the apartment.

Lily took the hint and squeezed onto the bed next to Sacha. But Benny accepted her chair without thanking her—or even glancing away from the two young lovers. He sat down and distractedly accepted a heaping plate from Mrs. Kessler.

Then he leaped up as if the seat of his chair had suddenly become burning hot. Then he sat down and stood up and sat down again.

Finally he raised his unused fork in the air and proclaimed, "I can be silent no longer! A guy's gotta say what a guy's gotta say!"

Everyone froze, forks stranded in midair and mouths hanging open.

"Mr. Kessler!"

"Yes, Benny?"

"I know I don't have duh best reputation of any guy on duh block. But I swear I'll take care of her. I'll treat her like a queen!"

Benny waved dramatically to underscore his point, but he had forgotten that he was holding his plate in one hand. The plate crashed into the wall behind him and shattered. Mordechai laughed, and Mrs. Kessler kicked him under the table and then buried her head in her hands. Meanwhile Benny picked up the shattered pieces of the plate somewhat sheepishly, frowned at them for a moment as if they had broken his train of thought, and then placed them carefully back on the table.

"Anyway, duh point is," he told Mr. Kessler, "no one will ever disrespect your daughter when she's my wife."

"Your wife!" Bekah and Moishe cried at exactly the same moment—and Sacha couldn't say who sounded more outraged by the idea.

Benny didn't seem to hear Moishe at all, however. In

fact, Moishe might as well not even have existed, for all the notice Benny paid him. Instead the gangster turned to Bekah, one hand laid upon his massive chest as if he were a medieval knight about to proclaim his undying love for his noble lady.

"Miss Kessler," he declared, "there's some things I just gotta tell you. First thing, I never met a girl like you, and as we have discussed prior to this time, I would like to take you home to meet my mother. Second thing, I'm not such a bad guy once you get to know me. Just ask Meyer. Third thing—"

But whatever the third thing was, Benny never got to tell Bekah about it. Because before he could open his mouth, Moishe dashed around the table, wound up like a fastball pitcher, and belted him in the nose.

There's lucky and there's lucky. And, truth be told, Moishe's punch was just about the luckiest one Sacha had ever seen in his life. If Benny had been looking at Moishe instead of Bekah, he would have ducked. And if he'd been standing up—or even sitting down for that matter—the blow would have bounced off him like rain off a duck's back. But instead it landed just as Benny was dropping to one knee. Moishe's fist was coming up. Benny's nose was heading down. And the two of them collided like a pair of freight trains running in opposite directions on the same track.

A resounding crack echoed through the room.

Bekah squeaked.

Mrs. Kessler gasped.

Benny stopped in midsentence, raised his eyes to the

ceiling, said, "Whu—?" and then toppled with the slow majesty of a redwood falling in the great forest wilderness of the Pacific Northwest.

Every woman in the room shrieked, and every man shouted. Bekah leaped up to tend to Benny's wounds, scolding Moishe all the while (but nonetheless looking flushed and a little pleased, or at least so it seemed to Sacha).

Benny sat up, holding his nose, and gave Moishe a mournful look.

"I didn't know she was your goil," he said accusingly. "And what's the point of hauling off and hitting a guy widdout any warning like dat, anyway? How'm I supposed to know stuff if people don't tell me nothin'?"

"First of all," Bekah began, "I am not 'his' girl—"

"Yes, you are!" Moishe snapped.

"I'm not anyone's girl!" Bekah cried. "I'm a human being, not a pound of pickled herring! And if you can't respect that, Moishe Schlosky, then—"

"I respect it! I respect it! But this is between me and Benny!"

"Some revolutionary you are!" Bekah huffed. "And then you men have the nerve to go around accusing women of being counterrevolutionary!"

Lily guffawed at this, and even Wolf looked blandly amused.

But although Bekah kept on fussing over Benny's nose, Sacha noticed that she didn't look nearly as mad as she sounded. Meanwhile, Moishe—who suddenly seemed to have forgotten that he'd ever disliked Benny at all—was helping Mrs. Kessler put ice on the gangster's nose, and Mr. Kessler and Mo Lehrer were dissecting Moishe's boxing technique, while Mordechai had started in on some ridiculous story about his adventures in high society that eventually had everyone laughing until tears leaked from their eyes. And when Benny's nose stopped bleeding and Bekah sat down to eat, Sacha noticed that she sat down next to Moishe—and maybe even a little closer than before Benny came in.

And then at last the meal was done, and people were patting their full stomachs and pushing their chairs back from the table, and it was time to pour the fourth cup of wine.

Sacha's mother began to pour. But then she gasped. "We forgot!" she said. "How could we have?"

Sacha knew immediately what she meant—and he could see by the tears shimmering in Bekah's eyes that she remembered too. And indeed, his father was already going to the dresser and carefully opening the bottom drawer and unwrapping the silver cup that had traveled so far with the Kessler family and survived so many dangers.

Lily and Inquisitor Wolf didn't know all that the cup meant to the other people in the room, of course, but they could see the reverent way Sacha's father brought it to the table and the effect that it had on even the irrepressible Mordechai.

They drank the fourth cup. And then Mrs. Kessler

handed Sacha the old *Kiddush* cup, and he carried it around the table so they could all pour the last sip of their own wine into it to make the fifth and final glass.

As he carried the cup to the door, he heard his father explaining to the guests that this was Elijah's cup and that they opened the door on Passover to invite the prophet Elijah in to the feast.

Sacha opened the door and stood with the cup in his hand looking out into the dark hallway. The night seemed to have crept into the stairwell, and he could smell the earthy bite of green leaves and budding trees on the air. As he turned back into the bright room, a gust of wind blew through the open door to flutter the curtains and the tablecloth and set the flames dancing atop the candles.

Suddenly Sacha felt tears stinging behind his eyes. He set the cup back on the table. Then, instead of sitting down himself, he stepped out onto the fire escape for some fresh air. After a moment, the window opened and Wolf climbed out after him. They stood for a moment, side by side, saying nothing.

"It's just how easily Morgaunt got away with it that bothers me," Sacha said savagely.

This time it had been even worse than after the fire at the Elephant Hotel. Morgaunt's cover-up had been as perfect as it was effortless. He controlled the police force and the newspapers too completely for the deadly confrontation at his mansion to ever become anything more than one of those vague unfounded rumors that blew clean out of people's minds at the first hint of a newer and juicier scandal.

And as for Rabbi Kessler, he never made it into the papers at all, except as an anonymous victim of an unfortunate accident.

The dybbuk, meanwhile, had vanished yet again. This time Sacha knew better than to fool himself that it was gone for good. His shadow would be back. And it would be stronger, much stronger. But it wouldn't be under Morgaunt's control—or anyone else's. Sacha didn't know what that meant, but he didn't think it could mean anything good.

"I've changed my mind," he blurted out to Wolf. "I do want to learn magic."

Wolf didn't answer. He just gazed north at the glittering skyline.

Finally Sacha couldn't bear it anymore. "Aren't you happy?" he snapped. "Isn't that what you've been pestering me to do? I thought you'd be dancing for joy."

"I guess I don't have to ask why you changed your mind."

"Morgaunt killed my grandfather right in front of me. And I couldn't do a thing to stop him."

Wolf turned to look at him. He seemed to be frowning, but his face was lost in shadows, like everything else on the deserted street.

"Your grandfather sacrificed himself to save you. Do you think he would have wanted you to throw your life away on a pointless act of revenge?"

"Then what about Morgaunt? We just let him get away with it?"

"He's going to get away with it whether you 'let' him or not. At the moment, I'm more worried about keeping you alive."

"Why bother?" Sacha asked bitterly. He gestured at the rundown tenement building, the sagging fire escape, the garbage-strewn street below them. "Look around. In case you haven't noticed, I'm nobody. Who the hell's even going to notice if Morgaunt kills me? What difference will it ever make to anyone?"

"Your grandfather thought it made a difference," Wolf said simply.

Sacha buried his head in his hands.

"I don't know how to say this," Wolf began. "I'm not even sure what I'm trying to tell you, or if it's a good idea for you to think about it too much. But when I said your grandfather sacrificed himself for you . . . well, that isn't the whole story, is it? Everyone else the dybbuk has killed has gone unwillingly, because it fed on the darkness and fear and emptiness inside them. But your grandfather gave the best of himself to it. Including his love for you. In a way, I suppose, he gave the dybbuk the very things it thinks you stole from it."

Sacha spoke haltingly about what his grandfather had told him. "Do you think part of *his* soul is in the dybbuk now?"

"How should I know? I don't even know what a soul is!"

"My grandfather knew. And he tried to tell me. But I

barely listened to him—I thought he'd always be here to tell me again."

Wolf was silent, waiting. Something in his silence made Sacha remember that Wolf's own fate might be wrapped up with the dybbuk's. Morgaunt had once asked Sacha to betray Wolf and work for Pentacle. Wolf had charged to Sacha's rescue just in time to keep him from having to answer Morgaunt. But how would he have answered if he'd had more time? And how could Sacha say whether the dybbuk was good or evil when—in the darkest reaches of his own soul—he couldn't even answer that question about himself?

"What do we do now?" he asked, hardly knowing whether he was asking about the dybbuk or about Morgaunt.

"We do the best we can," Wolf said simply. "That's all we *can* do."

Suddenly there was a squeak and a thump as the window opened. Bekah leaned out onto the fire escape. "How long are you two going to sit out here, anyway?" she said. "Dessert's on the table, and you better get inside if you want any. Mordechai's already asking for seconds!"

Sacha and Wolf stared at each other for another moment. Then Wolf smiled. "Your mother's a really good cook. I was sort of looking forward to that cake."

"Yeah, me too. So . . ."

"So nothing. Just eat your cake. And go to your lesson with Shen tomorrow. You don't have to decide the rest of your life right now, Sacha. In fact, I'd much rather you didn't."

Wolf turned away, fumbled for a moment with the

unfamiliar window, and then opened it and stepped inside. Sacha began to follow him, but turned back for a last glance at the city.

Night was coming on, the sky darkening to a regal blue above New York's dazzling skyline. Morgaunt was out there somewhere. He hadn't been seen in public since the dybbuk attacked him, and Sacha had no idea how badly he'd been injured. But he couldn't have died—even he couldn't have covered that up. The dybbuk was out there somewhere too. Perhaps slipping down some shadowy side street. Perhaps deep in the warm, echoing darkness of the subway tunnels. And there were millions of other people out there, busy with their own lives, for whom one old man's death wasn't worth noticing. Suddenly he felt confused and overwhelmed and unable to even begin to understand his life.

"Sacha!" Lily said, poking her head out the window. "What are you doing? It's freezing out here. You're shivering."

She was right, he realized. He was shivering.

He let her take his hand and lead him through the window into the warm kitchen. There was still one piece of cake on the table, and someone had set it in front of his place, where Bekah was now ably defending it against the encroachments of Uncle Mordechai.

"If you want it," Bekah warned him, "you'd better eat it now."

"It's really good," Lily echoed. "You should have a piece."

Sacha sat down on the foot of the feather bed and looked at the cake in front of him. Then he looked around at the faces of his friends and family.

"Actually," Uncle Mordechai said, "it's terrible. You should have a bite—just a little one—to make your mother feel better. But then you should give the rest to me."

"Mmmmph," Sacha said. But his mouth was too full of cake to say more.